A REFLECTIVE WORLD

Many thanks to Chad, Jason, Nicole, and Sara. And, of course, Shona.

Thank you to the good people at Scribendi https://www.scribendi.com/for their professional editing services.

Thanks to Damonza https://damonza.com/ for their cover art and formatting services.

For Mona Sneddon

A REFLECTIVE WORLD

KEVIN LAMPORT

Singularity – A point smaller than an atom, having infinite density and mass, which expanded rapidly at the moment of the Big Bang, creating all the space, time, matter, and energy of our physical universe.

Cosmic Inflation – An explosive scaling-up of spacetime a tiny fraction of a second after the Big Bang. Some parts of spacetime expanded more quickly than others, creating "bubbles" of spacetime that then developed into other universes… the multiverse.

Multiverse – The hypothetical set of possible universes, including the universe in which we live. Together, these universes comprise everything that exists: the entirety of space, time, matter, energy, and the physical laws and constants that describe them.

"Two possibilities exist: either we are alone in the universe or we are not. Both are equally terrifying."

Arthur C. Clarke

March 1, 1954
Corporal John "Jack" Taylor

PROLOGUE

CORPORAL JOHN "JACK" Taylor had one job: shoot to kill any person who approached the huge metal cylinder on the opposite side of the room, if that person was not named on the access list. He stood guard with an M3 "grease gun" in his hands and a Colt M1917 holstered on his hip. He didn't expect he'd need either weapon. Everyone on Bikini Atoll was there in support of Operation Castle, either directly or indirectly. The idea that a spy or saboteur might have learned about Castle, made his way to the Marshall Islands in the South Pacific Ocean, and then somehow infiltrated the American military machine to a point he could sabotage the cylinder… well, the idea was ludicrous. But the government paid him to guard the cylinder, so that's what Jack did, short-shifting two hours at a time with several other marines in order to prevent complacency on a detail that was critically important but probably unnecessary.

He transferred his weight from side to side. Standing on the concrete floor made his feet ache inside his leather combat boots, which, upon reflection, didn't matter much. His supervisors didn't care, the other marines would have laughed with scorn had he mentioned it and at a lean and muscular one hundred and eighty pounds, his minor aches and pains disappeared the moment he started moving again. More annoying than tired feet was the tropical heat. Blonde and fair of skin, he was susceptible to burning beneath the pitiless equatorial sun. He dripped constant sweat under his uniform. Although his "utilities" were comfortable, eighty-six degrees was too hot for everyone on Bikini except those permitted to wear T-shirts and shorts. Everyone, in other words, except those tasked with security. Thankfully, his final shift was almost over. The evacuation of the atoll had begun almost two full days before, at H minus forty-eight hours. Other than the firing party on the island of Enyu twenty miles away and security personnel such as himself, most everyone else was already on board the USS Curtiss, or one of the other ships that were part of an operation that would see the detonation of five thermonuclear devices over the following ten weeks. Today's shot, Castle Bravo, would be the first.

Jack heard the distant sound of a Jeep's engine, the growl growing noticeably louder. He wiped the sweat off his forehead with the back of his hand. He eyed the cylinder, wondering how something that appeared so innocuous could produce such immense destruction. Suspended from the ceiling and supported on both ends in a steel framework, the cylinder reminded him of an oversized propane tank lying on its side. Named "Shrimp," it was five feet around, twenty feet long, and covered with the signatures of people named on the access list. His own name was scribbled on the right-hand side, near a collection of pipes that fed the device. He'd overheard a scientist say the expected shot would be equivalent to five million tons of TNT, a staggering amount of explosive that would have overfilled one of the arched steel storage facilities on Bikini Atoll.

A voice behind him said, "Sir, I'm here to take you to the helicopter."

Jack nodded his acknowledgment, turned his back on Shrimp, and followed the driver out to the jeep. Forty minutes later, he stood on the deck of the USS Curtiss among top brass, scientists, and fellow marines twenty-three miles distant from ground zero and the forthcoming explosion.

When the countdown hit ten seconds, fearful anticipation raised the hairs on the back of his neck. Goose bumps stippled his arms, giving the porpoise tattoo on his forearm a three-dimensional appearance.

With his back to Bikini, he settled a pair of blackout goggles over his eyes, turning the midday sky an inky black.

At three seconds, every breath came in shallow, nervous sips.

At zero, the device detonated.

Day turned so incredibly bright that Jack saw the bones in his arms through his own living flesh as if he were looking at an x-ray. A wave of heat, like a blowtorch applied directly to his entire body, washed over the ship's deck. The blonde hairs on his knuckles and the backs of his hands turned black and shriveled. Even with plastic ear defenders and cotton stuffed in his ears, the sound was a physical blow that made him stagger. He recalled an argument in which two scientists disagreed on whether it was the colossal noise that could kill a human, or if it was the soundwave assaulting the eardrums that was lethal. He thought they were splitting hairs.

He turned around. Facing Bikini Atoll, he pushed the goggles onto his forehead and stared at Armageddon. A boiling black and orange storm surrounded the USS Curtiss. Fireballs plunged out of the nightmarish cloud, splashed into the ocean, and sent geysers of steam and water back into the air. The shockwave pushed a tsunami toward the ship, and the Pacific Ocean was painted in all the flaming colors of hell. Several combat-hardened veterans dropped to their knees and prayed. Jack had time to think of his young son Richard, all pointy elbows and bony knees, and his slim-as-a-willow wife, who preferred Oklahoma winters with the snow and frigidity, "...a place with seasons," over continually warm and sunny Honolulu.

The shockwave struck the side of the Curtiss. The five hundred and twenty-seven-foot ship heeled over like a child's bathtime toy. Jack grabbed a gun mount and set his feet as the ship listed and the angle of the deck steepened. Men less prepared lost their balance and yelling, tumbled toward the ship's gunwale and the long plunge into the burning ocean. He caught the flailing arm of a seaman sliding backward down the deck and held on tightly, one hand clinging to the gun mount, the other clamped around the sailor's wrist. The muscles in his shoulders strained, and the veins in his arm bulged.

The mighty ship reached an apex. It paused, as if deciding whether or not to right itself or roll over and show her belly to the world. Slowly, it leveled, revealing a fiery column of dust, smoke, and debris churning rapidly skyward. At the top of this poisonous stem, encircled by a glowing red halo, an awful mushroom cloud bloomed and swelled to an impossible size. Horrified, Jack looked at the end of the world and thought God alone should have that kind of power.

The twenty-eight-year-old corporal didn't know he'd just witnessed the detonation of the largest manmade destructive force the world had ever seen. He couldn't imagine the immense ramifications it would hold for himself and for the entire planet in the years that followed.

January, 2028

CHAPTER 1

"YOU LIKE, MR. STEVE? Is nice, yes?"

Steve Quinn swept his eyes from the cinder block wall on the left side of the charitably described living room to the cinder block wall on the right. He ignored the dirty beige carpet, heavily dimpled by more than one careless nicotine addict. He ignored the muddy gray stains on the tips of the popcorn ceiling. Demanding they be cleaned was too much to expect. He pointed at the window-mounted air conditioner. Its frayed cord dangled down the wall and coiled like a dead snake on the floor beneath the appliance. Without hope, he asked, "Does it work, Elaina?"

Elaina Cosma laughed. She slapped at him playfully with ring-adorned fingers. Nails painted blazing scarlet lingered on his forearm a beat too long. "You make this lady laugh, Mr. Steve."

He gave her a brief smile, pretending not to notice her drawn-out touch. She wore black high heels, snow-leopard yoga pants, a white mohair sweater, and a silky black headband that held her dark hair on top of her head in a thick bundle. She should have looked overdone. Somehow, Elaina pulled the disparate elements into an attractive package. Maybe it was his overtired, grief-stricken mind, but Steve found her slightly intimidating. He didn't want her hand on his arm any more than he wanted the previous manager's sweaty, sausage-like fingers on his arm. Of course, that never would have happened.

Charlie Houston seldom got out from behind his desk. Walking his considerable bulk up thirteen floors to show the apartment was out of the question. He would have handed Steve the key and said, "Take a look. Let me know."

For the third or fourth time, Elaina said, "Nice view, yes? Is on the fourteenth floor. Thirteenth, really, but here, thirteen is called fourteen." She shook her head. "Foolish North American superstition. Where I come from, we don't have that. We have other superstitions."

For the third or fourth time, Steve agreed. Yes, the view out the single window was… nice. From this height, he had an unobstructed view of the rain-soaked streets and the stream of tired commuters exiting the Metro station a block away. They'd pause to pull up a collar or open an umbrella, giving the afternoon dabs of cheerful color before rushing away with their shoulders up and their backs bowed. Had the brownish smudge of perpetual pollution not obscured the horizon, his view of the suburbs and the distant Cascade Mountain range would have been nice, too.

Steve circled the apartment once more. He peered into the empty cupboards, opened a refrigerator with a burned-out light, and turned the taps on and off. The linoleum curled up along the baseboards under the cabinets at the toe kicks. A seat on the toilet would have been more civilized than cold porcelain. There was a rusty stain in the cabinet beneath the dripping bathroom sink. They were all easy fixes. Steve was handy that way after growing up with a father who made a habit of repairing things rather than buying them.

"You think a plumber is smarter than you?" his father would ask and shake his head. "He's not. He knows what to look for. That's all. Figure out what's broken, and fix it. What's the worst thing that'll happen? You're not going to break it worse."

Standing with his fists on his hips, Steve gave the empty cube another left-to-right appraisal. He would have preferred a room lower in the building. On the up side, however, a room on the fourteenth was easier to secure than the two-bedroom on the second floor in which he used to live. Way up here on the fourteenth, there'd be no need to bolt a sturdy metal screen to the window frame, as was common on floors closer to the ground. He wouldn't need to stash Tamara's pistol in the night table for easy access or stow his shotgun close at hand, in a storage device known as a "Couch Cradle" that attached to the back of the sofa. Although once he moved into the tiny apartment and filled the closet and drawers with normal household trappings, he was unsure where else he'd store the weapons.

As if reading his mind, Elaina said, "I sorry, Mr. Steve. Everybody wants lower floor. It could be worse. It could be on fifteenth." She smiled, cracking her heavy red lipstick. She gestured toward the nice view. "Is cheaper for you on the fourteenth. And romantic. Not like on two."

Steve was tempted to ask how Eastern Europe superstitions differed from those in America—he guessed her accent was Romanian—but decided not to. He didn't want to get more personal, to open a more intimate door. Not with a word like "romantic" floating in the room, as conspicuous as the lady's acrylic fingernails. He stared at the street. Below him, the city spread out in a perfect checkerboard. Several blocks reflected light off the low-hanging smog. Several blocks on either side were dark. The electrical grid hadn't been able to keep pace with demand in close to a decade. In a couple of hours, the checkerboard would reverse itself: light would go dark; dark would go bright.

Many people would have been overjoyed with a scabby, one-bedroom apartment, such as this. Vacancy rates in the city were less than one percent. Steve only had a chance at it because it was located in the same high-rise as the two bedroom in which he used to live with Tamara; people in the building were given first dibs when a vacancy opened up. The price was right, cheaper than two bedrooms, as Elaina had mentioned. He saw no reason to spend his savings on square footage. He didn't entertain prodigiously, like the happy couples on home improvement shows, all with dozens of friends who dropped in every weekend with food, drink, and fun that appeared forced, even by reality television standards. Cheaper, too, because the elevator was paralyzingly slow and, therefore, usually uncomfortably full of tenants from every floor of the building. Steve didn't mind taking the stairs down to street level, but when he went out for groceries, he would have to do a certain amount of planning. He wouldn't want to forget a single thing; nobody enjoyed climbing up thirteen flights of stairs or taking twenty-minute elevator rides more often than absolutely necessary.

Steve slowly scratched his cheek and came to a decision. Other than lousy aesthetics, he saw little downside to the apartment. It ticked the most important box: he needed a change that took him away from Tamara's memory. Everything else was gravy.

"You like, Mr. Steve? You take?"

"I'll take it." Then, knowing he didn't have much in the way of bargaining power but unable to stop himself, he added, "But—"

Elaina's happy smile slipped a fraction. Her plucked and carefully redrawn eyebrows rose questioningly.

"—I want a new air conditioner." Stretching a dollar, haggling, was a habit his never-pay-retail mother had instilled in him. He started ticking off defects on his fingers, shaking his head, and frowning. He said, "I can fix the broken stuff. For that, I get three months free."

Elaina's questioning expression turned into exaggerated, wide-eyed incredulity. He thought he saw a glimmer of fun in her eyes. Shaking her own head, she said, "Oh, no, no, no, Mr. Steve. Is impossible."

Eventually, stricken and worried, assuring him that her bosses would dock her pay and her nieces and nephews wouldn't get birthday gifts this year, she gave him the first month's rent free, as long as he allowed her into the apartment at the beginning of the following month to confirm he'd fixed all the broken stuff he said he'd repair… perhaps one evening when they'd both finished work for the day? She also said that if he carried the inoperative AC unit downstairs, he could swap it for the functional unit in the apartment he was leaving. He'd have to do all the carrying himself.

Steve held back a smile. An air conditioner and a free month's rent. He figured his coupon-clipping mother would have nodded her approval.

Pretending he didn't understand Elaina's not-so-subtle suggestions, he said it would be better if he picked up the AC unit today, while they both had free time and their agreement was fresh in their minds.

CHAPTER 2

WITH THE HANGAR doors closed and blackout blinds covering the windows, not so much as a sliver of illumination escaped the cavernous building. None of the usual lights—green taxiway lights, blue edge lights, or white runway lights—that identified an airport environment were turned on. All the overhead sodium arc lights surrounding Niger Airbase 201, such as those over the employee parking lot, were also dark. Soldiers wearing night vision gear patrolled the perimeter in Humvees, armed with .50 caliber guns. As a final precaution against curious eyes, twin razor-wire fences, both of which were electrified and alarmed, circled the airfield.

On the tarmac in front of the hangar, a drone similar in size to a Boeing 737 slowly came to life as Captain Clint Atkins remotely worked through his startup procedures. When all the pre-takeoff requirements were complete, Atkins contacted ground control. He received his instructions and, under a moonless sky, taxied to a pitch-black runway, following virtual lights projected onto the simulated windshield in front of him through the HUD, or Heads-up Guidance System.

Over thirty miles away from Niger Airbase 201 in the Nigerian city of Agadez, Atkins advanced the thrust levers. The drone under his control, serial number DSDv3-14903, more commonly known as a Diablo by the select few who knew (with certainty) of its existence, began its takeoff roll.

Heavily loaded with fuel and cargo, the Diablo needed most of the 14,000-foot runway to get airborne. Climbing through two hundred feet, Atkins engaged the autopilot. Automation flew the drone while he managed its speed, altitude, and heading using small dials on the glare shield—the Mode Control Panel—according to the air traffic controller's instructions.

Vacating 10,000 feet, the ground-based controller transferred Atkins to a controller in an Airborne Warning and Control System E-2 Hawkeye. The AWACS, with its powerful onboard radar, vectored Atkins clear of the scant traffic occupying the airspace over Central Africa. With the sky around him empty, Atkins accelerated in earnest, reaching over three times the speed of sound, some twenty minutes after takeoff.

Cruising at 50,000 feet, well above civilian traffic, the Diablo was invisible to the naked eye, even during daylight hours. The sonic-boom cone traversing the ground below the aircraft was fifty miles in circumference and weakened by terrain. Unless a person knew exactly what he was listening to, the drone's passage could easily be mistaken for the indistinct rumbling of a distant motorcycle. Had there been a country in central Africa with ground-based radar capable of tracking it, the Diablo's stealth technology made detection virtually impossible. With its transponder turned off, no airborne radar could find it. For all intents and purposes, it did not exist. Given the assignment with which it was tasked, absolute deniability was exactly what the top secret organization operating it required.

Atkins slid his chair back a couple of clicks. For the next forty-five minutes, he had only to monitor the drone's flight, ensuring everything about the complex machine's performance remained optimal. Strictly speaking, he couldn't relax, but he dropped from high-alert to a state of active monitoring. This was when people who thought they understood a professional pilot's job said, "Not much to it, is there? Turn on the autopilot. Get a coffee."

Atkins, a former Air Force captain and presently a Delta Airlines widebody captain, had quit responding to dozy remarks such as this.

After thirty-plus years in aviation, with thousands of hours of flying time as well as a degree in military history and a bachelor's degree in aeronautics, his well of patience had run dry. He'd reply brusquely. "There's more to it than that."

A decade earlier, he'd told his oldest friend that the stupidity of the average person had worn him out. He and Paul Moore were grilling strip loins at the time, lubricating their vocal cords with Pabst Blue Ribbon before upgrading to a bottle of Palm Breeze amber rum. They'd slammed rum and Coke ever since high school, long before they were of legal drinking age. Way back then, what seemed like a century ago, they got their booze from a twelfth-grade entrepreneur named Chris Angelos. Chris financed his weed habit by charging commission on the alcohol and cigarettes the less swarthy teens in Pinecrest High wanted on a Friday night, but were too young to purchase. Atkins would dump out half the Coke, refill the bottle with the newly attained Palm Breeze, and then drive the wheels off a tired sixty-nine Camaro he owned at the time, he and Paul passing the bottle back and forth between them. If Atkins managed to talk Martina Donato into the back seat (never a long or complicated negotiation), Paul drove, sipping from the bottle and pretending like nothing was happening behind him.

Atkins never made it much past second base with Martina. He never much minded. At the time, second base felt like the entire world.

Paul, who'd become a detective on the Denver City police force (a fact that amused them both, the Air Force captain and the police officer, authoritative roles they spent their youth rebelling against), understood Atkins' cynicism. Jaded as a young man and as cold and jagged as a slab of shattered Canadian Shield granite after twenty-seven years dealing with societal dregs, Paul told Atkins the most common question Joe Public Dipshit asked him was, "You ever shot anyone?" He continued, "All the possible questions a person could ask, that's the one he goes with?"

The two men had shaken their heads, bumped PBR cans, and laughed disbelievingly and without humor.

Atkins wished he could return to those golden days of simplicity.

As for tonight's flight, very few people knew about this—his second job, flying part-time for a company called Dark Sky. Had someone known and asked questions, pinching off verbal diarrhea was his only permissible choice. He'd signed a highly classified nondisclosure agreement. "Top secret" in this day and age was a questionable concept. Before he signed, Atkins had asked his recruiter, "How top secret can it possibly be?"

His recruiter, a solidly built Bostonian who introduced himself with an overly aggressive handshake but not his name, had answered, "You've got a degree in military history. Surely, you know how dark the development of the A-12 Oxcart was? Secrecy can be done." He wore blue jeans and a collared shirt, an outfit that appeared pedestrian until one looked closely and realized the shirt was tailored and the jeans were designer. He had a fastidiously trimmed goatee and a meticulously shaved head. Atkins noticed a faint ring of black and gray stubble, suggesting that the man suffered from male-pattern baldness.

The Oxcart was the CIA's version of the Blackbird SR-71. The CIA had flown the high-altitude reconnaissance airplane for years without the Air Force's knowledge, never mind the public's. Atkins knew his history. He replied with speed that bordered on disdain. "1963 was a long time ago. Today, everyone has a phone with a video camera." He was having a difficult time taking the Bostonian seriously. As a squared-away ex-air force pilot, he was highly suspicious of someone he perceived as shallow and vain. At the same time, Boston had referenced Oxcart and Top Secret in the same breath. That meant he was an individual who *had* to be taken seriously. The juxtaposition made Atkins curious. He adjusted his tone. "Who am I talking to? The CIA?"

Boston looked at him without blinking. He said nothing.

"You can neither confirm nor deny the name of your employer?"

A quick smile touched the man's mouth. Amiable and friendly, it invited Atkins to relax. Instead, his wariness ticked up a notch. After years of training with type A individuals in the civilian and military world, Atkins recognized the intensity underscoring Boston's smile; it hadn't reached the man's eyes. This was not someone with whom he should let down his guard.

After five or six long seconds, Boston wobbled his cell phone back and forth. "You're right. Everyone has access to more information than ever before." His eyes narrowed into a thoughtful squint. "Consider this: every large, really large company, is so interwoven into the public consciousness they're practically invisible. Take Verizon, for example. Imagine if it disappeared. Overnight, it's gone. People wake up one morning, and everything 'Verizon' no longer exists. Technology, infrastructure, research, so on, and so forth… all of it, gone." He moved his hands rapidly back and forth, like an umpire calling a runner safe, emphasizing his point. "Suddenly, everyone is talking about Verizon. Suddenly, everyone is paying attention. Before, as long as they had a strong Wi-Fi connection, they barely noticed the company existed. That's why Verizon advertises. To remind people they're more than four bars on a cell phone screen.

"Dark Sky's contribution is as real as Verizon's, but we work inconspicuously. Most people are sheep. As long as they have access to their social media streams, they're deaf, dumb, and blind. 'As long as my Instagram is getting likes, I don't care.' For us, that's a good thing. Dark Sky is happy to remain invisible. We *want* to remain invisible. Secrecy can be done."

Put in those terms, Atkins supposed Boston had a point. Had the public known about the creation, cost, and operation of stealth drones the size of Southwest passenger jets, they probably wouldn't have reacted with more than mild interest; shoveling unprecedented amounts of money into the military was firmly within the president's character. Paradoxically, where the money went once inside that ponderous complex was anyone's guess. Maybe the offices in the Pentagon were being redecorated in colors "guaranteed" to encourage creative thought. Maybe it went into training, maintenance, or support. Or maybe it went into the development of a new way to keep track of the nation's enemies. It had been done before. More than once.

Three decades after the Oxcart, Northrop Grumman developed the B-2 Spirit, commonly known as the Stealth Bomber. It operated for years without the public's knowledge. The B-2 became the progenitor of the B-21 Raider. With Grumman's substantial experience and knowledge at its foundation, the aerospace company went on to develop the B-28S Diablo drone. Atkins had no problem believing that a branch of the CIA had been given the responsibility of operating it. The agency's mission statement, "... conducting effective covert action as directed by the president..." meshed perfectly with a stealth drone program.

If the Diablo was a well-kept (albeit much speculated upon) secret, Dark Sky's use of it was a file so dark that it wasn't even a twinkle in the world's most fervent conspiracy theorist's eyes. Had the whack-a-doddles found a scab at which to pick, the information they discovered would have been so insignificant, their only explanation would have been the same as it had been for decades, the same as it had been when the CIA was flying the Oxcart. Blame it on UFOs, weather balloons, or the secrets hidden behind the razor wire fences surrounding Area 51.

In Agadez, Atkins sipped his coffee and watched the Primary Flight Display screen. At the speed it was traveling, his Diablo would cover the nearly 2300 nautical miles to Lusaka, Zambia, in an hour and forty minutes. The smart people at Dark Sky, those individuals with the sharpest pencils and pointiest heads, had waited for a night when the forecast indicated rain and cloud would cover the city and the winds would be calm.

The Lusaka weather was ideal when Atkins pulled the thrust levers back and, under the direction of a different AWACS Hawkeye, began his long descent. He controlled the heading, speed, and altitude and leveled out six thousand feet above the one hundred eighty square mile city. Small compared to Tokyo or New York, Lusaka was still too large for the Diablo to adequately blanket in a single pass. Atkins had therefore programed a route similar to those flown by search and rescue flights into the Flight Management Computer. Under cover of night and weather, he piloted the drone from one edge of the city to the opposite edge, did a one-eighty and backtracked, parallel to its previous course. From twenty-three hundred miles away, he monitored the drone's performance with careful eyes, as the liquid contained in five 1000-gallon bladders slowly emptied out of specially designed nozzles developed in a purpose-built R and D facility in Shenyang, China. The nozzles aerosolized the liquid. The drone's wake turbulence effectively mixed the resultant vapor into the heavy atmosphere. The poisonous blend settled at ground level soon thereafter, swathing the city's three million sleeping inhabitants.

When the bladders were empty, after a fourth and final pass, Atkins pushed the thrust levers forward and pointed the Diablo home toward Agadez.

He didn't ask the men in white hazmat suits what they'd loaded into the Diablo before it took off. He didn't ask why he'd been ordered to empty the bladders over top of one of the planet's most violent, disease-infested, and crime-ridden cities. After he landed the drone safely at Niger Airbase 201, he wouldn't hang around and watch the same men carry out an intensive and complicated decontamination procedure. He wouldn't ask because he didn't need to know. That information was *way* above his paygrade. As the humorless Bostonian with the goatee had made perfectly clear at the end of their meeting, curiosity earned men lifetime sentences in secure military prisons, and by that point, Atkins was taking the man very seriously, despite his stylistic choices.

"Consider my offer," Boston had said. He checked the time on an elaborate-looking wristwatch, pushed back from the table, and stood. "We're not hiring you to think about the mission. It's not your job to speculate. 'Why' is irrelevant. I'm hiring you to fly. Keep the ND agreement in mind."

So that's what Atkins did. As a student of history, he was familiar with the decades-old rumor suggesting that the captain of the Enola Gay, Colonel Paul Tibbets, had committed suicide after witnessing the death and destruction the atom bomb he dropped on Hiroshima had wreaked. The rumor was unmitigated bullshit, the truth much less melodramatic. Until the day Tibbets died in 2007, he viewed the assignment as his patriotic duty…

… which was exactly how Atkins chose to view his mission to Lusaka. Retired or not, much of his personal identity came from the twelve years he had spent in the United States Air Force. In his mind, carrying out his orders remained his patriotic duty. Two weeks after his Lusaka flight, he didn't believe there was any reason—no incontestable reason—to associate the flight he'd operated with the unfolding humanitarian disaster in the city. Nine hundred thousand deaths, if early reporting were to be believed.

He took the healthy signing bonus his Dark Sky employers paid him and bought a Honda Supersport motorcycle. If he rode the insanely overpowered motorcycle with more than reckless regard, it wasn't because *ordering a man not to think about a certain subject* was a surefire way to make him do just that; it was because he was a risk taker. An adrenaline junkie. A man whose years of military training had instilled in him a best-of-the-best attitude and a sense of immortality that left no room for doubt or remorse.

Twelve weeks later,
May, 2028

CHAPTER 3

IF GETTING FUCKED up is the goal, nothing rivals tequila poppers.

Steve Quinn had never heard of a tequila popper before he met the woman three stools to his right. He overheard her order a cocktail containing coriander—coriander, for fuck's sake—and grimaced when the bartender placed the drink on the coaster in front of her. Herbs and vegetables didn't make salads taste good. He couldn't see how they improved cocktails. Vegetable-based cocktails were to be avoided, including Caesars, the granddaddy of them all, although avoiding Caesars was more about spurning clam juice than an aversion to celery. He had to give Canadians and their strange cultural habits a modicum of begrudging respect. Who couldn't admire a nation that thinks…

… let's combine tomato juice, vodka, and the salty brine from inside a clam shell and see what happens…

Steve quietly asked Linda the bartender (according to the brass name plate pinned to her white button down) to repeat the name of the coriander cocktail so he'd know what to avoid in the future. Linda told him, "It's called a 'Mrs. Enough.' It's interesting and refreshing. Not an everyday drink—"

"Mrs. Enough?"

"All I do is mix them. I don't name them," Linda said. "You'd prefer another beer, I guess?"

Steve looked at the half-empty pint in front of him. He didn't need another beer, but saying "No" to Linda's cuteness was difficult. The ruby red lipstick, the curly brown hair, and the way the white button down made her appear proficient and alluring at the same time. He remembered an eighty's movie trope: an attractive but reserved young lady removes her oversized glasses and tugs out the clip controlling her hair. She straightens her posture, whips her head around, looks over her shoulder with sleepy eyes, and parted lips. Suddenly, a reserved professional has become a provocative femme fatale. A white dress shirt in a nondescript bar was probably excessive—this wasn't a Michelin restaurant in which service workers were meant to be seen and not heard—but Steve couldn't deny loving the look.

He ordered another beer.

"With or Without You" began playing on the club's sound system, U2 singing what was generally accepted as the band's best song. Steve's uncle had given him, among other things, a compact disk containing the song when he moved into a retirement home and ran out of personal space. Steve couldn't play the CD—nobody had bothered with CD players in at least thirty years—but his internal geek got a kick out of having something from a time when people owned physical items instead of storing ones and zeros in the cloud.

He was going to have to do something with his uncle's boxes as well as the boxes he'd filled with his and Tamara's second-floor possessions. The fourteenth-floor apartment wasn't a storage facility. Even for a single guy, there wasn't enough room to treat it as such. But unpacking didn't interest him much. Nothing interested him much. He'd roll into work, put in his time, and then leave at the end of the day, filled with the optimistic motivation that came from doing an interesting job among people he enjoyed. By the time he got home, the motivation had turned to ambivalence. Instead of unpacking, he'd flop into a chair and scroll through headlines on his iPad without reading the articles, or surf the television channels without watching a program from start to finish. Something had to change. Grief was fine, but how long would he allow himself to drift like garbage on the surface of a river, letting the current carry him along without purpose? Hadn't the time come to swim in a direction of his own choosing?

A female's accented voice, an appealing blend of Indian and British, interrupted the random track his thoughts had traveled down.

She said, "You questioned my cocktail of choice?"

Steve glanced left and right to ensure the woman was talking to him and then rotated ninety degrees and faced her. Head tilted, he looked at her through curious eyes, wondering why she'd joined him. Zak's wasn't busy. There were other seating choices available. Sitting in a contemplative slouch (some might have called it a morose slouch), with both hands wrapped around a pint of warm beer, didn't normally invite conversation. He said, "Pardon me?"

"You prefer a drink with more snap, crackle, and pop?"

Steve didn't think beer was a "snap, crackle, and pop" kind of drink. He supposed his other go-to, an Old-Fashioned, when he was feeling spendy, qualified. He said, "Uhm, I guess?"

The woman smiled. She showed Linda two upraised fingers. "Two tequila poppers, please." She faced Steve and offered her hand. "Paige Patel," she said.

Steve shook automatically.

"And you are?"

"Steve. Steve Quinn."

After two poppers and the remainder of his beer, Steve forgot her name. He couldn't understand why she'd sat down beside him. Or why she hadn't moved on when she recognized his gloominess. Or why she'd bought the poppers, although he considered her brilliant for introducing them to him. Since her name escaped him, he called her Hermione, on account of the British shade in her accent and the fact that he had a secret love affair with the all-grown-up Emma Watson. The trick with a name, he'd read, was to repeat it three times immediately after meeting a person, thereby cementing it in your mind. It sounded like an excellent strategy, except he only remembered the strategy after the fact. If he couldn't remember the strategy, he couldn't be expected to remember the name, could he?

She said, "How do you know I sound like Hermione?"

"My brother has six kids. My sister has four. With all those nieces and nephews, Harry Potter is pretty much the curriculum."

She said she liked the movies well enough and really enjoyed the books. She added, "I prefer Paige over Hermione, though."

"Paige," Steve said out loud. He dropped his voice to a bare whisper, "Paige, Paige, Paige."

"Paige Patel," she said, and then, "Six kids?"

"My siblings enjoy amateur piano concerts and endless dance recitals." He shuddered theatrically.

"Why?"

"Someone has to."

Paige said nothing. Possibly, she was too polite to state the obvious: nobody enjoyed amateur piano concerts and endless dance recitals, not even grandparents who were contractually forced to lie and say they did.

Because he felt like he needed to fill the silence, he said, "Do you come here often?"

Her eyes widened, and her forehead wrinkled. "Really?"

It took two or three seconds to realize he'd inadvertently used a tired old pickup line. Embarrassed, heat rushed up his neck, burning the tops of his ears. He stuttered something about living nearby and stammered something about having never seen her in Zak's before. Finally, he threw in the towel and settled on, "The classics never die."

"Sometimes they should."

Steve laughed, surprising himself. He couldn't remember laughing in several weeks. Some of the tension left his muscles. The world took on a soft-focus cast, much different and more welcoming than the dark listlessness of earlier. The good feeling made the conversation that followed easy.

Paige asked about his job.

He said, "I work for a company that builds fluid management systems."

"Okay," she said, drawing the word out and turning it into a question.

"We designed a system that automatically transfers ocean water in and out of ballast tanks inside container ships. It keeps the ships balanced in constantly changing conditions. There's more to it than a few strategically placed gyroscopes and floats that turn pumps on and off."

This was the point when most people nodded politely, mumbled, "Interesting," and then changed the subject. Paige, however, did not turn away or cross her arms. Her dark eyes seemed curious. Encouraged, he said, "Most recently, I spent my time working on a project for Northrop Grumman."

She raised her eyebrows and swiveled to face him more directly. "The aerospace company?"

He answered with a nod. "A few years ago, they hired us to build the hydraulic and fuel systems for a new aircraft. Supposedly for the US Air Force. Although, that's a guess. Nobody knows for sure." The downstream customer was one of several mysteries surrounding the subcontract, including how CompuTech had landed such a lucrative deal in the first place. Rumor was, key personnel had attended university together. They had downed pitchers of draft in the same pubs and threw darts at the same dartboard. The job specifications were also unusual. For no elucidated reason, Grumman wanted a fluid delivery system incorporated into the new aircraft, similar in principle to what small crop dusters and large water-bombers utilized. Steve was as curious as everyone else who had speculated around the CompuTech water cooler. Ultimately, however, the answers were irrelevant. The contract paid his rent. That was all that mattered.

Paige continued to appear interested, so Steve kept going, telling her about noteworthy projects and answering her questions. She appeared to lose interest when he said, "Another team is working on a system that processes raw sewage into something that can be safely exhausted into the ocean. If a few more coastal cities bought our tech, maybe one or two of the ocean's species wouldn't be extinct."

She broke eye contact and stared into the bottom of her glass, apparently finding something more thought-provoking than politically correct chatter in its depths. Belatedly, he realized he'd killed the conversation. Discussing human effluent with a complete stranger was akin to pounding an oaken stake through a vampire's heart.

Embarrassed once more, he let his gaze roam from the ceiling tiles to the empty tables to the darkened stage. He shifted his weight from side to side. The silence grew heavy. Finally, he said limply, "If fluid management is required, CompuTech is an interested bidder." Then, in a desperate rush, he asked, "What do you do?" He didn't particularly care—he didn't know her—but anything she said *had* to be more enjoyable than the excruciating silence.

CHAPTER 4

PAIGE SAID SHE attended LSE in London, majoring in political science. He asked what kind of employment opportunities an education like that got her. Without elaborating on how she ended up in the Pacific Northwest after living in England, she answered, "I work in the HR department for a tech company. Boring stuff to everyone but me."

Steve wasn't sure about that statement. He worked for a tech company, too. Different department for sure, but there'd be some common ground. He said nothing. *Boring to everyone but me* implied an unwillingness to discuss specifics. He sipped his beer, listening as she described her life and asking questions when it was expected of him. He laughed when she leaned hard on the Indian part of her accent in order to make a point. She said her mother used to sound that way when her children started working her last nerve. Despite having traveled extensively with her job, she'd never been to Mumbai or Delhi, or anywhere else on the Indian continent. When he asked why, Paige laughed and said in her mother's heavy accent, "There's nothing there for me," which seemed to be the general consensus of anyone who'd been to India, including a great number of Indians.

A plump Indian girl with huge black eyes and skin, the color of a creamy café mocha, Paige didn't look anything like Hermione of the movies or the novels. She wore her hair in the same messy bun as Meghan Markle did, back when the Duchess of Sussex was a younger woman. She had a gold ring in her left nostril. Usually, when he saw something like that, Steve wondered what kind of statement the person was trying to make. With Paige, the ring was as noticeable as a tiny pair of stud earrings, which was to say, hardly at all. Her perfectly straight posture was much more interesting. Weird thing to notice, but the arrow-straight manner in which she held herself made her scoop-neck T-shirt cling to her in all kinds of tantalizing ways. It also showed off a soft roll around her waist, what kids called a muffin top. She wore a filmy, billowy skirt that ended at her shins. When she crossed one leg over the other, Steve saw a kick-ass pair of high-heeled boots. A spark of interest ran up and down his spine. He liked a lady who wore high-heeled boots with a skirt…

Or a dress.

Or pants.

Or shorts.

Or nothing at all.

Once, when Tamara and he were getting busy, before the accident took her away from him, he asked her to put her boots back on after he slid her undies off. That was the worst thing about high-heeled boots. Maneuvering a filmy scrap of silk past a pair of boots was delicate work, if a guy was being careful and doing his best not to rip them. The last time he asked, Tamara rolled her eyes and said, "Oh for… How 'bout I don't wear underwear? Would that be easier for you?"

"Is that an option?" Steve asked, excited. "If it is, then, fuck yeah it would be!"

Tamara was the shit. He missed her like a drowning man misses oxygen.

"Separate Ways" by Journey played unobtrusively in the background, another majestic ballad that sounded as smooth and thought-provoking as an aged red wine or a vintage single malt. The lights in Zak's dimmed, and the bar grew considerably darker. Although the music didn't rise in volume, they moved closer together to hear each other better. Tamara was never far from his thoughts, but after two pints and three poppers, her memory had taken a blessed step into the background. He wasn't seeking company when he stepped out for a drink, but Paige was doing a welcome job in that role. Since switching apartments, he hadn't enjoyed much in the way of companionship, other than his second-floor neighbors, and that community had happened slowly.

One day, in front of the mailboxes, a guy nodded at him, raised the Home Depot bag he was carrying, and grumbled, "Probably have to wait two months for the Super to install it."

Steve looked in the bag, saw a garburator and answered without thought, "Nothing to it. I could have it hooked up in an hour." Basic small talk, in other words, but Lorne Ramsey's eyes widened behind his black rimmed glasses. He adjusted the brim of his suede driving cap. In the lobby's cracked mirror, it appeared as though two men with hopeful white-whiskered faces were standing at the foot of the stairs with Steve.

Ramsey said, "Really?"

Steve realized he'd unwittingly volunteered his time and skills. "Really," he said. "Saturday morning, if you want?"

A day or two after he installed the garburator, Ramsey bought him a thank-you bottle of bourbon. He must have told Jamie Clark in 207 about Steve's help, because Clark knocked on Steve's door and asked—if it wouldn't be too much trouble—could Steve help him mount some ornamental curtain rods? His wife wanted to hang new curtains, but after recent bypass surgery, the doctor had forbidden Clark from doing any heavy lifting. Clark's wife thanked Steve with a huge pan of lasagna, which he and Tamara enjoyed for several nights in a row.

Concerned about roving bands of rapists, Maria Bell in 216 asked him to install a heavy-duty security chain. Steve said he'd never heard about roving bands of rapists, not on TV or online news feeds. Maria countered in her airy voice, "Goodness gracious, Steve. You need to pay more attention. The mainstream media…" She shook her head.

The frown lines on her forehead deepened. "I'll give you a website or two. They tell the truth." With bushy graying hair that had never seen a brush, oversized multi-colored clothes, and intensely fierce eyes, Steve thought Maria would have scared potential rapists away had they happened to get too close.

He installed the security chain at waist height, telling her that if an intruder tried breaking in, he'd expect to see the chain at eye level where they were normally attached. If he didn't see it, he'd probably try to push the door all the way open. It would come to a loud and unexpected stop. That noise was a warning. It bought a person time.

"In this city, an intelligent intruder would know enough to run. If he didn't," Steve said, looking up at Maria from where he kneeled, winding in the last screw, "the next thing he'd see in my place would be three bright lights. Two muzzle flashes when I gave him a twelve-gauge double tap. After that, heaven's white glow." He shrugged. "Or the red fires of hell."

Maria said, "Goodness gracious, Steve." In heavy thought, she tapped pursed lips with an index finger. Then she whipped a nine-millimeter Ruger out of the cutlery drawer beside her oven and said, "This will do, right?"

Steve winced and ducked as she waved the weapon in the air, sweeping the room from right to left with the barrel.

A week later, Maria presented Tamara with an extravagant flower arrangement.

"What did *you* do?" Steve asked. "I installed the chain."

With her nose buried in the bouquet, Tamara answered, "Poor, poor hard-done-by you."

When he moved to the fourteenth floor, Steve told his new friends that he wouldn't be far away. Eleven floors up, is all. Text if they needed him. But the first time he pulled the apartment door closed on the fourteenth, he realized he was a stranger in a new neighborhood and even more alone than he'd been on the second floor after Tamara's death.

Somewhere around popper number four, his body stopped processing the tequila. He began re-thinking the genius of the drink. He ordered another round.

The conversation degraded.

He said, "I'd have an exotic car in the garage. Something stupid fast."

"If I was super rich, I wouldn't bother with a car. I'd go everywhere in a helicopter." Paige paused. "I'd want a place with a view, wouldn't I? You know, for the thirteen days a year it stops raining in this part of the world."

"It rains a ton in Gotham, too. I'd move there, if I could."

"A panoramic view is mandatory in the Pacific Northwest. The mountains are there for a reason."

"Why does it rain so much in Gotham? Gotham is on the East Coast. Every picture I've ever seen—"

Paige held up a palm. She looked confused. "What are you on about?"

"I'd live in Gotham. Despite the rain."

"Gotham isn't real."

"In a different world, New York City would be called Gotham. You know, if there was a multiverse." He leaned in, and stage whispered, "Batman wouldn't be a comic book hero. He'd be real! I'd know his secret." He pressed his index finger on his lips.

Paige said, "Okay, Sweet Pea," and patted his hand.

Despite his drunken state, Steve didn't think she was mocking him. She'd spoken thoughtfully, giving him the impression that the "secret" was valid with her. Later, he'd have to acknowledge that the Batman bit was not what she keyed on, but rather, his statement about a multiverse.

After the fifth popper, Paige's eyelids started drooping. Her accented voice became slurry. Steve was no longer capable of paying attention to anything she said. He liked the idea of inviting her back to his apartment, but the fact was, the mechanics would never work. Puking and sleeping had risen to the top of his priority list. Both sounded like more fun than sex.

An old song played on Zak's sound system, burrowed in and took hold...

A-weema-weh.

Hardly classic rock, but memorable all the same.

Even if the mechanics hadn't been questionable, Steve wouldn't have invited her home. Three towers of unpacked boxes from the two-bedroom lined one wall of the new apartment. Leaning against the boxes were a row of framed photographs and prints he hadn't bothered hanging. Short stacks of books, acting as end tables, supported a collection of unwashed dishes. A damp, funky smell oozed off the bath towel, even when it was fully dry. He hadn't used Scrubbing Bubbles in the shower in two weeks, hadn't changed the bed sheets in three. Half the time he fell asleep in front of the television, beneath a blanket that never left the sofa. He was storing dirty clothes on the floor rather than in the laundry basket he'd used as an extra moving box.

Among this apathetic landscape were his uncle's treasures. Filled with an eclectic mix of CDs, DVDs, magazines, comic books, and photographs, these boxes were stacked carelessly against a different wall. One box contained an unopened bottle of mezcal. His uncle brought it home after a drunken week in Cancun in the eighties. Famous for the fuzzy, segmented worm floating forever in the amber liquid, he considered the tequila an interesting keepsake. "No way I'd drink the stuff," he said. "Probably taste like burning piss."

He'd bequeathed Steve a small amount of cash, as a reward for his interest in his "collectibles," and written in his will, "At least you pretended. Would it have killed the other nieces and nephews to throw me a thumbs-up on Facebook? A heart on Instagram?" Steve was grateful for the cash and was learning to appreciate the memorabilia, but the result of all the trash was an apartment that looked like the inside of a dumpster. He didn't want Paige to see it, which surprised him. He hadn't cared for several months.

A-weema-weh,
A-weema-weh.

The empty glasses on the bar orbited in gentle clockwise ellipses. Blinking rapidly, he swayed in the opposite direction, in an impossible effort to counteract their motion. He said in a distant-sounding voice, "It's time to go." He stood, staggered, caught himself on the edge of the bar and thought inanely, *good thing I'm not driving. I shouldn't even be walking.* He was way more hammered than he realized before he stood up.

"I think you're right," Paige answered. She asked Linda for a glass of water. While she waited for it, she opened her purse, took out a pill bottle, and shook a red gel cap into her hand.

"What's that?" Steve asked.

"Hangover helper."

"Does it taste like noodles and ground beef?"

It took her a second to process the pun and then they both laughed manically, the way drunks do when even the weakest joke seems hysterical. Scientists say the line between genius and madness is thin. That was probably true. Every day, Steve felt as though hysterical laughter was only a breath away from unrestrained despair. Hysterical laughter felt good.

Paige dried the watery corners of her eyes with the side of a finger. "It doesn't taste like anything."

"Does it work?"

"I don't know, do I? A friend gave them to me. They're supposed to help clear the fog, so-to-speak. Gatorade and aspirin are probably more helpful, but at this point, I'm willing to give it a try. Want one?"

Two pints and five tequila poppers?

"Hell, yeah," Steve said, already knowing the hangover would be demonic. Hoping she was right, he held out a cupped palm and took a chance on the red pill.

CHAPTER 5

THE BOEING 787 was seconds from landing. Nose high, wings level, landing gear extended. Nothing indicated that the aircraft's final few seconds of flight were in peril. The main wheels touched the asphalt with twin squawks and puffs of blue smoke. The nose wheel touched down a moment later. With almost two miles of runway in front of it, the widebody had plenty of room to slow to a manageable taxi speed...

... but suddenly, impossibly, the runway shrank to half its former length. Then it shrank again. Instead of shoving both thrust levers fully forward for maximum power and going around, the captain slammed on the brakes and pulled full reverse thrust. For a panicked piece of a second, passengers flew forward in their seats before their seatbelts snatched them back with gut-punching force. Under aggressive braking, the tires burst with loud rapid-fire explosions. Without rubber tires, the aluminum alloy wheels scraped the runway surface, slewing the cumbersome widebody sideways. A storm of phosphorous yellow sparks trailed behind the wings. The screams of terrified passengers and the screech of rending metal performed a discordant symphony. The end of the runway filled Captain Clint Atkins' vision and then disappeared as the airplane careened off the asphalt surface, wiping out the lead-in lights at the runway's threshold. The engine nacelles and landing gear carved trenches into the earth, flinging soil, vegetation, and debris into the air. The Boeing continued its uncontrolled slide down a steep ravine several hundred feet past the end of the runway. Orange flames licked out the top of one wing. A plume of smoke stained the blue sky a sooty black. The reek of melting plastic filled the morning air.

Covered in a slick layer of nervous sweat, Atkins awoke with a jerk, as he always did when the aircraft he was piloting in his dream crashed. The blankets were a tangle around his feet. His heart stuttered high in his chest. His breath came in shallow dry pants that did little to reoxygenate his blood. He cursed softly, knowing that his traitorous mind would keep him awake for the rest of the night. Four rum and cokes on the flight from Frankfurt to Agadez, plus the bottle of duty-free Bacardi Anejo Cuatro he'd bought on the stopover (some of which he had tipped back before bed), had helped him fall asleep. Regrettably, the alcohol hadn't done anything to help him stay asleep. Nor had it blunted the dreams.

He switched on the bedside lamp, swung his legs out of the bed, and planted his feet on the floor. Elbows on his knees, face in his hands, he closed his eyes and focused on inhaling slowly and deeply, in through his nose, out of his mouth. He'd dated a teacher for a short time, a looker with red hair, an adventurous streak, and a sarcastic sense of humor. She had two little dogs, yappy pull-cord-toys that, unfortunately, she liked more than she liked him. During the August they spent together, a few weeks before the new school year began, she'd awakened several times dreaming about an exam hall filled with hundreds of students, knowing she hadn't studied and was about to write a test she'd surely fail.

Most people experienced stress dreams at one time or another, but not Atkins. Not anymore. Not since his early days in the Air Force, when the pressure of intense training, impossibly short time frames, and the judgment of instructors with little interest in his success or failure had all conspired to wash him out of the program. Now, years later, the dreams had returned with all their confidence-draining, soul-shattering insidiousness. The cause didn't require any psychobabble.

He was back in Agadez. His fourth Dark Sky mission was planned for the following night. He knew exactly what would happen after he piloted his Diablo over another African city…

… hundreds of thousands of people would die. Feverish and delirious, aching deep in every muscle and joint, they'd drown in the phlegm filling their lungs. The World Health Organization would make statements seemingly designed to terrify rather than calm. The locusts in the media would gravely devour the story, while secretly hoping the crimson chyron on the bottom of the television monitor continued counting the dead. Unsurprisingly, the story the locusts would tell with such manufactured concern would draw parallels between the dying African cities of today and the Covid-19 crisis of 2020.

As with most people whose lives cartwheeled into chaos, Atkins hadn't forgotten the misery of the pandemic, the lockdowns, the job losses, the economic devastation, and attacks upon personal freedoms the sanctimonious politicians deemed necessary for the greater good. Unlike many, however, Atkins didn't waste time deluding himself with foolish statements, such as, "It wasn't that bad." 2020 was every bit "that bad," so when the media started reporting on a fresh new horror in Lusaka, Atkins found his thumb glued to the television remote, cycling between CNN, Fox News, and BBC, hoping against hope that a new pandemic wasn't beginning. Hoping against hope the mistakes the people "in charge" made in 2020 wouldn't repeat themselves. Logically, his interest held an additional element of curiosity. He found it morbidly coincidental that Lusaka was the first city attacked by the new flu-like virus mere days after his first flight for Dark Sky.

After two more missions, one to Luanda, Angola, and another to Harare, Zimbabwe, he could no longer claim coincidence between the flights he operated and the unfolding humanitarian catastrophes. Whatever was in the Diablo's bladders was responsible for the suffering and death of untold millions. This knowledge was a peculiar relief. The world did not appear to be on the cusp of a devastating new pandemic. It was also an unimaginable nightmare. The patriotic statement that

I was just doing my job was no longer valid. Lusaka wasn't Hiroshima. Paul Tibbets may have considered the A-bomb his patriotic duty, but the African cities Atkins dosed with the Diablo weren't major players in a world at war.

The stress dreams began after his third flight. Not content to accept them, Atkins dug in. He started looking for answers, for cause and effect, for everything the bald Bostonian with the goatee and oversized wristwatch explicitly warned him against. Before long, Atkins knew everything there was to know, and in his own mind at least, he'd turned that which he didn't know (the vagaries and coincidences) into certainties.

Despite persistent rumors and much anecdotal fact, Western epidemiologists and virologists were never able to conclusively determine if the Covid-19 pandemic had been concocted in a lab. Wuhan scientists were never forced to confirm the West's suspicions, nor were they held accountable by the Chinese government. Whenever foreigners raised the issue, Chinese leaders reacted in their favorite time-honored manner: they pretended to be grievously offended and then loudly accused the West of racist paranoia.

Inside the secretive country, the regime's reaction to what was generally considered fact, took a two-pronged approach.

First, in true Chinese tradition, the government tightened the flow of information leaving the country. Most world leaders assumed the Chinese president knew about Covid-19, authorizing not only its development but also its release into the world. Other, more naive leaders, such as the woefully unqualified Canadian Prime Minister, an individual who openly admired the Chinese dictatorship, chose to believe Xi Jinping's claimed ignorance. Either way, information out of China became too scarce to form irrefutable conclusions, thanks to Beijing's aggressive media control.

Second, in response to a crisis they denied creating, and in a futile effort to show the world they were treating the situation seriously, the Chinese government overreacted spectacularly. They initially quarantined their citizens for over two months and subsequently made aggressive public shows of containment and cleanliness (complete with hazmat suits and face shields) whenever international cameras were filming, or when foreigners such as air-crew members or businessmen were present.

These heavy-handed measures effectively redirected the world's attention, concealing the small, well-funded circle of scientists in Wuhan tasked with synthesizing the respiratory disease, *not to find a vaccine as is typical but rather to make it more potent.* Releasing Covid-19 into the world provided the team with the real-world data they needed. However, to fulfill their mandate, drastic improvements were required.

The benefactors who supplied the money and, therefore, got to issue the orders—the unknown "they" who issued the mandate—wanted a virus that killed more efficiently and died more quickly than Covid-19. They did not want it to create another unnecessary global pandemic similar to 2020. The social and economic fallout was far too unpredictable.

The Wuhan scientists worked tirelessly. In 2025, when the mortality rate of Covid-19 nudged sixty-five percent (in a controlled environment), and the transmission rate dropped to less than two percent, they declared the reengineered virus ready. Ready for what? None dared ask. Nobody in the lab wanted to suffer the same fate as the Chinese whistleblower who made "false comments on the internet" and who, although young and healthy, allegedly succumbed to the virus in February 2020. Much like the individuals involved with the Manhattan Project in the forties, the Wuhan scientists assumed they'd developed a weapon. They agreed the use of the weapon was somebody else's concern. They'd achieved (however morally questionable) success.

Mass-producing Covid-25, as the new virus was creatively named, was only a matter of time. Figuring out how to store and deliver it in large quantities before its half-life rendered it ineffective was a more complicated process. Covid-25 was renamed Covid-28 three years later, when scientists perfected a means of enveloping fragile

Covid molecules inside a protective barrier that remained intact when suspended in a proprietary mixture of temperature-controlled water and chemicals. When the temperature changed and the liquid passed through nozzles designed to aerosolize it, the Covid-28 virus survival rate dropped to as little as four hours, depending on a variety of external factors, including UV exposure and atmospheric pollutants. Given the safe harbor of the human respiratory system and the high mortality rate, four hours were deemed long enough. It only took minutes to fall from six thousand feet, settle at ground level, and, like a silent black mamba, strike anybody in its path.

Western scientists realized within weeks that the virus killing the cities of Lusaka, Luanda, and Harare was a Covid-19 hybrid—after 2020, they had a great deal of knowledge and intel on which to draw—but Covid-28 acted much differently than its predecessor. Although Covid-19 traveled between humans with relative ease, the death rate was minimal on a global scale, despite the media's voyeuristic reporting and what the politicians wanted the public to believe. Covid-28 reacted in exactly the opposite manner.

Outside the perfect incubator that was the human body, the virus died so quickly that transmissibility remained low. If a person caught it, however, the chances of dying rose to a shocking thirty percent. In affluent areas, where professional healthcare workers were readily available, that number dropped a few percentage points. It rose precipitously in African slums and shanty towns where people lived in close proximity, where medical resources were scarce and where sanitation was negligible.

Most of these facts read like Hollywood fiction, but Clint Atkins had no problem believing them. After all, China was a country that painted stripes on donkeys and assured everyone who visited the zoos that they were looking at zebras. He remained mystified as to China's involvement in the mass euthanasia project; how did a sub agency of the CIA and a communist country align? He suspected Dark Sky was a much larger entity than the bald Bostonian had alluded to. He would never learn the full truth of Covid-19 nor discover why African cities were deliberately being poisoned with the improved version, Covid-28.

Neither did Atkins know—couldn't know—that forty-three minutes into his fourth mission, with thousands of miles to fly before he reached the city of Cazenga, a silicon chip would fail inside the Diablo he was piloting. Perhaps a less than perfectly pure grain of sand had been used in the manufacturing process. Perhaps a technician sneezed at a crucial moment during the aircraft's construction. Perhaps failure is inherent in a fragile world. Drone DSDv3-14903 was far more technically advanced than the first unmanned aerial vehicle used in a targeted killing, but, ultimately, it was still subject to the same vagaries as all man-made devices. The defective chip would allow a random, unexplainable electrical surge to overload a resistor within a solid-state black box, which in turn would melt a conduit many times thinner than a strand of dental floss. In the city of Agadez, inside the drone's flight deck, a red LED would begin flashing. An aural warning would sound. Despite all of Atkin's considerable experience and skills, he'd be unable to salvage the situation. His Diablo would crash in the vast Congo Rainforest, disappearing in an area that covered 264 million acres.

But that which Atkins didn't know, didn't concern him. When he sat down in his pilot's chair, the niggling Bacardi hangover was gone. The stress dream was nothing but a dim, uncomfortable memory. The former Air Force captain, now a widebody captain at one of the world's premier airlines, had a job to do. He prepared his Diablo for takeoff as conscientiously and professionally as he always did, as he'd been imprinted to do through years of second-to-none training, while deep in the back of his mind, he wondered how quickly he could escape Africa. He'd take a head-clearing leave of absence from the airline and go for a long, hard ride on the Honda Supersport.

Maybe he'd journey west into the mountains, leave Denver early and beat traffic through the Bruce Blainey Memorial Tunnel, and then push on, all the way to Las Vegas. Maybe he'd blow a month's wages on a Bellagio baccarat table with an escort named Brandi, and a bottle of Mount Gay. Maybe he'd suffocate his burgeoning guilt and self-loathing with the immoral sins considered ubiquitous in Vegas. Afterward, he could ride south through Albuquerque and then loop home from there, north, all the way to Denver. Or maybe he'd keep going, keep putting time and distance behind him. He'd figure it out. The Supersport wasn't a touring motorcycle. Atkins didn't care. He wasn't looking for a relaxing, leisurely cruise. He wasn't going sightseeing. He needed a distraction. On a bike as outrageously fast as the Supersport, when you're weaving through oncoming traffic, when you're accelerating through one hundred-sixty miles per hour, or leaning into a corner with your knee an inch off the ground, praying a scrap of rubber from a trucker's blown tire isn't lying on the road, or a mule deer doesn't dance out of the brush in front of you, concentration is paramount. There's no time to think about how, although you may not be the root cause of millions of deaths, you are the vector. There's no time to think about how nothing can be done to fix the situation. There's definitely no time to think about how your only option is to keep your mouth shut and cash your paycheck.

CHAPTER 6

STEVE AND PAIGE walked out of Zak's side by side, with a magical, anticipatory tingle jumping back and forth between their loosely linked fingers. They paused on the wide concrete step that led from the bar down to the sidewalk, enjoying the deceptive feeling of sobriety the fresh May temperature and physical movement brought about. Paige did a slow, right-to-left scan, possibly to get her bearings but more likely, as a way of deciding where the evening was going next: her place or his.

Steve put the question to bed, asking her, "Can I call you an Uber? A cab?" He couldn't have claimed with complete assurance that she would have come home with him had he invited her, but given the flash of surprise on her face and the way her eyes widened, he was positive she expected him to ask. Her surprise was flattering. Everyone enjoyed the occasional ego bump. This one came at the right time. When a nine-year relationship has ended abruptly and with finality, no matter the circumstances, a guy tended to ask questions of the universe, including whether or not he could still be attractive and appealing to someone new. He wasn't blind to the unlikely spark that had flickered to life between them. Knowing she felt it too, was gratifying.

In answer to her surprise, he asked, "Have you ever seen *True Blood*?"

She shook her head. "What is it?"

"A TV show about vampires. Came out in the late 2000s. It has a good theme song. *Bad Things*." In a voice that wouldn't win him any talent contests (nor make people wince and dogs howl), he sang a couple of lines.

When he finished, Paige nibbled her lower lip and then said in her deliciously blended accent, "You want to do bad things with me?"

"Do I ever. Just not tonight."

Paige gave him a full-body hug, the kind that fills in a body's curves, dips, and hollows. The kind that makes a promise. She said, "The Metro is fine. It's not raining, for once. We can walk."

"You sure?" he asked, scratching his cheek, already mapping the simplest way to the closest stop, and how to best circumnavigate the vacant alley even the street denizens chose to avoid. If he and Paige stayed on the opposite side of the road, they could walk past the alley and circle left, around an abandoned warehouse, back to the street where the Metro was located. They'd end up walking an extra city block—maybe a little more. The route would take them past a crumbling sort of shanty town on the dark side of the street, and the four or five individuals his deceased grandmother would have labeled "Toughs" who called it home. He didn't think they were dangerous. However, he preferred not to put his belief to the test.

His grandmother's memory put a lump in Steve's throat as it always did. She used to try out words like "Toughs" in an effort to better relate with her grandson. He'd shake his head, slightly embarrassed on her behalf. Back then, he thought she sounded silly. As time passed, embarrassment became guilt. Today, he would have listened to her say funny words all day long, if he could have wrapped her in his arms and kissed her powdery cheeks one more time. He missed her that much.

A-weema-weh.

A-weema-weh.

In the jungle...

As good a song as "Bad Things" was, it couldn't kill an earworm like "The Lion Sleeps Tonight."

They walked side by side, in a more or less straight line, coming together, bumping shoulders and hips, moving apart, singing in decent enough harmony, Paige doing a better job with the high notes than Steve.

A yellow labrador retriever with dirty patches of skin showing through his mangy coat appeared out of the shadows. It crabbed along beside them in a sideways trot, snuffling the sidewalk with its snout in a relentless, hopeful arc, seeming to enjoy the company of people who were happy together rather than having to avoid bored kids throwing rocks. His rack of ribs shone in the overhead streetlight like a row of worn piano keys. Steve slowed, bent, and gave the lab a scratch between the ears. Tongue lolling happily out the side of his mouth, the dog looked over its shoulder with what Steve imagined was a contented grin. He said, "What's your name, dog? Going to have to give you a name."

A denizen with matted gray hair, a curiously well-trimmed beard, and a useless bundle of multicolored string attached to his belt loop materialized out of nowhere with an outstretched hand. Steve gave him the loose change in his pocket, and the denizen faded back to wherever it was he'd come from. Steve felt worse for the yellow lab than for the streety. After hassling pedestrians all day, the denizen would end up with coffee and a burger for supper. The hungry dog would have nothing but high expectations.

On the other side of the street, the Tough's shanties came into view. A mismatched collection of scarred aluminum siding, wooden pallets, and tattered weather-worn tarpaulins formed the walls and roofs. Wind-blown garbage had piled up against what would have been the footings of a real house. The structures were held in precarious place by remnants of frayed rope and treadless tires. The Toughs, dressed in dirty jeans and worn hoodies, stood around a fire contained in a large metal barrel. They watched Steve and Paige approach through hooded eyes. One of them, with the brim of his ball cap sticking out from beneath his hoodie, yelled, "Shut up," with something like exasperation in his voice.

Steve yelled back, "The lion sleeps tonight," before dissolving into another bout of hysterical laughter.

If getting fucked up is the goal, nothing rivals tequila poppers.

With the Toughs behind them and the yellow dog padding amiably beside them (Steve said, "Looks like I made a friend," and Paige laughed and said, "Looks like"), they reached the point where they had to decide: circle the block or cut through the alley. The abandoned warehouse towered over the alley's open mouth like some kind of prehistoric predator. Smashed upper windows and boarded-over lower windows glowered a warning at them. Steam exhaled from a subway grate. From deep underground, the sound of an approaching train rose, peaked, and fell, the rumble making him imagine the alley was alive and clearing its throat.

Paige nodded down the alley. "That way."

"The long way around," he countered.

"Look at my boots. I don't care what the song says. These *ain't* made for walking."

The reference made him like her a little more than he had a second before. His resolve slipped. He said with reluctance, "I guess." He didn't move.

He'd made a habit of avoiding the alley and the inexplicable malevolence it emitted, although how an alley could be malevolent was beyond him. All he knew for certain was that the closer he got, the worse he felt. It was more than unease, more than instinct, or an actor saying, "I've got a bad feeling about this." Once, when he'd stopped and stared into the alley's mouth in an effort to identify what was so repellent, his mouth had gone dry, and his eyes began watering. Gooseflesh had rippled his arms. His stomach had rolled in sluggish waves, forcing pebbles of oily sweat to bead on his forehead and sheet the small of his back. He'd seen nothing unusual. Just empty beer cans and grease-stained takeaway cartons, a battered dumpster tight against a pollution-black wall, and a rusty, long-forgotten shopping cart.

Except when he was being completely honest with himself, "nothing" wasn't accurate.

On a different occasion, at the height of a rare, sun-filled day when shadows were all but impossible, he'd spotted a rectangle of shimmering darkness halfway down the alley. Unlike a luminous mirage lying across a desert highway, this mirage stood vertically. To his moist eyes, it resembled a jagged door, a broken remnant from a condemned building. His knees had weakened, and the familiar sick feeling filled the pit of his stomach. Clutching a nearby light standard, bent at the waist and sweating something sour, he'd jammed the heel of his hand between his teeth, stopping himself from puking in the gutter. When his liquid gaze returned to the alley, whatever he'd seen was gone.

Ever since, he'd steered a wide berth around the alley.

"What?" Paige asked. "What's the matter?"

"Nothing," Steve said warily. The malevolent force that insisted he hurry past all those many times before was quiet.

"Come on, then," she said. She clutched his arm with both hands. "Let's go."

He sighed, checked for crossing traffic and then side-by-side, they J walked across the street. At the entrance to the alley, the dog whined. He cast a sad, disapproving look at them across the arch of his rounded back, and then, with his tail tucked firmly between his legs, he shambled away.

Telling himself everything would be all right, Steve stepped into the alley. A pool of broken glass crunched under the soles of his sneakers, reminding him of the roaches he crushed with his toe when they skittered out from behind a baseboard in his scabby apartment. Blocked by the warehouse on one side and a tall cinder block wall on the other, the light from the street behind them disappeared. From the street at the distant end of the alley, a sick yellow glow bounced off serrated shards of glass in the upper windows, highlighting them like shattered, spit-shiny teeth. Long forgotten and never used, the dumpster didn't stink. The gutter paralleling the warehouse, on the other hand, emitted the mingled stench of rotted food and urine, possibly the waste left over from the Tough's little community. Steve didn't think anyone would dare live in the warehouse, but with every step, the boarded-over windows felt more and more like hungry eyes. He lengthened his stride.

Ninety seconds after entering the alley, he and Paige walked out the other side. The malice that usually gnawed the back of his brain and the churning sickness he expected never came. Relieved, he shoulder-checked, expecting… what?

The alley remained empty. Nothing evil had materialized out of a shimmering rectangular patch or oozed out from beneath a locked door. Nothing flitted along behind them, from shadow to shadow, waiting to pounce. He shook his head at his own foolish fear, halfway annoyed the alley hadn't done something to prove him right.

With Paige snuggling his arm and humming contentedly, they turned left. Half a block later, they stopped and embraced outside the well-lit entrance to the Metro station. She broke the hug, stepped onto the escalator, and gave him a wave as she descended into the depths of the station. An unexpected sense of loss struck him, making his next several breaths shallow and ragged. He was about to call her name, but she stepped off the escalator, turned a corner, and disappeared without looking back. The sudden sense of loss became more profound. How could he miss someone so much whom he knew so little? They'd enjoyed a spontaneous evening. They'd made a connection. His intent ended there; there was no road forward for them. Asking for her number was pointless. He wouldn't have followed through. He liked her too much to waste her time that way, and Tamara was too close. Still, he had a feeling he'd remember her for a long time to come, particularly the last thirty seconds, as the escalator carried her away from him.

CHAPTER 7

STEVE TURNED TOWARD his apartment. Now that he was no longer concentrating on good behavior for Paige's benefit, he weaved a crooked route along the sidewalk, tonelessly singing "The Lion Sleeps Tonight" for no other reason than the need to concentrate on something other than his roiling stomach and the way his brain sloshed from side to side in a shallow pool of tequila.

Returning home from the Metro station meant approaching his apartment building from the back. He could have walked all the way around to the front door and entered the building through the lobby. Instead, he took the shortest route possible, and chose the lower-level fire exit at the rear, near three leaking dumpsters lining the outside wall. Strangely, their stench didn't assault his senses like it normally did; typically, it caught in the back of his throat and made his eyes water. He enjoyed the difference but didn't spend time thinking about it. He stabbed his key into the door lock, keeping a foggy eye out for the curious rat who lived beneath one of the dumpsters. He didn't spot the furry little freak peeking out at him from its pebble-black eyes, like it often did when he returned home. This late at night, it was probably tucked away, as snug as a rodent in a rug.

He laughed quietly as he pulled open the door; *rodent in a rug.*

Once inside the building, he thumbed the elevator's Up button. During off-peak times, when the need for the elevator was small, it operated marginally faster than usual. Tonight, he was in luck. The doors slid open without delay, as if the elevator was waiting for him. He selected his floor, leaned back against the mirrored wall and closed his eyes, dreading the psychological and physical pain the morning would bring. Tamara's death struck hardest in the mornings. The mammoth hangover that would attack with the rising sun would make her loss feel much, much worse. The pain usually faded throughout the middle of the day because work was a place he didn't associate with her, and his job required concentration. Alone in the evenings, her absence hit him with Tyson-sized combinations.

That's when his heart felt like a wrung-out facecloth.

If the sun always shone and the flowers always blossomed, Steve would have described his job as the one positive in his life. As he had explained to Paige, he did interesting work for adequate wages at a company called CompuTech. Not a bell-ringing endorsement, but he'd come to believe that most jobs were, if not pointless, then at least unimportant compared to most other things in life. And if a guy had to do interesting work for adequate wages, it was nice doing it in the company of people he enjoyed. Tomorrow, when he left two hours before normal quitting time (to make up for arriving two hours late), nobody would complain. When he told his colleagues on the third floor of the CompuTech building how bad the hangover was, not only would he be forgiven, he'd be given rock star status for an hour or two, as long as he made up the lost time. Nobody wanted to carry someone else's water.

The elevator doors opened. He shoulder-shrugged off the mirror and ping-ponged down a hallway that for some reason, did not reek of ethnic food, pets and unwashed humanity. He was surprised to see, for the first time in memory, every light bulb in the wall sconces glowing brightly. It appeared as though Elaina Cosma had spent the day being a busy little beaver. Not only were the bulbs all present and accounted for—the building's inhabitants hadn't yet gotten around to breaking them or stealing them—it appeared as though she'd cleaned the carpet. Various stains that might have been grape juice from a child's juice box, or, to a more pessimistic individual, blood from a severe head wound, were gone. Steve smiled appreciatively. Tequila colored glasses made everything look nicer than it had over the last several months. Drinking poppers more often might be a good idea.

At the door to his apartment, he poked at the deadbolt with the tip of his key. Like a bad day at the shooting range with his shotgun or Tamara's pistol, it took a long time to zero in on the bullseye. He got there eventually, slotting his key into the lock, where, despite his best efforts, it refused to turn. "Son-of-a..."

He focused his alcohol blurred gaze on the key,

the lock,

the numbers on the door and realized...

... he was on the wrong floor.

He was on the fifteenth floor, not the fourteenth.

Swearing under his breath, he tugged his key out of the lock. With only one floor to descend, he ignored the elevator and headed for the staircase, moving like he was five minutes late for an appointment. Whoever lived inside the apartment was probably already on the phone to the cops, or more likely, checking how many rounds were loaded into his preferred weapon of home defense. Before smart people began upgrading to metal, intruders had been shot through wooden doors for doing what Steve had just done.

Eighteen months earlier, a home invader had crowbarred his way into an apartment on the first floor. The tenant, a woman in her late thirties, had opened up with a .45 1911. She put two holes God never intended into the would-be intruder, along with three in the walls, two in the ceiling and another in the door frame. The woman's hysterical screeching woke her neighbors, not the gunfire. Gunfire wasn't unusual in the city, and therefore, it was easy to ignore. The cops took one look at the scene and shrugged. *He got what he deserved.* They took some photos, made some notes, and interviewed some neighbors. Before they left, they suggested she consider practicing her muzzle control.

Trespassers learned (as if there'd been any doubt) how little tolerance and sympathy their bad behavior would be given by the authorities.

After that incident, Steve decided he needed to learn how to shoot accurately. He and Tamara became members of a range called the Firing Line. They bought weapons and had fun accessorizing them. Tamara went with a laser sight that attached to her pistol below the barrel. Steve bought a Shake Awake red-dot sight for his shotgun as well as the "Couch Cradle," a storage device that reminded him of a hammock. Every Saturday morning, they turned different shooting drills into a mild competition. The loser got to wash *and* dry that night's dishes.

As he hustled down the hallway, he couldn't help tossing a couple of apprehensive looks over his shoulder at the door he'd mistakenly tried to open. He didn't feel completely safe until the fire door at the top of the stairs slammed shut behind him.

Four minutes later, and one floor down, his key worked properly. He entered his apartment and locked the door behind him. As Paige suggested, he thought about Gatorade and considered aspirin. One or both were excellent ideas. He didn't make it as far as the refrigerator or medicine cabinet. Instead, he headed straight for the sofa without turning on a light or kicking off his shoes. Seconds later, buried beneath a blanket that in his drunken stupor felt larger and cozier than ever before, he passed out. Had tequila not dragged him under so quickly, he might have noticed how comfortable the sofa was compared to what he was used to.

July, 1954, three months after the Castle Bravo explosion
Corporal John "Jack" Taylor

CHAPTER 8

CORPORAL JOHN "JACK" Taylor sat on the topmost step of the staircase that led into the front door of the Honolulu tract house the US military provided him. His feet were planted one riser down. His forearms rested across the top of each knee. An unfiltered Camel burned between the fingers of one hand. In the other hand, he swirled a tumbler of bourbon in gentle circles. A half-empty bottle of Jim Beam sat between his feet.

From behind, Jack heard lightweight footsteps approaching and then seven-year-old Richard sat down beside him. Mimicking Jack's position, he put his feet on the lower step and supported his skinny arms on his bony, freshly scabbed knees. He asked, "What-cha doing, Pop?"

Jack pulled hard on the Camel until the glowing red tip became the brightest point in the deepening dusk, the crimson fire filling his eyes like the Castle Bravo explosion had filled his world three months before. He blew out the smoke and sipped the bourbon, washing the velvety liquid around in his mouth, almost like he was chewing it. The warm alcohol was a welcome change to the stomach upset he'd felt over the last three or four weeks. He was down thirteen pounds thanks to nausea that had stolen his appetite, dropping from his lean, muscular one-eighty to a gaunt one-sixty-seven. He wondered if the blonde hair littering his pillow in the morning and clogging the shower drain at the end of the day were somehow related to the weight loss and queasiness. He didn't think it likely. As he recalled, his father had begun losing hair at a young age too, although he wasn't sure of that either. To a boy, a father was strong, wise, and always much, much older than he was in actuality. More concerning than nausea and hair loss were the sores on the top of his feet. The skin had rubbed off where the laces of his shoes tightened down, leaving weeping wounds the size of pennies.

"Just sitting, boy," Jack answered, his voice friendly and conversational. "You learn anything in school today?"

"No, sir. Nothing."

"Don't tell me nothing." Jack's tone didn't change. Instead of talking down in the manner of so many adults, he spoke as if to an equal, another marine perhaps, over dinner in a mess hall far from home. He wasn't home enough of the time to know his son. Consequently, he didn't have much practice speaking to the boy.

Richard scratched his head with four vigorous fingers. His nose and forehead wrinkled, and his eyes narrowed in concentrated thought. He said, "We learned to 'Duck and Cover.'"

"Duck and Cover?" Jack prompted.

"If the commies attack with nuclear bombs, we get under our desks and cover our heads with our hands." Richard leaned forward, pressing his chest to his knees. He laced his fingers together behind his neck, demonstrating the drill he'd practiced at school that day, when the air raid siren went off after lunch...

... a pretty darn good deal, as far as Richard was concerned. Lunch break and then, instead of Mrs. Cunningham's arithmetic, they practiced their Duck and Cover, which was almost as good as playing outside in the yard, especially when Donald Lawson dropped to his hands and knees and crawled beneath his desk because Donald had let go a series of rattling farts. Gary Parker pinched his nose and said loudly, "Something stinks," and everyone had laughed pretty darn hard, except for Mary Hanson, who said, "Ehew!" in her snottiest voice and Mrs. Cunningham, who said sternly, "Ladies and gentlemen, enough!" She must have been extra miffed, because usually all she said was, "Boys and girls, please."

Thinking about Donald's jiggly butt in the air and that rattling sound made Richard laugh all over again, that rattling like the ace of spades running over the spokes of his bicycle before he bent the front wheel coming around a corner too fast. He was looking over his shoulder at the time, searching for his two best friends instead of paying attention to where he was going. He rode straight into a telephone pole. John and Gary had laughed when they caught up with him and saw his twisted bicycle and bleeding knees.

Now, sitting on the front stoop, Richard's Pop was laughing too, and although Richard didn't understand why (nor did he realize there wasn't much humor in his Pop's mirth), he sure enjoyed sitting there, side by side in the twilight, him and his Pop laughing together.

Jack didn't laugh long. He asked, "You learn anything *useful*?"

"Mrs. Cunningham gave us an air raid handout to study."

"She did, huh?"

"And I learned roy-g-biv. That's the colors in a rainbow. Red, orange, yellow, green, blue, indigo, violet."

"Good to know," Jack said. "You dry the dishes for your mother?"

"Yes, sir."

"Good boy." Jack inhaled the last of the Camel. He flicked the butt toward the street and watched the arc of red embers flare brightly before vanishing like they never existed.

"Pop?" Richard said, "My bike is broke."

"Broken. What's the matter with it?"

"Front wheel is bent."

"We'll fix it tomorrow, okay?" Jack reached out and gave his son's shoulder a tender squeeze. "Promise."

Richard said, "I love you, Pop."

In a slightly raw, slightly choked voice, Jack said, "Go on, now. Get inside. Get to bed."

Jack sipped the Beam. When the level of bourbon in the tumbler dropped, he topped it up with the bottle between his feet. Overhead, the stars popped out one silver pinprick at a time. In the dry grass lining the fence, the crickets chirped their nighttime song while up and down the street, lights blinked to life behind curtains in bungalows identical to his.

Eventually, Shirley sat down beside him.

Knees together, she smoothed her dress with a swipe of her palms, tucking it in primly beneath her legs before leaning back and propping herself up on the landing with her elbows. She saw him sneak an admiring look at her calves, and she wiggled a little bit, pretending to find a more comfortable position. Her dress pulled up two or three inches, exposing more of her legs.

"Trollop," Jack said. He leaned over, bumping his shoulder gently against hers.

Shirley smiled.

He lit another Camel with a battered Zippo that he pulled from his breast pocket, snapping it open and closed with two practiced flicks. When he had the cigarette burning and he'd inhaled and exhaled, Shirley reached for it with index and middle finger parted like a peace sign. He gave it to her. After she'd taken a drag of her own and coughed daintily behind the back of her hand, she handed it back. She said, "When do you go back?"

Jack said, "Ten days."

"I'd like to take Richard home to see his grandparents when you're gone."

Jack nodded. As difficult as it was for Shirley to live so far away from her parents, it was harder for the boy's grandparents. The boy was only three when Jack walked into the Oklahoma City recruiting office and was subsequently told he'd be posted to Honolulu. The boy's grandfather understood, or said he did. A marine himself, he'd spent World War One in France. He'd come home to the young bride he married the day before he deployed. Fractured families were a fact of wartime life. Even so, Jack had seen disappointment behind the old soldier's stoic smile. He approved of Jack's military choice, but Richard wouldn't be sitting on his knee, "helping" him drive the Farmall tractor. He wouldn't be "sneaking" the boy the occasional Tootsie Roll or Turkish Taffy when they stopped at the general store, warning him in a conspiratorial whisper not to tell his mother.

"Makes sense," Jack said. He emptied his glass and shuddered. Wiped his mouth with the back of his hand. He sighed more audibly than he intended, and Shirley said, "What's the matter, Jack?"

He said nothing for a long time and then, hesitantly, "I've seen things, woman. I've seen the end of the world."

Unaccustomed to this level of communication, it took Shirley a surprised second to answer. In a feathery voice, she said, "The end of the world? I don't understand."

"The bomb went off, and all hell came up around me. When it pulled back, it took some of the world with it. It left something behind, too. I've been guarding it all this time."

"What, Jack? What have you been guarding?"

"A tunnel. They call it the Passage."

Dark unease crept up and surrounded her. Her arms speckled with sudden gooseflesh.

He poured a generous portion of Jim Beam into his tumbler, swallowed a large mouthful, and then took a long draw on the Camel. After exhaling, he said, "There's another world out there. We were in it. Guarding the president at the time. Me and some of the lads."

She leaned into him, careful not to touch him, lest her presence break the spell and end his nightmarish story before it began. As much as she didn't want to hear it, she didn't want to miss a word. "You met President Blainey?"

"Him. Two from the CIA. Some government big-wheels with fancy yellow braid on their hats. We walked through the Passage to the other side, me and Georgie Harelip. Our M1s locked and loaded. The president came behind me and Georgie. The big-wheels and one of the

CIA guys were tight on him. The second CIA guy, young, lean like an athlete, least that's how he looked, had a briefcase chained to his wrist. Two more, like Georgie and me, came last, securing our tail." Jack shivered, remembering the way the cold wind in the Passage sounded like a thousand whispering voices, the way the diaphanous white vapor in the air looked like the ghosts of his long-dead comrades. "It was like walking on nothing," he said. "If man ever goes into space, it would be like that, I guess. Darkness everywhere, except for the Passage. And it was just a different shade of black, pointing toward a rectangle of light. Like a door hanging there, not connected to anything."

Under the porch light, Jack's damp lips shone. His eyes were distant now, his murmured voice the precisely controlled monotone of a man on the verge of intoxication, which Shirley assumed was the reason for his unprecedented monologue. The military didn't permit him to tell her what he'd seen, what he'd done, or where he'd been, although when the wives got to gossiping over afternoon coffee, they were usually able to make accurate guesses, based on the dark tans their men returned home with and the occasional careless comments they dropped.

With the tumbler clutched in one trembling hand, Jack raised his arm and swiped away a trickle of bourbon from the corner of his mouth. In his other hand, his cigarette smoldered, forgotten between his fingers.

He and Georgie Harelip had walked side by side, one slow step after another, toward the door-shaped light, Jack questioning how perfect geometric proportions could exist in an environment so blatantly unnatural. A sick feeling settled into him. His eyes watered, and his breath came in shallow, fragmented gusts. Every time a white cloud misted over him, desperate spectral whispers begged him to stay in the Space Between forever. The spirits' lonely despair infected him with an almost uncontrollable terror. Acting as though he were checking the president's progress, Jack looked behind him, down the length of the Passage to the light they were walking away from. How long would it take to return to safety if he turned and ran, *sprinted*, toward the world he'd left behind?

He risked a sideways glance at Georgie.

In the Passage's black light, the sweat on Georgie's forehead shone like gasoline on water, despite the cold air rushing past. His forearms, poking out of the rolled-up sleeves of his fatigues, were ropy with tension. His eyes, watering and intense, remained resolutely focused on the Passage in front of them. He may have felt as miserable as Jack, but it didn't appear as though he were thinking about running like a terrified little girl. Of course, Georgie had walked into the Space Between before, exploring it after its initial discovery. Presumably, he was more accustomed to their surroundings. More capable of handling them.

Georgie must have sensed Jack's silent question because he said, "Carry on, Jack." He licked his lips, turned his head, spat. The glob of saliva, spinning and frolicking like a dot of silver mercury, traveled less than an arm's length before the relentless wind snatched it and carried it away. "It don't get easier 'til the other side."

Ashamed of his fear, Jack loosened his fingers and then, with fresh resolve, rewrapped them around the walnut grip of his M1. He blinked the water from his eyes and mumbled to himself, "Enough of that cowardly shite."

The incongruous rectangle of light grew with every step. However, without anything in the Space Between providing scale, Jack couldn't tell if the rectangle was the size of the front door into his Honolulu home, or that of a garage door into one of the steel Quonset huts on Bikini.

And then a couple of guys stepped out of the light with their own rifles aimed at Jack and Georgie—and the president too—and Jack's heart did a loopy startled somersault and he exhaled a heavy, "Fuck," and he socked his rifle into the pocket of his shoulder and tightened his finger on the trigger, even though for no reason he could articulate, he doubted the rifle would work in the Space Between, and then Georgie flung out a hand and pushed the barrel down and said, "Easy, Jack. They're Americans."

Georgie's rifle was pointing down at a forty-five-degree angle, toward what would have been the floor had the Passage been substantive. After giving him a look and receiving a short nod, Jack reluctantly lowered his rifle, although doing so made him more apprehensive than he already felt. Walking toward armed, unknown soldiers with his rifle pointing uselessly at the floor didn't seem wise.

Visibly relaxing, the soldiers facing them lowered their own weapons. They back pedaled into the light, and Jack realized they were only a few yards away from a regular-sized door. Several steps later, tight on Georgie's heels, he exited the Passage and entered a well-lit room the size of a two-bay garage at a Shell service station. He sidestepped right, effectively putting a cinder block wall between the Space Between and himself. The seething nausea vanished. He cut a glance over his shoulder. Behind him, and off to the side, the opening in the wall formed a frame that was undoubtedly responsible for the precise geometric shape he'd seen from the Passage. Gossamer-like phantoms swam within the frame. Sparks of light blinked to life and died just as quickly. Jack blew out a quiet, tormented breath. Returning home through the Space Between would be a sickening experience, made worse now that he knew what to expect.

A small crowd of people, one of whom sat at a heavy oak conference table situated dead center in the room, looked back and forth between him and Georgie in silence. A moment later, President Blainey exited the Passage through the door between Jack and Georgie. With scarcely a pause, Blainey took several steps toward the man sitting at the table and to Jack's astonishment, he extended his right arm and said, "Mr. President."

The man behind the table was already pushing himself to his feet, straightening a maroon tie over a white shirt. Reaching out, he shook the hand Blainey offered. "Mr. President," he replied in a voice that held a slightly southern twang. He gestured to the empty chair opposite him. "Welcome. Please have a seat."

Later, Jack would come to appreciate the peculiarity of the

situation. He was in a different world from that in which he'd eaten breakfast, standing inside a room that couldn't possibly exist, witnessing a meeting between two *simultaneously sitting* American presidents. In that moment, however, the peculiarity didn't dawn on him. The other president had fully captured his attention; the briefing he'd received before entering the Passage had not indicated that the presidents were not the same in both versions of America. He'd expected to see another President Blainey on the opposite side of the table. Two Blaineys. Twins. But that wasn't the case. He wondered why, and decided the chances of Bruce Blainey becoming president in both worlds was astronomically slim. In a world of millions, how many people claimed sports icon or literary genius status? Or president of a nation? Less than one percent. Most of the population existed from beginning to end, without doing anything remarkable. They lived simple lives of predictable routine. Logically, then, their lives would be similar between worlds. Similar but not identical because even the most miniscule variance amplified across an infinite universe was bound to create differences. Blainey would have a twin, yes. That one of them became president defied most odds. That both became president at the same time was impossible.

The room smelled overwhelmingly of fresh paint and, to a lesser degree, of furniture polish and floor wax. An American flag on a gold pole stood in one corner. The burnished oak table and the chairs surrounding it reflected catch-lights from the overhead fluorescents. The ceiling and walls on one side of the table were painted the same pale blue as the tiles on the floor. Halfway into the room, blue became green. The demarcation line circled the room. Blue on one side, pale green on the other. The conference table straddled the line. Even when pulled tight to the table, the five chairs on Jack's blue side wouldn't encroach into the green zone. The manner in which the other Americans had secured their entrance into the Passage impressed him. There was no doubt about the location of the border between their two countries, which, he thought, made the Space Between kind of like the newly established Demilitarized Zone between North and South Korea.

The delegation on the other side of the table represented an identical complement to Jack's group. The meeting had been carefully choreographed on one of the previous exploratory trips through the Passage. Four unsmiling, unblinking soldiers stood with their backs against the green wall, two on either side of what appeared to be an unbreachable steel fire door, the only way into the other version of America, Jack assumed. Two gray-haired, iron-jawed men with yellow braiding on their sleeves and colorful ribbons on their chests sat down at the table to their president's right. Two suits (Jack guessed they were that America's CIA equivalents) sat down to his left.

Blainey introduced his two CIA men: Mr. Green and Mr. Brown. Then he introduced the bigwigs who'd come through the Passage with him, Secretary of Defense Robert Gray, and Chairman of the Joint Chiefs of Staff, Michael Black.

Jack kept his face carefully impassive. The SecDef and the Joint Chief were not named Gray and Black, respectively. They were the second and third most powerful individuals in the United States, behind Blainey himself. They were Jack's bosses, several steps removed, so he was well aware of their real names. Treading a cautious path, Blainey had lied. The men on the opposite side of the table may have been Americans, but at the same time, they were foreigners. Trust, it seemed, would start slowly.

While Jack and the other soldiers in the room maintained a mute and rigid stance, the bigwigs at the table exchanged guarded pleasantries in the politest of tones until the other president, who'd introduced himself as President Dwight Eisenhower, said, "As proposed, we've prepared a preliminary schedule. We've also listed five goals we'd be interested in exploring going forward."

"As did we," President Blainey replied. He held an open palm out to the side. Mr. Brown, the athletic CIA man, lifted his briefcase off his lap, thumbed the combination lock, and popped the latches. He extracted a red file with a Top-Secret banner printed in bold white letters on the cover. Blainey took the file and handed it across the table to Eisenhower. He said, "For you. In short, I propose we meet semiannually. Our representatives will meet quarterly." He nodded at the bigwigs to his left and the CIA men to his right.

Eisenhower tapped pursed lips with his index finger, seemingly thinking hard about the proposal. He said, "As you'll see," he nodded at the file Blainey had taken from him, "I suggested quarterly meetings. However, if these men speak for you, a face-to-face is not strictly necessary. Semiannually is acceptable." The finger, that moments before was tapping his lips, was suddenly pointing toward the ceiling. "Provided you make yourself available sooner should an urgent situation develop and the need for such a meeting is required." He added in a more conciliatory tone, "Obviously, I would make the same allowance for you."

"Agreed." Blainey nodded, stood, and shook Eisenhower's hand. "I need to get back. It was a pleasure meeting you. We'll talk again in six months' time. If not sooner."

"Until we meet again," Eisenhower replied.

Jack Taylor would never return to alternate America. If asked, he would have claimed he was damn glad he never went back. He didn't want to spend another second in the Space Between, what with the nausea and the ghosts and the crushing loneliness. Had he known the Castle Bravo explosion had already killed him, and the time he was borrowing would end days after Christmas that year, Jack probably would have reconsidered. A few isolated minutes of misery inside the Space Between was better than the cancer liquefying his organs.

Beneath the porch light on the front stoop in Honolulu, Shirley asked in a whisper, "What else did they say, Jack?"

Jack flicked his burned-to-the-end cigarette into the street. He sipped the bourbon. "They want to use the Passage. They don't know how, or for what purpose, but they want to use it." He chuckled without humor. "If I was a cynical man, I'd say they'll exploit it. One thing's for sure. They don't want anyone to know about it."

"President Blainey doesn't?"

"Him. The CIA. The bigwigs." His voice became less solemn. "They."

Shirley heard the change in his voice. She nodded slightly. As much as she wanted to know more, she knew her husband had said all he was going to say. It seemed the word "they" had reminded him that he wasn't permitted to discuss his job. Perhaps "they" were his supervisors. Perhaps "they" were his supervisors' bosses. Whoever "they" were, she guessed he'd suddenly remembered the consequences of breaking their rules. "Okay," she murmured and put a reassuring hand on his arm.

He tensed, and then after a moment, relaxed. "Skin hurts." Louder, he said, "What did your folks have to say?"

"A man from Mobil wants to put a drill on the farm." She traced her fingers around the blue porpoise tattoo on his forearm, feeling the soft hair beneath her fingertips. "He said there might be oil in the ground under Pa's house."

She kept talking, getting him caught up with the news that her mother had shared in this week's letter. Jack sort of paid attention. Mostly, he thought about the maladies he was suffering—the nausea, hair loss, and lesions—and wondered if they were related to each other and hoped they weren't symptoms of something dire.

When she'd run out of things to say, Shirley asked, "Who's Georgie Harelip?"

Jack smiled. He swallowed a mouthful of Beam and offered her the tumbler. She took it, raised it, and with her lips sealed, tilted her head back. A dribble of bourbon leaked into her mouth, enough to make her shiver, which was enough to make Jack think she'd shared his drink with him. His smile turned into a laugh. "One of the lads," he said. "You should see that man's nose. Crooked as the Pacific Coast highway."

Nonplussed, Shirley tilted her head. How'd the man's crooked nose earn him such an unflattering nickname?

"Yeah," Jack continued. "It's been broken two, maybe three times. Fighting, you see? On account of his harelip."

May, 2028

CHAPTER 9

AGONIZING MORNING SUNLIGHT stabbed into the center of Steve's brain like ten thousand rusty broadswords clashing together in the largest medieval battle ever fought. How this much light could make its way through his apartment's single grimy window was a mystery he didn't dare open his eyes to investigate. His skull pulsed with the most diabolical headache he'd ever suffered. He sipped a small amount of air across cracked lips and kept his eyes clamped resolutely shut. He tried not to shift his position on the sofa, suspecting that any movement larger than breathing would result in unmitigated agony. Never before had he experienced a morning after of this magnitude. This was a fifty-caliber hangover, a nine-point-four on the Richter scale, a five-alarm fire. Paige's red gel cap had worked for shit.

Inevitably, he had no choice but to move. Lying face down, the weight of his body applied tremendous pressure to his tequila-tortured belly. Gingerly, he rolled onto his side. As he did, his guts twisted, forcing out a long, wet fart, the stench so incredibly noxious that it seemed to surround him in a substantiative gaseous cloud.

Remaining immobile was no longer an option.

He toppled off the sofa and landed on his hands and knees a microsecond before his stomach erupted. By the time he finished spraying puke all over the floor, he was weeping in abject misery. His temples pulsed like some mad doomsday concerto. His wildly spasming abdominal muscles shrieked with pain. His mouth tasted like the bottom of a septic tank.

He felt marginally better than he had two minutes before.

As unrivalled as tequila poppers were for creating a euphorically good mood, they were equally unrivalled at reminding him of how stupid he was for drinking them in the first place. Some people might have said, "If you drink like that, you deserve the consequences." Although it is difficult to make a strong counterargument, statements like those were drivel perpetuated by the terminally righteous. When drinking, Steve didn't get violent, obscene, or abusive. He didn't annoy other patrons with inappropriately loud laughter or coarse language. When he barfed, he did it politely, in private. He hadn't stiffed Linda on her tip. Truth be told, he probably over tipped her, and yeah, he knew looking good significantly helped her take-home pay. He didn't care. All that cuteness. All he'd done was meet a friendly face, drink too much, and walk home. That was all. He didn't think he should be suffering to the extent that he was. Expecting the punishment to fit the crime wasn't unreasonable, was it?

Closely following that somewhat philosophical question came another, far more rational query. Why was the floor a beautifully polished hardwood, rather than the age-stained no-color carpet it should have been?

Carefully avoiding the puddle of puke between his knees, Steve pushed himself upright and sat on the back of his legs. The reason for all the sunlight was immediately apparent. A grandiose glass wall allowed light to flood into the room, filling it to overflowing. Under the blue dome of the sky, the city spread out below him in a sharp panorama. In the distance, the ragged peaks of the Cascade Range poked up from the horizon. The view from the fourteenth floor of his scabby, one-bedroom apartment was perpetually reduced in a smudge of greasy brown smog. When he lived on the second floor, the view was further restricted by a heavy metal screen bolted over the window. In this apartment, wherever *this* was, all the open space on the other side of the glass made him feel faintly acrophobic. It reminded him of the time he had helped his father shingle a second-story roof without the comfort of a safety rope. His father had said, "No point. You'll bounce before a rope catches you."

Squinting against the sunlight, Steve looked around the room with uneasy curiosity.

The ceiling, held up with wide crown molding, was easily ten or twelve feet above him. A crystal chandelier took the place of the dirty popcorn he was used to seeing. The maple furniture was upholstered in muted floral fabrics designed to complement the window coverings. Walnut bookshelves contrasted wonderfully with the fabric, paint, and flooring. The ornaments separating the books on the shelves...

Startled, his unease spiked.

He recognized the ornaments.

He recognized the books.

Steve wasn't a blackout drunk. He had not entered the wrong apartment. He remembered trying the wrong door the night before. When his key didn't work, he had dropped down one level, from the fifteenth to the fourteenth (or from Elaina's point of view, to the thirteenth), and in the correct door, his key worked as it was supposed to. This, however, was not the run-down one-bedroom he'd moved into after Tamara's death. This was the home of an affluent professional with money to spare who evidently had similar taste to him and Tamara.

The more he looked, the more he realized that "similar" was a colossal understatement.

The artwork hanging on the walls (in all the correct spots for the room) were duplicates of those that leaned against the banker's boxes in the scabby apartment, minus one or two prints that he liked and Tamara had tolerated. He'd given many of their shared possessions to Tamara's parents after the accident, including a hideous vase painted the orange and green of a Royal Poinciana tree, a keepsake Tamara bought on a vacation to the Yucatan Peninsula. In this apartment, the vase sat on a shelf beside a chrome cocktail shaker shaped like an airplane, identical to the shaker he'd given her for Christmas the previous year.

The book collection was more definitive. The titles matched those stacked in the scabby apartment. They were more heavily weighted toward Tamara's chosen titles, but several of his favorites stood on the shelf as well: *The Power of One, I am Pilgram, The Ocean at the End of the Lane*...

From his position on the floor, he saw a worn leather jacket in an open hallway closet. It appeared indistinguishable from a jacket he'd owned for so long that it had gone out of style and then become popular again.

He spotted a framed photo of Tamara posing with her parents in a graduation gown.

He could no longer tell if the dizziness he was experiencing was from the hangover or a result of a growing mental chaos. Slowly and shakily, he stood. He saw a pair of oversized sunglasses on the walnut credenza near the front door. A handbag. A pair of earbuds. In a kitchen of white marble and stainless steel, he spotted a space-age coffee maker that sold for a couple of thousand dollars at Williams Sonoma. Gooseflesh bloomed on his arms. Tamara had lusted after this exact appliance. Buying it would save them ten or fifteen bucks a day at Starbucks, she'd argued. He'd countered with a statement about new-age math only working if a person had money to spend. They didn't buy it.

Already running double time, his heart rate seemed to kick up a gear every time his eyes landed on one of these identifying markers. Tamara was all over the apartment, from the style in which it was decorated to the lists with crossed-off items on the kitchen counter and the dining room table to a fashion magazine he didn't recognize lying open on the armchair.

This was her place.

It was his, too, but much less so.

"It can't be," he whispered. He closed his eyes and forced himself to inhale deeply and exhale slowly. When he reopened them, he'd pushed back the rising fear. Ignoring the space-age coffee maker, he grabbed the refrigerator handle, hesitated, and then yanked the door open. Glass jars and condiment containers jangled. There was no way to know exactly what he'd find on the shelves…

chardonnay, iced tea, Gatorade,

… but all the same, he knew exactly what he'd find.

The refrigerator was almost empty, aside from the chardonnay, iced tea and sports-beverages he expected. There was also a selection of pre-mixed protein shakes with flavors like mango and field berry sitting beside a Tupperware container holding what appeared to be leftovers. There were condiments in the door and nothing else. With a shaking hand, he tugged a radioactively blue sports beverage out of a plastic retaining ring. He cracked the top. As with the fashion magazine, the brand was unrecognizable, but the flat, overly sweet flavor tasted identical to Gatorade. Leaning against the counter, he stared into a living room he didn't recognize and forced himself to drink the entire bottle.

Beneath the kitchen sink, he found an assortment of cleaning products, none of which he recognized, but all whose purpose was plain. He snapped a pink rubber glove on each hand. Kneeling on the floor, he bent over the puddle of puke. With a cleaning rag in hand and a pail filled with hot water and something that smelled like Pine-Sol, he came close to heaving up the sports drink. He held it down, while a barrage of questions he couldn't answer threatened to unravel his tightly contained fear.

He remembered house-sitting for a friend. He'd walked into the man's empty home the first time and experienced an odd feeling of disquiet. Everything about the apartment was familiar, from the carefully displayed ornaments on the shelves to the untidy tangle of blankets tossed on the sofa. Everything was the same as it had been on countless previous visits. He'd seen it all before. There were no surprises. This time shouldn't have felt different…

… except, it did.

For the first time, he was alone inside his friend's space. Nobody was watching him, neither overtly nor covertly. If Steve did something unusual—if he opened a kitchen cupboard to see what his friend warmed up for lunch—nobody was there to question his nosiness. Only Steve would know. He could have opened the medicine cabinet, the linen closet, or a bedside table. Had he wanted to get creepy, possibly a little pervy, he could have peeked inside the girlfriend's underwear drawer to see what color of undies she preferred.

Alone in this unfamiliar apartment, a place that looked like his and Tamara's thanks to the contents, a place that tasted like theirs given what he found inside the refrigerator, a place that smelled like Tamara's soap and his leather coat, there was no need to feel like an interloper. He could rummage through any cupboard he liked. Open any drawer, including the one on the top right of her dresser, without guilt or illicit feelings because, by every indication, the apartment was his as well as hers, and he already knew what kind of underwear Tamara wore and the colors she preferred; he did the laundry in the apartment they shared.

So, why did he feel as out of place as when he house-sat for his friend, like a stranger who didn't belong?

The answer was obvious. He *didn't* belong. He didn't live here as much as it appeared as though he did. He lived in a one-bedroom unit in a polluted, crime-infested city over which the sun seldom shone.

When the maple hardwood was as glossy as it was before he had defiled it, he wrung the cleaning rag out in the pail and peeled off the pink gloves. Yawning, he slumped on the sofa, wiped the back of his hand across his eyes, and felt what little remaining energy he had drain away. Maybe if the hangover hadn't been so monstrous, he would have tried working out what was happening but, exhausted and scared, with diamonds of sweat beading his scalp and his stomach flip-flopping horribly, he was incapable of rational thought or deductive reasoning. He picked up a remote control he'd spotted earlier and tabbed a button labeled "Blinds: Close." With a soft whir, a blackout blind rolled down, covering the huge window, hiding the spectacular view. As the dazzling blue day disappeared and the room darkened, a digital readout appeared on the ceiling, telling him that the time was eight-fifty A.M.. His colleagues at CompuTech were probably asking the same question as he was: "Where are you, dude?"

His body went limp. In the seconds before sleep took him, a crazily impossible idea, a delusional fantasy, nudged its way to the front of his alcohol-weakened brain. Maybe Tamara didn't die in the crash. Maybe when he woke up, she'd be alive, and he'd be with her again, under the day's warm blue sky, instead of alone beneath the smog and acid rain where she was gone and never coming back.

CHAPTER 10

IN A CITY known for limitless entertainment catering to every taste, the arrival of ten well-dressed government officials from different countries around the globe, all of whom checked into different Las Vegas hotels, was as inconsequential as the Strip was garish. The next day, when, one by one, they arrived at the Plutus Hotel and Casino and asked the concierge where they'd find the room hosting the Global Solutions convention, nobody would remember who they were, least of all the concierge himself. Annually, he cleared several thousand more than any one of the officials (legitimate income from tips he'd never claim, and illicit cash from side hustles involving cocaine and escorts), so the pomposity of people like these made absolutely no impression on him. They were as unmemorable as every other lamb who walked through the front doors of the casino, all wide-eyed at the mermaids swimming among the sharks in the one-million-gallon salt water aquarium behind the front desk… and didn't they all beg to know how the Plutus pulled off that illusion, these sheep who came to Vegas eager to be fleeced by the slots or table games, or willing to believe they *weren't* being fleeced by extravagant, overpriced shows and boundless high-end shopping centers.

Global Solutions had booked one of the smaller conference rooms at the Plutus. Compared to the concierge, the event planner in charge of the casino's two million square feet of convention space was vaguely more aware of who GS was, although he had no interest in their crusade. Something in the world always needed saving. There was always a charity specific to the job. His sole concern was ensuring Global Solutions' complete satisfaction. He wanted them to rebook the next time they returned to Vegas. So far, they were making his job easy. They were paying several thousand dollars for a three-day weekend, but only required the room for a single day. He'd already double booked the space (as he'd done twice that year under similar circumstances), effectively guaranteeing himself a healthy year-end bonus. GS had only one non-negotiable stipulation. They would arrive with their own security detail to provide an extra layer of protection when their meeting was in session. For all the event planner cared, they could show up with their own sequined showgirls. Conditions and requests, no matter how unusual, were always accommodated in Las Vegas; money solved every problem. The decades-old campaign, "What happens in Vegas, stays in Vegas" was every bit as factual as it was a catchy marketing tagline.

Not one of the government officials had considered meeting virtually. It was Vegas. One or two attendees had come from inclement locations. One or two had arrived from countries with less liberal forms of entertainment. All ten wanted to over indulge in the excesses many people found obscene: nonstop buffets in a starving world, dancing fountains that wasted more water in a day than entire African communities could access in a year… More significantly, GSs' head of security had insisted upon an in-person meeting. Emails could be hacked, internet traffic monitored, conversations overheard, notes taken and lost. Locked in a conference room, Ethan Turner had a level of control that couldn't be attained online.

Arms crossed, he watched the preparations with a careful eye. Five-foot-ten and built like he spent plenty of time in a gym, he eschewed the stereotypical suit in favor of a pair of PT Torino Jeans that cost two and a quarter a pop, and a collared shirt tailored to fit. That was his privilege, much to the vexation of the ten government officials who didn't like being subordinate to a person they believed to be a security guard. Turner didn't care. His boss lived in Washington, in an ornate house on Pennsylvania Avenue. *That man* had more important things to worry about than Turner's choice of clothing.

When the breakfast buffet was fully stocked and the room was polished to a shine commiserate with the quality for which the Plutus was known, Turner had two of his men escort the hotel employees out of the room. They then placed themselves in front of the doors, shoulder to steroid-enhanced shoulder. No unauthorized hotel guests would get past them. He had another team member scan for bugs. A fourth man, an audio-visual expert, placed audio and ultrasonic omnidirectional speech protectors around the room, so nobody could eavesdrop with a parabolic microphone, or record the meeting through an opening disguised as a nail hole. The blinds were closed to thwart anyone who might have found a way to see through the reflective coating on the windows.

Had anyone noticed all of these precautions, they might have considered them excessive. After all, Global Solutions was a charity created to alleviate human suffering in the face of an emergency. How much security did such an organization need? As it was, nobody was paying attention. Nobody knew who the officials were or why they were in Vegas in the first place.

With the preparations complete, Turner looked at the oversized watch on his wrist, an antique Oakley Fuse Box manufactured back when Oakley, with their imaginative product names, still made watches. He had a penchant for extravagant wristwatches. Some of his female subordinates speculated that they were compensation pieces. In actuality, they were nothing more than a collector's obsession. The Fuse Box had cost a pretty penny on eBay, nowhere close to a Rolex or Patek Philipe (neither of which he could afford and told people he didn't want, a ten-thousand-dollar piece of jewelry instead of something that told time with style and panache), but it was a favorite. It told him that he was thirty minutes ahead of schedule. He smiled with satisfaction through his goatee. Thirty minutes...

... which was really only ten. Olivia Hall, the attendee from New Zealand and Global Solutions CEO, usually showed up early.

Today was no different.

The elevator dinged. The doors split open. Oliva walked out, low heels silent on the deep blue carpet. Twenty pounds overweight and expansive across the hips, she wore black dress slacks and a plain silk blouse, over which she'd buttoned a light cashmere sweater. Her brown hair was pulled back in a simple ponytail, displaying large diamond studs in each ear lobe.

Ethan Turner did not care for the woman. That did not prevent him from admiring her prowess as a CEO. Pedantic to the point of irritating, she ran Global Solutions with the same brutal efficiency as Genghis Khan had run the Mongols. Truth be told, successfully controlling an empire fractionally smaller and vastly wealthier than the Red Cross required pedantry. As annoying a trait as it was, it was largely responsible for Olivia's success, a fact Turner appreciated in silence.

Olivia gave him a perfunctory smile. "How are you, Ethan?" She asked the question with neither warmth nor animosity. "Are we ready?"

"Good morning, Oliva," he replied carefully, returning her smile with a cordial smile of his own; there was no reason to start the morning on unfriendly terms. Those would come soon enough. They always did. "We're ready," he said, not bothering to answer her first question. Asking, *how are you* was nothing more than Olivia's version of "Hello." She didn't want to know. He'd learned that after trying to answer once in the past, and watching the polite interest slide off her face the instant he began speaking. Apparently, she liked him as much as he liked her.

Turner would have been surprised to learn that their mutual disdain represented two sides of the same coin. She considered his choices—the shaved head and trimmed goatee, the designer clothes, and flamboyant wristwatches—nothing more than a strategy designed to camouflage a superficial, arrogant personality. As for the diamond studs in her ears, when she became Global Solution's CEO, her insanely proud husband had bought them for her as a congratulatory gift.

With the pleasantries out of the way, Turner said, "I'm going to need some time at the end. After you're done with the day-to-day."

Olivia frowned with thin-lipped disapproval at the Glock 20 in the holster on his hip and the stun gun holstered beside it. "The room is secure. Are the weapons necessary?"

Turner didn't bother responding to a question she'd asked and he'd answered many times in the past. She dropped a slim leather briefcase on the seat of the chair at the head of the table. At the buffet, she filled a mug from an urn labeled Tea and dressed it up with sugar and milk. With both hands wrapped around the steaming mug, she looked over the rim at him. "How much time?"

"You have somewhere to be?"

"Shopping this afternoon. Taylor Swift at Caesars Palace tonight."

Turner didn't allow her to see him shudder. He admired Swift. She was talented, wealthy, and rockin' hot. A smart and savvy businesswoman, she was a billion-dollar economy all on her own, worth more than the GDP of most small countries. Too bad her music made his ears bleed. An infant of the early eighties, Turner listened to the antithesis of Swift during his late teens and early twenties. Red Hot Chili Peppers. The Offspring. Linkin Park. Like that.

He said, "Don't worry. I have a flight to the coast at one. I don't plan on missing it." His actual departure time was irrelevant. He wasn't flying commercial. Not with airline schedules. Not with the constant line-ups and inevitable delays. Not with TSA arrogance and restrictions. They became goddamn agitated when people showed up at passenger screening with Glocks and stun guns in their carry-ons. Mostly though, he'd booked the corporate jet because time was critical. He needed to get back to the home office for a mid-afternoon meeting that was bound to challenge his amiability and patience.

"What's come up?" she asked. "How bad is it?"

Turner hadn't yet pinned down how the crash of the Diablo in

Africa would impact Global Solutions' operation, but he had to give Oliva something. As CEO, she'd require an answer as to why the next mission wouldn't take place. The rest of the Global Solutions' cortege would want to know the same. They'd want to know they weren't in the crosshairs going forward. They would demand assurances. That said, none of them needed more than broad strokes...

A passenger on a commercial flight looks at his watch, sees departure time has come and gone. He wants to know why they haven't pushed back from the gate. The aircraft captain says over the PA system, "Sorry for the delay, folks. Unfortunately, we have a minor mechanical issue. Our talented maintenance personnel are sorting it out. They tell me we'll be ready within fifteen minutes." Now the passenger in the back of the airplane is happy. He thinks he's informed. He thinks he knows what's happening. He doesn't need to know about the number two hydraulic system, and so on, and so forth. That's superfluous information.

In answer to Olivia's question, Turner said, "Unclear. At this point, I estimate three out of ten on the bad scale. I'm handling it. You don't start a mission this sensitive without a contingency plan in mind. I've got a couple of people in place. A couple of moves in play. They should mitigate our exposure to essentially zero. I'll know more definitively in two or three days."

"Will it touch us?"

Turner hedged again. "As of right now, I don't see how."

Olivia selected a sticky-looking cherry Danish from the buffet. She showed neither stress nor relief at his response. Turner appreciated her reaction. Most of the attendees would have gone pale and asked, "What's my liability?"

"What will happen to me?"

"Will you protect me?"

Me, me, me.

Olivia took her Danish and mug of tea to her place at the table. Studiously ignoring Turner, she removed a yellow legal pad from her briefcase. Then she uncapped an oversized, onyx pen inlayed with gold.

Arms crossed, Turner eyeballed the pen and gave his head a small shake. He said, "Do we have to do this dance every goddamn time?"

Her gaze snapped up. She glared at him out of hard gray eyes. "The pistol, Mr. Turner. Do I have to put up with the pistol every goddamn time?"

With tightly contained impatience, Turner dropped his hand to the grip of the stun gun. He drummed his fingers on the distressed leather holster. "Don't worry. I won't shoot anyone in this room. I'll electrocute him."

"I don't find you amusing, Mr. Turner."

"I wasn't joking." He strode toward her, pointing at the yellow legal pad. "You want to make notes. Keep your briefing on track. That's fine. I'll destroy them when we adjourn. But not with your pen. Use this one." He handed her one of the complimentary Plutus hotel pens, made of plastic and paint instead of resin and gold. "Let's go. You know the rules."

There'd be no official minutes, no record the meeting ever took place. Turner was in control of everything in the room, including Olivia's attaché case and fancy Mont Blanc or whatever the fuck it was. He doubted it recorded the notes it took like some smart pens did, but he wasn't taking any chances.

Over the following thirty minutes, nine more attendees arrived. Briefcases, backpacks, and purses were all confiscated and stored outside the room under the tight control of the two men guarding the entrance doors. Inside the room, the nine new delegates filled their plates with bacon and eggs, shrimps and cocktail sauce, fresh fruit, rolls, sausages… piling it on like they hadn't seen a meal in three days simply because it was free, which it wasn't. Global Solutions was footing the bill.

When everybody had their drink of choice (everyone complaining there wasn't a bartender mixing mimosas in the room), Olivia stood, clanged her teaspoon against her mug and said in an authoritative voice, "If I could have everyone's attention, please?"

The small talk died quickly.

"Ladies and gentlemen," she said. "Today's meeting is an unofficial recap of Global Solutions' African mission and where efficiencies and improvements might be found, should we decide to continue our efforts. If that turns out to be the case, we'll follow the same protocols as before. We'll readjourn in an official capacity at the appropriate time. Against my objections, today's meeting is 'unofficial.' Our head of security," she cast a furious glare in Turner's direction, "doesn't feel our conversation is important enough to reference at some point in the future."

Turner stared back at her without expression. How many times did he have to remind Olivia, or any of the others in the room, for that matter, that GS was nothing more than a public face, the legitimate mask that concealed Dark Sky and the work the bleeding hearts and left-wing cry-babies considered unpalatable? Seen in that light, she worked for him, as did the other nine people in the room.

Ten people who represented ten heads of state, all of whom agreed that the world was in trouble. Pollution, a lack of clean water, food insecurity, and overpopulation were existential problems that needed to be dealt with. Ten presidents, prime ministers, and royals who agreed that something had to be done, something more aggressive than the endless talk and hand-wringing that took place every night on the eleven o'clock news. These visionary leaders even agreed on the methods to make improvements happen. The problem being, none of them could be seen as endorsing, sympathizing, or associating in any way with the CIA, not even when it was as arm's-length and independent as Dark Sky. If they wanted to remain out of prison, they needed unqualified deniability.

They needed a front.

A shield.

An Iron Dome.

Global Solutions was the backstop that gave these ten world leaders the ability to make "thoughts and prayers" appearances on television while simultaneously allowing tangible change to take place without their direct knowledge. Their emissaries in the Plutus conference room facilitated these objectives. When it came time to get their hands dirty, however, it was Dark Sky who got things done. When Olivia, or any of her associates forgot that, as pompous mid-level government officials often do when their egos aren't being stroked, Turner reeducated them.

He scrubbed a hand down his face, trying to wipe away the frustration. Directing his gaze at the ceiling so as to address everyone in the room without signaling anyone out for special attention, he said, "I don't care what you consider important. We don't write things down unless it's required. When required, we delegate to mid-level managers. We hide behind overworked secretaries. We rely on uninterested aides. Keeping paper to a minimum is in your best interests." He dropped his gaze from the ceiling. Looking briefly at all the attendees in turn, he said, "I shouldn't have to remind you of this."

Olivia carried on as though he hadn't spoken. "The numbers in Lusaka and Luanda have firmed up over the last several days. The success rate in Lusaka has settled down to approximately nine hundred thousand. In Luanda, the number is 2.7 million. The slums in both cities have been all but wiped out. It's too early for hard numbers out of Harare. There's no reason to expect different results out of Cazenga. These numbers represent approximately thirty percent of each city's population. Thirty percent is less than half what the lab created in a controlled environment. Recall, however, that we were told to anticipate this. An accurate number was indeterminable in a real-world setting. I think we can all deem this project successful."

Leaning against the wall, arms and ankles crossed, Turner tuned her voice down to a low drone. With his chin on his chest, eyes closed, he sighed, anticipating the questions he'd face when he told them the Cazenga mission had failed. The asshole from Houston would come out of the gate hard. He fancied himself a direct, get-to-the-point kind of guy. As a way to reinforce his don't-mess-with-Texas persona, he wore snakeskin cowboy boots instead of dress shoes and a bolo tie in the shape of a steer's head instead of something from Hugo Boss. He was unaware that his time with GS was winding down. His personal conduct outside the conference room was devolving.

Turner knew things about people. He had a dossier on every person in the room.

In the background, Olivia said, "I'm going to turn over the meeting to our treasurer. Arnold?"

Turner tuned back in. As the head of Dark Sky, he wanted a clear idea of where his funding came from and how much it amounted to. Arnold Fischer worked for the German Federal Ministry of Finance, the Bundeszentralamt fur Steuern. A couple of years ago, he'd made mouth noises about leaving government for more lucrative employment in the private sector. Turner found out how much he'd been offered. He added twenty percent, convincing Fischer to remain an employee of the German state. GS needed highly competent people in high levels of government.

As with every charity, Global Solutions' operating capital came principally from donations, everything from small public donations that typically spike after any catastrophe to enormous corporate donations from the likes of Gates and Bezos. Because a charity always needed more money than it had, GS had an active in-house investment department that placed money in areas that made sense for a charity: medical supplies, drug manufacturers, construction materials. It was a safe, boring, proven way of investing.

It worked, but it was slow…

… which made the accounting and income streams on which Global Solutions *actually* relied upon a little sketchy. A little less than lawful.

GS owned, through offshore accounts and shell corporations, many of the companies in which it invested. For instance, eighteen months prior to the Lusaka mission, they bought several commercial refrigeration companies in different parts of the world. The timing was seen by the world's stock markets as fortuitous. Covid-28 bodies in Lusaka were piling up. There was an urgent need for temporary cold storage.

The investment paid off enormously. When GS put boots on the ground in Lusaka, they hired these refrigeration companies. They vastly overpaid for the service, thereby recouping the purchase price at the back end and profiting handsomely on an investment that had suddenly become an appreciating, in-demand asset. The accountants were happy. Refrigeration could be shown as an operating expense, the cost of which GS wrote off at tax time. The refrigeration company itself earned even more money from the other charities operating in the disaster zone. Red Cross, UNICEF, and all the others needed the same supplies and services as GS. It didn't matter which refrigeration company they chose because, in all likelihood, GS owned it too, albeit several times removed.

GS did the same thing with several other industries, buying into heavy equipment manufacturers, medical equipment suppliers, and high-efficiency incinerators, industries that predictably exploded in valuation after Lusaka.

Fischer had studied the 2020 market trends and placed money in the same industries that profited so handsomely during the Covid-19 pandemic. The way he described it, GS was manufacturing money as though from a printing press. He fully expected the trend to continue with the rising death toll in Luanda and Harare.

The donations and legitimate investment returns (the visible up-front income) were used to pay genuine operating expenses. Refrigerating a hockey arena in Canada wasn't difficult. Cooling a similarly sized building in Africa was much costlier. The money that came in through the backdoor, however, the real money, was redirected into Dark Sky. Stealth drones, an R and D facility in Shenyang, a medical research lab in Wuhan… These were infinitely expensive endeavors, and crucially, none could be funded (or suspected of being funded) by the US taxpayer.

Fischer wrapped up his financial update, and Olivia thanked him.

Coffee mugs were emptied in single gulps. Someone slapped his hands on the table. Chairs scraped as attendees pushed back…

… everyone was anxious to get to the entertainment they'd come for: a Taylor Swift concert for Olivia Hall and, in all likelihood, something similarly innocent for most of the other attendees. For a select few, proper Vegas debauchery.

Olivia said in a raised voice, "We're not done, people. Sit down, please. Mr. Turner needs a few minutes of your time."

CHAPTER 11

WHEN STEVE WOKE up, the clock projection on the ceiling told him it was twelve-ten PM. Although he was nowhere close to one hundred percent, he felt physically and mentally sharper than before he lay down. Physically sharper was good. He didn't want to barf on the floor again. Mentally sharper wasn't saying much. A butter knife was never going to be a straight razor; he didn't know where he was, and he didn't know what to do next. The uncertainty amplified his earlier fear, buzzing in the back of his mind and gnawing in the bottom of his stomach.

He pushed the button on the remote control labeled "Blinds: Open." The black-out blind wound up, and a day as sunny and pristine as it had been before his nap spilled into the room. He squinted past the silver pain stabbing the back of his eyes and watched as the Cascades' serrated snowy peaks slowly revealed themselves. He remained on the sofa without moving and considered lazily wasting the afternoon, recovering in comfort while waiting for Tamara to return home. As tempting an idea as this was, he entertained it only briefly. Waiting for Tamara was irrational. She was dead. Something else was happening, something he didn't understand for lack of information. Remaining indoors was akin to hiding under the bed. Venturing into the larger world outside the apartment made more sense. He'd open himself up to a wider number of potential answers. And, as a purely practical consideration, exercise would help with the hangover.

He sat upright and then rose to his feet with a groan of pain. He shuffled into a chrome and marble bathroom, wondering with every agonizing step what unknown third ingredient had been mixed into the tequila poppers. Something had to account for the severity of his hangover. Could the glasses have come out of the dishwasher improperly rinsed, covered in a film of soap? Could tequila go bad? One of Tamara's friends had returned half a case of beer to the liquor store, claiming it had spoiled and consequently made her sick. Miraculously, the store accepted the return; somehow, a liquor store employee had never heard of a hangover.

He opened the medicine cabinet in search of Pepto-Bismol. As with the sports-beverage and cleaning products, he didn't recognize any brand names, but the pink tablets with the embossed V he found in one bottle were easily identifiable. The description on the bottle read, "… for temporary relief of intestinal distress…"

Good enough.

Unsurprisingly, the double vanity was covered in a wide selection of bottles, tubes, and makeup. A small bottle of Estee Lauder's Private Collection gave Steve a start. Tamara's father gave her a bottle of the eau-de-toilette every birthday because, at one point in the distant past, she mentioned liking the scent. There was a straightening iron, hair dryer, and a scattering of jewelry. It was every bit a female's bathroom, with one exception. A bottle of men's cologne stood in a corner, separate from the worst of the clutter. He didn't recognize the name on the bottle, but when he spritzed a squirt into the air, he knew the scent. It was the same as what Tamara had bought him for Christmas the previous year, the same year he'd given her the airplane cocktail shaker.

The shower looked overly complicated—too many handles and knobs—but he guessed the rainfall shower head would help sort out his hangover. First, though, he needed fresh clothes. Every indication suggested that there'd be an outfit or two that would fit and appeal to his personal style in the master bedroom closet.

He hesitated before entering the bedroom as the previous feelings of belonging and intrusion reared up and collided. It took several seconds to talk himself into walking through the door. As with everything in the apartment, the bedroom was "designed," an oasis of muted colors and textures. The view was every bit as spectacular out the bedroom window as it was through the living room window. His eyes roamed across the top of the dresser. It held a collection of items that didn't interest him any more than they had in the apartment he used to share with Tamara. He swiveled away from the dresser…

… and froze in place.

His gaze snapped back to a photograph in a silver frame. His breath caught. He took two slow steps toward the dresser, staring at a memory protected behind glass: he and Tamara laughing together at a party in Cancun days before the airplane carrying them home had crashed.

Something deep inside his head slipped. There was no other way to describe the sensation. His brain lost traction, as though on a piece of ice. He felt as though he was no longer tethered to the Earth, like he'd fallen into another universe. With a rapidly beating heart and violently shaking hands, Steve picked up the framed photo and stared at it through huge eyes. As much as his presence was hinted at in the apartment, nothing had categorically proved it. The photo in his hands changed that. How could he and Tamara be together in this photo, here in some reality he couldn't define?

He had no way of answering that question.

He replaced the photo and backed up one slow step, and then another, as if trying to distance himself from something as incomprehensible as aliens or sea-monsters. He tore his eyes away from the photo and turned toward the closet.

As he expected, he found three men's outfits hanging off to one side, almost completely hidden by a long row of clothes that a young female professional might wear: pant suits, blouses, and dresses with unrecognizable labels that reminded him of Gucci and Dior. The men's clothes (he assumed they were his) were of much better quality than what he normally wore, nicer by far than anything lying on the floor of the scabby apartment. He chose a shirt and a pair of jeans. As he did, he brushed the back of his hand across Tamara's dresses and blouses. The small ruffling motion enhanced her scent in the room. His breath caught in a wave of memory and melancholy. He swallowed the sudden lump in his throat and blinked away the mist in his eyes. When the moment passed, he headed into the bathroom for a shower. As he approached the bedroom door, he slowed. Paused. Cast a guilty glance at the top right-hand drawer of the dresser.

Why not?

The drawer was filled with brightly colored briefs and color-matched brassieres, exactly as he knew it would be. He also found a startling camo-patterned thong and matching camisole that he didn't expect but kind of liked.

Feeling like a creepy pervert, he slammed the drawer shut.

Steve had never experienced a rainfall shower. He wasn't particularly impressed. The shower in his apartment didn't have a water conservation head. The volume and force of the flow were powerful enough to scare the sweat off his body. Under the rainfall, he had to scrub with an orange loofah because he couldn't find a washcloth. A loofah was next to useless at the best of times, never mind when trying to wash away a Titanic-sized hangover under an anemic shower head.

While he dressed in the outfit he'd taken out of Tamara's closet, he thought about the life she was living in whatever fucked-up hallucination he was experiencing... Before the accident, she worked as a passenger service agent for San Juan Airways, an Oceanic Airlines connector. At CompuTech, he was one among many who collectively drove the organization. Together, they made enough to cover their rent, a Netflix subscription, their membership at the Firing Line, and little else. They were comfortable, but far from wealthy. Combined, their salaries wouldn't have come close to covering the rent on an apartment as nice as this.

Had her job improved that substantially?

Had his?

Had she been gifted the apartment?

Or how about this: wherever *here* was, maybe this apartment was slumming, similar to the two-bedroom in which they used to live? In other words, rich people lived in even nicer places.

He laughed and said out loud, "Yeah, right." That was a mindfuck he couldn't wrap his head around. It was also a doubtful hypothesis. He couldn't imagine an apartment nicer than this one.

How did he fit into the mix, given that the apartment was more hers than his? Maybe this was heaven? He died holding off the Toughs when they jumped him and Paige? She escaped into the Metro… He shook his head. Melodramatic nonsense. Given the amount of misery he was in earlier in the day, and how lousy he continued to feel, there was no way he'd been reborn into some benevolent afterlife.

Of course, that was the only way in which Tamara was alive, so who knew?

As in the apartment they used to share, there was a jumble of sneakers, boots, and high heels lying in a messy pile just inside the front door. Somehow, they never made it into the entrance closet where they belonged. Straddling them, Steve grabbed the leather jacket from the closet. May was a contradiction. If it wasn't overcast and raining, it was sunny and bright and tricked a person into believing he could leave the house without a coat. Creased and worn at the cuffs and collar, the leather jacket fit as perfectly as he knew it would. He pushed assorted junk around in the credenza drawer—pens, sunglass cleaner, dental floss, a shoe horn—in search of a spare key. His key had allowed him in the previous night; he wasn't sure it would work again. With luck, when he returned, he wouldn't need either key to get back in. Until then, he didn't want to leave the apartment unlocked.

As he slid the drawer closed, his eyes fastened on a handful of loose change stored in a polished wooden bowl he imagined had been turned on a lathe and sold at a local craft fare. He picked up the bowl and shook several coins into his hand. They were labeled, but without examining them closely, he couldn't have guessed their value. They did not look like the change he'd given the street denizen the previous night. An unexpected thought occurred to him. Since the coins were different from what he was used to, could he reasonably assume paper money was different, too? The answer was undoubtably, "Yes." Another wave of sick heat washed over him. Now, in addition to whatever unfathomable fuckery was happening, the cash in his wallet was useless. In the time it had taken to open a drawer, he'd become as impoverished as the denizen.

Steve blew out a couple of deep, stabilizing breaths. When his whirling mind settled, he emptied the bowl into his pockets. The coins didn't add up to much, but now he could honestly claim he wasn't destitute.

Before he walked out the door, he thought about the yellow dog, possibly because he associated the beast with the denizen, and since he'd given the streety something, why not the dog as well? He took the plastic container he'd noticed earlier out of the refrigerator, opened it, and removed what he guessed was a chicken burger. As he wrapped it in plastic wrap, he smiled at how much the hungry mutt would enjoy it.

Without knowing what to expect, he walked out of the apartment.

CHAPTER 12

ETHAN TURNER SHRUGGED off the wall, stepped forward, and clutched the back of a chair. Leaning into it, tattooing his fingers on the backrest, he nodded a thanks in Olivia's direction and waited until he had everyone's full attention, which didn't happen straight away.

The representative from China was inhaling shrimp with such studious concentration and mechanical efficiency that he wouldn't have noticed a topless chorus line draped in red feather boas singing "New York, New York" at the head of the table. Turner watched with revolted fascination as China seized a shrimp off his loaded plate. Pinching the shrimp's tail between his thumb and index finger, pinkie pointed out like a British royal sipping High Afternoon Tea, he dipped the crustacean up and down in red cocktail sauce. He dropped his chin to within a few inches of the table top, popped the shrimp into his mouth, and then sucked the body out of the shell. He chewed so fast that his entire face got into the act. His nose wrinkled, his eyes squinted, and his cheeks bounced. The extra flesh under his chin wobbled. With every noisy slurp, audible above the air conditioning in the cavernous room, Brazil shot China an increasingly hostile glare and huffed out an exaggerated breath. Her overly dramatic reactions attracted amused glances from the other delegates. China remained oblivious. He was too busy washing his sauce-stained fingers in a small bowl of lemon water and preparing his next mouthful.

Turner's grip tightened on the back of the chair. He closed his eyes. "Goddamn," he muttered. "They've never seen a buffet?" In the future, he'd instruct the hotel event planners to refrain from including shrimp cocktail on the buffet, like he'd done with the Alaskan King Crab legs after the San Diego meeting. One hundred bucks a leg, and the delegates had devoured them like they were unlimited Olive Garden breadsticks.

He rapped the tabletop several times with his knuckles. "Hello, people! You might be here for the food. I've got business to attend to. Listen up."

Several people stiffened in their chairs. Heads rotated. Eyes met. A couple of people leaned forward attentively. The Canadian smiled slightly and raised an eyebrow. Unsurprisingly, Texas squared his shoulders, puffed up his chest, opened his mouth...

Before the bombastic asshole had a chance to object, Turner interrupted him with a lethal glare. Texas deflated. Turner kept him eye-locked for a long two seconds before saying to the room, "We need to discuss two separate, seemingly unrelated events. First, in December, a San Juan Airways commuter jet crashed in Portland. It was raining heavily at the time. The flight hydroplaned off the runway, broke apart, and caught fire. The plane was carrying eighty-eight souls. There were thirty-one fatalities. One of the casualties was a CompuTech employee. You might have seen the story on the news?" He paused in case someone at the table, someone less self-involved than the others, had seen the news and whispered a silent prayer, or at the very least, given a passing thought to the deceased's family and thanked their goddamned good luck they weren't on the airplane when it burst into flames.

The expressions looking back at him ranged from curious to indifferent. Someone muttered, "What's CompuTech?" A couple of individuals nodded, acknowledging the question.

What was this unknown entity?

Where was it based?

What did it do?

They knew the answers mattered, otherwise the bald Bostonian with the goatee wouldn't have detained them. But why was this one death important?

Predictably, Texas spoke up. He said in his nasal voice, "What does this have to do with us?" He gave his watch a pointed look. "Why do we care?"

In stark contrast to a moment before, the glance Turner leveled at the Texan this time was mild. He was no longer annoyed. The Texan's two questions had popped the fragile bubble on which he'd been standing. He didn't know it yet, but in that instant, his time with Global Solutions officially came to an end. Ethan Turner knew things about people.

He knew, for instance, that the Brazilian delegate enjoyed boring the shit out of anyone who'd listen with supercilious stories about the many marathons she'd run. She never mentioned the part where she had her chauffer pick her up in a Cadillac sedan with blacked out windows, and drive her most the distance between the start and finish lines.

He knew the French delegate, a building inspector in Paris, ignored substandard construction in exchange for hefty cash deposits into secret bank accounts, accounts that a second cousin and his stepdaughter's son had never set up and didn't know they had.

After the Glasgow convention, Turner knew the Canadian delegate had spent every cent of next month's alimony on rare scotch at a whiskey bar. He could afford the whiskey and the alimony but took perverse pleasure in telling his spiteful ex-wife that he was tapped out. Forcing the flaky bitch into her lawyer's office, shrilly howling for every penny the leech claimed she was entitled, apparently amused the Canadian.

Turner appreciated that kind of savoir faire. He wondered in which offshore banks Canada stored the money his ex couldn't find, but was confident he had.

God help him, he knew about Olivia Hall's love of Taylor Swift.

He knew everyone's secrets.

As of a few seconds ago, he knew Texas wouldn't leave Las Vegas alive.

The Texan's given name was Sean Caulder. Middle-aged, with the associated paunch that came from long lunches and short treadmill sessions, Caulder's once-black hair was thinning on top and showing the same gray as his beard. When he was younger, fitter, and on the rise, he'd married an ex-Dallas Cowboy's cheerleader, a stereotypical blonde who made the pages of a Playboy special edition, *Girls Next Door* or *College Girls*, or some such thing. The happy couple had twin daughters, two over-indulged twelve-year-olds who acted like they were seventeen. Nothing atypical for a career politician, in other words. However, away from the public spotlight, Caulder's life got dark. He had two Thai prostitutes lined up after today's meeting. He'd guaranteed both of them double their usual fee if they dressed as though they were tweens and promised not to break character.

Normally, Turner wouldn't have given a shaggy sheep's ass who Caulder banged, no matter how debased the man's tastes. He had larger concerns upon which to dwell. But beyond the questions regarding the distance that Caulder would inevitably go when he lost interest in legally aged professionals, was Global Solutions and the increased scrutiny that would occur if the public discovered his immoral proclivities. An even larger concern was Dark Sky's potential exposure. Caulder's habits could be used as leverage. Turner had no doubt the Texan would buy his freedom with the information he learned in this Vegas conference room. That meant Caulder's immoral proclivities and Turner's "larger concerns" intersected.

Texas acknowledged Turner's look with a reluctant nod. He quickly dropped his gaze to the half-eaten waffle and the single breakfast sausage resting in a puddle of maple syrup on the plate in front of him.

Turner said, "As I was saying, we need to discuss two seemingly unrelated events. The first was the death of the CompuTech employee.

The second is potentially," he paused, choosing his next word carefully, "more worrisome. The Diablo crashed enroute to Cazenga. The fourth mission failed. Consequently, the entire African program is on hold."

Seconds crawled by, and then a noisy barrage of questions assaulted him as every delegate in the room simultaneously asked a version of, "What happens now?" Turner interpreted this to mean, "Are we vulnerable?", which he further interpreted as, "*Am I exposed?*"

While he waited for the room to settle down, he thought about logistics. Could he eliminate Caulder himself after he wrapped up his mid-afternoon meeting on the coast? Getting to the coast and back to Vegas before eight or nine P.M. wouldn't be difficult on the corporate jet. Two of his men were already in Las Vegas, busy with something unrelated to the GS convention. He could catch a ride home with them and give himself a solid alibi at the same time, should the need arise. He liked the idea. He'd be doing the world a favor. The Texan had a propensity for tweens? Turner would use that depravity and turn the execution into a symbiotic spectacle. Force the man to don clothing a tween would wear: white cotton panties, a pink Hello Kitty t-shirt. Like that. If possible, he'd use the man's steer head tie and stage the murder like an autoerotic asphyxiation thing. Allowing his dislike to get personal wasn't professional, but goddamn, Turner hated the bolo tie. He'd sell the scene with an adult movie off the hotel's in-house entertainment system. When the details hit CNN and Fox, the Republican good-ol' boys in the home state would have a collective fucking aneurysm. Imagining the front-page headlines standing bold and black and two inches tall, Turner had to restrain a smile.

Banishing these happy thoughts, he returned to the reason he was in Las Vegas. He said, "I doubt there'll be an accident investigation. Our work in Africa is unsanctioned. Very few people know the Diablo's capabilities. Fewer know it was based in Agadez. It took off without a flight plan. For all intents and purposes, it didn't exist. The crash site is hundreds of miles from the closest urban center. If a local jungle savage happened to stumble upon it, all he'd see is the remains of a wrecked aircraft. Word might travel from his village to a low-level government official. That person might run it up the chain of command. Someone might decide to investigate, assuming the Democratic Republic of Congo has the capability."

Turner spoke with a high percentage of doubt in his voice. He wasn't acting. He couldn't imagine anyone launching an investigation. Not on the fourth-hand word of a jungle savage. Not when the site was located in such a remote area. Not when there were no human deaths involved. If he adopted an extra-pessimistic outlook and conceded that the government might investigate, how diligent would they be? Would they even get there before jungle vegetation and extreme weather consumed the site?

He continued the briefing. "My concern is that a team of investigators *does* visit the site. As unlikely as that is, professionals will immediately identify more than a wrecked aircraft. GS has a window of time in which our personnel can reach the site before anyone else. That's crucial. There can't be any debris that links us, and by extension, Dark Sky, to the Diablo. If we're there first, we can conceal our involvement. The only way to accomplish this is with the help of someone who designed, built, or maintained the fluid management system. Someone who knows what he's looking at needs to go with us. He can identify anything that came from CompuTech, thereby eliminating any link between the drone, GS, and Dark Sky, no matter how nebulous."

Heads around the table began nodding. A high-paid consultant was *always* the answer in a sticky situation.

"The CompuTech employee who died in Portland would have been the perfect candidate. Sadly, he's not an option." Turner cut Texas a glance and said, "We care because we need someone like him. Ideally, we need someone with similar skills who worked on the Diablo project. We need another CompuTech employee. I think I've found the right person."

The politicians looked from left to right across empty glasses and scrap-littered breakfast plates. They met their equal's eyes, and with heads nodding more vigorously, they silently agreed. Ethan Turner made sense. They were in good hands. Their head of security had mitigated their liability.

Turner nodded along with them. Just like the airline captain dealing with a mechanical delay, he gave them enough information to allow them to feel informed while avoiding anything too specific. And, just like the passengers in the back of the plane, it seemed the politicians in the room liked what he'd told them. Vestiges of the truth, alongside elements that made incontrovertible sense, were integral to every good lie. This was especially true when they *wanted* to believe. Now, though, the time had come to cut them loose, to let them get to the Vegas depravity they'd come for, before they thought it through and realized that they hadn't asked the questions they should have asked... because what he knew and they didn't was that no matter how essential it was to utilize a knowledgeable consultant, convincing a CompuTech employee to go to Africa, was stupid in the extreme.

Who would he choose?

Why would that person agree to go?

How many people would that person tell about the trip before he left? Once he returned?

The questions compounded at a merciless rate, and with them, Dark Sky's potential exposure.

He said, "Life would be easier if the Diablo had burned on impact. However—and this is ironic—the same reason there are remains left to examine in the Congo is the same reason fifty-seven people survived the Portland crash. In Africa, the liquid the Diablo was carrying contained the fire. In Portland, rain contained the fire. It's unfortunate that one of the Portland survivors wasn't our CompuTech engineer. Unfortunate, but not insurmountable." He paused and looked from face to face with what he hoped was an equally concerned and confident expression. He finished with, "That is all. Have a good day."

The delegates pushed back from the table, stood, brushed crumbs off their shirts, and tossed wadded-up napkins onto the table. They shook hands with their colleagues as if they had made big decisions and drawn important conclusions.

Turner slapped both hands on the back of the chair on which he'd been leaning. He straightened, and started thinking about Walmart, a store that had almost everything.

CHAPTER 13

MAYBE STEVE DID have an idea what to expect. He was only mildly surprised when he stepped out of the apartment into a well-lit hallway with clean carpeting and unblemished paint. Unlike his building, the corridor here didn't smell like a fusion of different ethnic foods or the pets that a third of the residents owned and expected everybody else to tolerate, if not love. If anything, the hallway smelled lightly of lilies. He assumed the barely detectable fragrance was mixed into the HVAC system, which brought another revelation. Tamara's home wasn't unbearably hot behind all those glass windows, so along with the other luxuries, it had central air conditioning.

The hallway was as silent as a coffin. Absurdly, he found himself walking softly so as not to disturb residents he wasn't sure existed.

He pushed the Down button, hoping the elevator was close at hand. Usually, he gave it two or three optimistic minutes before heading for the staircase; at this time of the afternoon, the demand would be ramping up toward maximum. He wasn't holding his breath with expectation, but it arrived promptly. Less than a minute after the doors closed behind him, they reopened onto a lobby several times the size of his entire one-bedroom apartment. The floor, tiled in huge squares of marble, shone with a fresh coat of wax. There wasn't a hint of urine or garbage in the air. On one side of the lobby, leather sofas faced a skinny fireplace burning blue fire. Dominating the opposite side of the lobby, a billiard table sat in front of a gently bubbling aquarium. Steve laughed out loud—no flirty Romanian proprietor here. The property manager in this place probably had a full-time staff.

Wherever Steve was now, he never wanted to go back to where he had lived yesterday.

The laughter died when he walked through the front doors, out of the lobby, and into the dazzling afternoon. Confused, he looked left and right. His forehead creased in uncertainty. Getting out of the house seemed like a good idea a few minutes ago. Now he was outside, he didn't know where to go. He didn't know where he'd find any number of possible destinations. The grocery store, for instance. The bank. His favorite coffee shop. The Firing Line. Disorientation threatened to morph into the same private fear he'd experienced earlier. Trying to hold it in check, he did a slow three-sixty and felt some of the confusion slide away. The polished brass numbers above the building's glass entrance were the same as those at which his scabby apartment was located. Somehow, he was (and wasn't) in the same place he'd been the previous evening.

Steve scratched his cheek with thoughtful fingers, and decided for two rational reasons, and a third that he didn't want to examine too closely, that CompuTech was his best option. First, at a minimum, the familiarity of his work environment would feel reassuring. Second, a place in which he spent most of his waking hours would be the best place to find answers as to where he was and what was happening.

CompuTech housed itself in a nondescript cube identical to those that crop up in business parks on the periphery of airports around the world. Assuming that he'd find it in the same place it was located yesterday—a logical theory given the way various other similarities were stacking up—Steve started walking, shoulder checking now and then for a city bus, hoping the coins from the credenza drawer would be enough to pay his fare.

Tamara and he often went to work on the same bus. He'd get off after five stops. She'd keep going all the way to the airport. On her way home, she'd occasionally hop off a couple of stops early and join him at Ballers, a sports bar he and his fellow CompuTech employees gathered at after work. It delighted the computer geeks he worked with when three or four of Tamara's colleagues accompanied her. Although it seemed impossible in this politically correct era, San Juan Airways only hired attractive young counter staff, and it turned out there was some truth in the cliché that geeks didn't get out much.

Ballers was Steve's third reason for journeying to CompuTech. After he checked in at the office, he planned to stop at the sports bar. As utterly inane as the idea continued to sound, he hoped Tamara's appearance would be another similarity between the past and today.

As he walked, every step driving a nail of pain into his hungover brain, a question pushed its way to the surface. Why was the city so quiet? When he started looking for a reason, he discovered an answer almost immediately. The amount of traffic hadn't changed overnight, but the decibel level was much lower. It only took a single glance to see that the majority of the vehicles didn't have exhaust pipes.

Setting aside prohibitively expensive Teslas, Steve considered electric vehicles little more than wind-up toys. Where he came from, less than five percent of the hundreds of millions of cars on the road were electric. Their widespread use had peaked in the late twenty-tens, when the planet's three largest manufacturers realized (almost concurrently) that there was no viability in electric automobiles. Green energy zealots and virtue-signaling politicians had refused to acknowledge that uncountable billions would need to be spent producing sufficient electricity and improving antiquated infrastructure. They'd blindly continued their full court press, setting unattainable targets mandating electrical vehicle use. Predictably, the electric grid across North America, Europe, and Asia began failing. Rolling blackouts became commonplace. Toyota was the first company to give up on a system that would forever hamper their commercial goals. They pivoted, and began developing hydrogen-powered automobiles. Now, electric vehicles were little more than political talking points, pacifying self-righteous men spouting climate change statistics and women who didn't wear makeup or shave their legs.

Here, however, the green-powered automobile paradigm—as he knew it—was upside down; they appeared to be the norm, to the betterment of wherever "here" was.

A city bus arrived. He climbed on, asked the driver how much the fare was, and dropped the required number of coins into the hopper. Then he watched the city slide past the windows, marveling at how remarkably clean it was. Less automobile exhaust resulted in buildings and windows that were free from a film of black grime. The trees and grass were a sharper green than he'd ever seen. He'd never noticed the smell of the air before. Today, it smelled clean and fresh. He couldn't explain the lack of litter. He hadn't walked past a single garbage can or recycling bin into which he could drop the plastic-wrapped chicken burger in his pocket. There was no sign of the yellow dog, or any other strays, for that matter. Perhaps that wasn't particularly strange. A person didn't expect to see homeless mutts near the hearts of most cities. What was decidedly peculiar, however—and he had to admit pleasant—was the lack of street denizens. He hadn't seen anything as intrusive as the Tough's shanty town or as omnipresent as a solo panhandler in front of a donut store.

As wonderous as he found this strange utopia, Steve was too puzzled about his presence within it to fully appreciate it. He needed answers. With luck, he was about to get some. If CompuTech was situated where he expected it to be, he'd arrived at the bus stop nearest to the building in which he worked or, more accurately, in which he had worked yesterday. He pushed the red Stop-Request button on the nearest seat-support-pillar.

November, 1964
Daniel (Danny) White

CHAPTER 14

THE INDIVIDUAL FROM the Central Intelligence Agency who carried the briefcase through the Passage in 1954, the man that deceased marine John "Jack" Taylor knew as Mr. Brown and referred to as "...the second CIA guy, young, lean like an athlete..." was only three years younger than Jack on the day they walked through the Passage to the other America.

His name was Daniel White. Danny to his friends. At present, he was concentrating on the light snow falling over the iron-gray waters of the Potomac in an effort to avoid looking at his watch. Judging from the color and weight of the sky, there'd be several inches of the annoying white stuff on the ground by morning. Hopefully, his upcoming meeting would begin soon and end quickly, before the roads became too clogged with traffic, plows, and pedestrians. His girlfriend was cooking supper that night. She had something special in mind, something with candlelight and soft music. White found the idea disquieting. He hadn't found a way to talk her out of it. If the snow really accumulated, Ava would expect him to spend the night. There'd be no polite way to tell her that he'd prefer to go home.

He looked at his watch—couldn't help himself—and saw that ninety seconds had passed since the last time he looked. Apparently, falling snow wasn't much more effective at killing time than drying paint or growing grass.

Tall and slim, White had gone to Cambridge on a track and field scholarship, graduated three years later with a degree in communications, and then joined the marines in time for the Korean War. He continued running after basic training—the athletic gene refused to stay silent—but he did it on his own time. The military was far more interested in his aptitude for languages than his physical prowess. While other marines were deployed to Korea, White was placed into an intensive Morse code course and sent to Hong Kong. He spent the remainder of the war listening to, translating, and interpreting North Korean Morse code communications. He became so skilled that he could differentiate the Korean operators on the other end of the wire—he named them Kim 1 and Kim 2 and so on—by identifying the subtle differences in the way each man tapped his messages. To White, Morse code was nothing more than a language spoken with slightly different accents.

By the time the Korean conflict ended, White had attracted the attention of key personnel at the CIA. A young marine with exemplary language skills was seen as an asset to the agency. His inclusion with President Bruce Blainey on the mission through the Passage was logical. Including a linguistic expert on an expedition to an unknown land made sense. What made less sense in White's mind (which made him smile to this day) was his alias in 1954: changing his name from White to Brown was wholly unnecessary, given that his last name was already a color. But the agency had a way of doing things. It had procedures. Protocols. Who was he to challenge them? And to what end?

What made no sense (as of yet) was today's summons from President Jeffery Birch.

Birch had won the 1960 presidential election decisively. He earned himself a second term (not quite as handily) three weeks before today's meeting. Inevitably, during his first term, old faces had left the CIA, and new faces had arrived. Daniel White, however, had become a fixture in his ten-plus years at the agency. An invitation to a one-on-one meeting with the freshly minted president made him uneasy. Had his time finally come? Was he being fired? Sent to an Eastern bloc country on the strength of his language skills where the only available food was scarce and of low quality?

Worrying about something over which he had no control was illogical. White knew this. He seldom suffered from that irrationality. However, in this case, he was meeting the president. He could be forgiven a trifling case of the nerves.

When White was eventually shown into the room, President Birch flopped the top half of the Washington Post over and peered across it through glasses balanced on the end of his nose. Seated in a burgundy club chair, one leg crossed over the other, he said, "Daniel. Good to see you. Have a seat." He leaned forward, making the leather chair squeak, and tossed the Post on the coffee table. "Can I get you something?" He gestured toward a well-stocked bar, a wide selection of bottles on an elaborate rolling cart constructed of dark wood shelves and black metal pipes. An ice pail made of cut-glass and half a dozen matching tumblers reflected the fireplace's orange flames.

Anywhere else, White would have replied with an enthusiastic "Yes," especially after spotting a bottle of Johnnie Walker Black among the bottles. Alone with the president, though, he thought a more decorous approach was appropriate. Keeping his faculties needle sharp was his best choice, at least until the purpose of the meeting became clear. "Thank you, Sir," and "No Sir, I'm fine."

"Coffee?"

"No, Sir. Thank you."

Birch removed his glasses, folded them, and placed them in the breast pocket of his shirt. He pointed at the newspaper. "You've seen what's happening in Haiti?"

White picked up the paper and read the headline: "Cleo Cuts Destructive Path." He said, "Yes, Sir. I've seen this."

"Didn't they suffer a hurricane in '54? Hurricane Hazel? Another one in '63? Flora? It killed 8000 people. Now Cleo. Thousands dead. Massive destruction. They can't get anything repaired down there before it happens all over again."

"It's not just the storms, Sir. Three centuries ago, they started chopping down trees to plant coffee. For decades, their only export was timber. As of today, less than two percent of the country is forested. The country's hillsides are naked. They're unable to hold water. Floods and mudslides keep wiping out crops, not to mention transportation networks, shelter, and livelihoods."

Nodding, Birch said, "History has made it exceedingly difficult for the country to become self-reliant. Difficult becomes impossible with each subsequent act of nature."

"They aren't exactly on their own, Sir," White countered. "The country receives millions of dollars in foreign aid and resources."

"Yes, it does. And, as far as I can see, millions will never be enough. A report crossed my desk indicating that Haiti's government received as little as one percent of the humanitarian aid it was given. It received only twenty percent of the long-term aid. Possibly less. The rest of it was channeled into nongovernmental organizations and charities." He landed hard on the word "charities," paused a beat, maybe to cast more emphasis on his skepticism, and then continued. "The resulting projects are often impossible to identify. I have little problem believing the Red Cross and UNICEF are doing all they can. Who are these other fly-by-night charities and nongovernmental organizations?"

"It's chaos," White said. He didn't know who the so-called charities were, either.

Birch stood, walked to the fireplace, and leaned on the mantle. He shook his head. Scowled. "Millions in manpower and resources, and what happens to most of it?" He waved both hands above his head and waggled his fingers, as if to indicate invisible clouds of money vaporizing into thin air. "I'm expected to believe a mere one percent arrives in government hands? One percent? Hogwash. Chaos breeds corruption. I strongly suspect malfeasance. High-level politicians are banking the money and claiming they didn't receive it."

White said, "The aid is almost irrelevant. The next storm destroys what little infrastructure that gets repaired. There isn't enough food to go around. The people can't produce more on their own. Water sources are polluted with storm debris, garbage, and human waste. Cholera and typhoid are rampant. Locals keep having babies they can't feed, house, or educate. The country doesn't have a single way of generating its own revenue stream. No tourism, no resources…" White shook his head. "There's no scenario in which they can help themselves. They've been given too much for too long. It's too late to teach them how to fish."

"That's precisely why the rest of the world steps up." Birch's face hardened. "A good Christian will tell you that giving is its own reward. It doesn't matter how often or how much. It doesn't matter how 'irrelevant' the relief appears to an observer.

"In hard times, a man might provide a loan to a friend. If the man is wise, he calls the loan a gift and forgets about it. How the friend spends the gift is not the man's concern. The money is no longer his. Therefore, he can no longer dictate its use. Does that make sense to you, Daniel?" Birch fixed him with an intense stare. "Is giving its own reward? Should it come with a price tag?"

White kept his face carefully neutral. No matter what a politician believed, he could not publicly say anything except, "… our thoughts and prayers are with the citizens of Haiti…" Not if he had an eye on his future. However, if White's intuition was correct, he now understood the reason for this private meeting. It seemed President Birch wanted accountability. *Thoughts and prayers* had become a cliché. Writing a check and then turning his attention to other matters was no longer enough.

White did not look away from the president's stern gaze, but he took his time composing an answer. He sensed his response would pave his path forward, or earn him a dead-end posting to Albania. Speaking slowly, he said, "I could make a case that a simple, 'Thank you,' spoken with genuine appreciation is expected, and therefore a type of price tag. That viewpoint is probably too esoteric for this discussion. In reality, forgiving and forgetting a loan to a friend is the right thing to do. But," he raised his voice to stress the next thing he said and prevent himself from sounding indecisive, "if the friend returns time and time again with an outstretched hand, I would either stop loaning the money or insist on accountability. Sir." He held his breath, waiting for the president's response, suddenly wishing he'd accepted a fortifying shot of Johnnie Black.

"You'd attach conditions, Daniel?"

"At a certain point, yes, Sir. I would. Otherwise, nothing good comes from the loan. The money is wasted. The generosity behind the gift becomes a thing taken for granted."

"Thank you for speaking candidly," Birch said with a nod. He spoke briskly. "You said, 'At a certain point.' Well, we've reached it. The situation in Haiti has become untenable. Much of the strife and suffering that follow a storm is not because of the storm. It's because fly-by-night organizations arrive on the gravy train and leave when the money slows to a trickle. I won't continue dumping resources into the situation. Not without accountability. Not while the Haitian government actively steals from its citizens. Not while gangs victimize their next-door neighbors. Not while the populace suffers through their own poor choices, be those choices ignorant or deliberate. I cannot *publicly* attach conditions to the aid we give. However, since so many organizations and people are taking advantage of the situation, we will, too."

A tingle of excitement straightened White's spine. He leaned forward in the club chair, very interested in Birch's next sentence.

Birch smiled at White's curiosity. "Is it time for that drink, Daniel? Was it the Johnnie Walker you had your eye on?" Using the tongs, he plucked an ice cube out of the cut-glass pail and dropped it into a crystal tumbler. He did it again, and then poured a generous dram into each glass. He handed White the whiskey. "You have one month, at which point I want a report on the feasibility of an arms-length charitable organization. It will be legitimate and, above all, beyond reproach. After the first year, it will fund itself. I don't want the Democrats to question its budget.

"You will be the CEO. You will staff it with a small, discrete group of handpicked people. They'll have America's interests in mind, not those of the Haitians. We're going to put boots on the ground, with two goals in mind.

"Alleviating human suffering is goal one. That's what the public will see. That's what we'll do. Let me be clear on that point. We're creating a charity." He sat down and crossed one leg over the other. He pinched the sharp seam running down his thigh and then smoothed the fabric with the palm of his hand. When he looked up, the intense expression was back.

White guessed they'd reached the trickiest part of the conversation, the part where talk that could be denied with a dismissive wave of the hand became actions with consequences from which a person couldn't hide.

"There will be a private, equally important goal. Let's figure out how we can resolve the problems that develop after a disaster, such as Cleo, in *a way that will benefit America.* Reach out to your Cambridge alums for ideas. See who they know. Meet with think tanks for help. Look to consulting firms for inspiration."

Birch picked up a file folder from the end table beside his chair. Leaning over, arm outstretched, he handed the file to White. "The initiative described here will give you a starting point. Help you understand my thinking. Briefly, a team in Sweden is developing a high-efficiency incinerator. Designed to burn garbage, it repeatedly reburns the smoke until the waste out of the chimney is less than one percent pollutant. It seems to me this would work well in a country awash in garbage and detritus. The heat could be harnessed and used to purify polluted water. Wouldn't that help lessen widespread disease?" He hiked his shoulders. "If it doesn't work, we'll know it isn't a technology worth pursuing. If it works, it would be a useful way to control pollution, especially in our colder, northern cities. Minneapolis and Fargo and such." He swished his whiskey around inside his glass. He said contemplatively, "What else could we do, Daniel? If the conditions in Haiti represent a snapshot of human suffering and misconduct, what else could be done to make the world a better place? Let's find out. Let's make Haiti our experiment."

White sipped his drink and acknowledged his own foolishness. All the doom and gloom thinking. He wasn't being fired. Nor was he being sent to Budapest, as he halfway feared when he stepped into the room. Instead, he'd been given a project that would literally change the world. Ideas, strategies, and concepts collided faster than he could consider or dismiss them. A blizzard of questions swirled like the snow thickening over the Potomac. There'd be time to sort them out, but one question needed an immediate answer, if for no other reason than that his first meeting with the president was drawing to a close, and he didn't know if he'd ever get another chance to ask it. He said, "Thank you for the opportunity, Sir. But I'm curious. Why me?"

Birch smiled. He held his glass up to the light and stared through the golden liquid. "When administrations change," he said, "especially between parties, all the top-tier people change with them. Let's face it: a president's shelf life is only eight years. Less for his inner circle. On the other hand, a mid-level government employee can last decades. How many bosses have you had in your tenure with the agency?"

"Three, Sir."

"My point. The dynamos who put in twelve hours a day but get paid for eight, the minions who wait all year for a two-week vacation to the Grand Canyon, the bureaucrats who make government happen without ever being acknowledged for their efforts... These are the people who outlive administrations. You're one of those people, Daniel."

Despite trying to control his reaction, the insult must have shown on White's face.

Without sounding the least bit sorry, Birch said, "Don't be offended. The fact that you are one of those people is the first reason I chose you for our burgeoning organization. I don't want someone who will disappear with the next election. I want someone who'll outlast me and hopefully several administrations into the future. With consistent leadership and quantifiable results, the charity we're creating will stand the test of time. If it funds itself, how could the Dems shut it down and reasonably defend that choice?"

He chuckled, apparently enjoying the idea that his proposal wouldn't be something the other side could undo when his final four years ended. "The second reason is your resume. It's not enough to be a workaholic. I need an intellectual. Your ivy league education, your talent with languages, your people skills… All of it will be necessary to get this thing started and to keep it operating in the future."

Birch stood, emptied his glass, and said, "One month, Daniel. Have a proposal ready. Keep it to yourself. I'll be in touch."

White emptied his own glass. He'd forgotten about the snow and what would surely be a hellish drive home. Ava's romantic dinner plans were a distant memory. He hadn't yet considered how he'd complete his normal day-to-day tasks at the agency in addition to writing the proposal that Birch wanted. He had, however, already come up with a name for the charity.

He'd call it Global Solutions.

CHAPTER 15

DANIEL WHITE BEGAN work immediately. Two hours after meeting President Birch, his kitchen table was blanketed with paper. He scribbled down ideas and thoughts that came too fast to arrange mentally. The right side of the table was devoted to notes regarding the charity. The left side was dedicated to future projects that could ultimately benefit the US. He was jotting down complications that he'd predicted concerning the incinerator project on a notepad he'd placed in the middle of the table.

His phone rang at six-forty-seven. The sound didn't register.

It registered at nine-twenty when it rang, but he didn't answer, choosing instead to treat the interruption like a recess bell, a signal to stand up and stretch. He circled the table, rolling his shoulders and head and shaking out his arms. He was hungry. After yawning a couple of times, he realized that he was also mentally fatigued. Still, he didn't consider turning off the lights and calling it a day. There was more work to complete. More ground to cover. The task that Birch had given him was the most exciting thing on which White had ever been involved. He foresaw it as the most impactful as well. He poured himself a whiskey (nothing as upmarket as the president's Johnnie Walker Black), and opened a box of Ritz crackers. He munched the crackers, sipped the whiskey, and mulled over a troublesome pattern that his notes had revealed: money and people.

The president wanted the charity to be self-sustaining within a year. That was an impossible goal. It would take longer. The public needed to become aware of Global Solutions and subsequently recognize the good work it did before they willingly handed over their hard-earned cash in the form of donations. Audiences had to be built and groomed. People had to *want* to choose GS over Red Cross or UNICEF. GS would require a marketing budget for the short term, at least.

Funding charitable work on donations alone would be a challenge, never mind financing endeavors that would benefit the United States. Birch would push back strenuously when White presented him with a bill and insisted that he fund the charity (however discreetly) until the end of his term. Clearly, GS would also require a more robust source of revenue, along with a top-notch accountant and an investment guru, to manage the money.

Getting the incinerator project up and running in Haiti would take time, research, and knowledge of the subject matter, none of which White had. So, in addition to money and a full-time staff, he'd need several part-time consultants and a deal maker to convince the Swedes of the benefit of perfecting their technology in Haiti. White figured they'd get onboard quickly if he offered them a large bag of money to help fund their groundbreaking work.

The consultants would be easy. White was certain that he knew someone who'd know someone who'd be qualified and enthusiastic about an all-expenses paid trip to Scandinavia. Birch had surmised correctly during their meeting. White regularly met several of his Cambridge University alumni for Friday afternoon cocktail hour. He kept in touch with people with whom he had served in the military. He socialized with people in his running group. None of these people were "contacts." They were friends and acquaintances with whom he enjoyed spending time. He tried to remember a simple fact about each person, so his greetings were personalized.

"Hey, Donny, is your piano protégé still melting hearts?" or, "Dianna, is your son still tearing up the lacrosse court?"

He'd ask with honest curiosity and respond to their answers with genuine sincerity. Without realizing it, they'd react in kind to his affability. Within days of meeting him, they'd be calling him "Danny," because "Daniel" sounded too formal, and "Dan" came across too casually. "Danny" hinted at a closer, more personal relationship that everyone unconsciously wanted with him.

White leaned back, rocking on the rear legs of his kitchen chair. Smiling, he dipped his hand into the Ritz cracker box, and then washed the cracker down with a sip of whiskey. The bizarre mixture of simulated cheese and liquid barley probably wasn't what the master distiller in Scotland had in mind when he tapped a carefully selected oaken barrel and declared the decade-old spirit ready for consumption. White was coming down off his galvanized high and was capable of absurd thoughts such as these; his hours-old charity had an imaginary staff working in a nonexistent office for wages he couldn't pay…

He smiled.

When the phone rang the third time, its stridulant clang startled him. He sucked in a sharp breath and rocked forward, slamming the chair legs on the floor. He glanced at the clock hanging over the kitchen sink. Five minutes to midnight. Without an inkling as to who he'd hear on the other end of the phone, he picked up the handset and said tentatively, "Hello?"

"What did you eat for supper tonight?" Ava asked, her tone if not icy, then certainly frosty.

The memory of Ava's dinner plans rushed back. White exhaled heavily, a noise that sounded like guilt. "Ava. I'm sorry. I had a meeting with the president. He wants me to head up a new project—"

"And you forgot about us?"

The rage that should have underlined her voice was missing. Several weeks ago, in the middle of a telephone conversation with her, he'd fallen asleep. He'd woken up in his recliner, with the phone dangling on the cord, a judgmental beep-beep, beep-beep coming from the handset. The next time they spoke, Ava had let her fury loose.

She'd thrown about a great number of words like "disrespected" and "unimportant." White absorbed them all with passionless silence. He understood and deserved her anger. Tonight, in anger's place, he heard resignation. It sounded much worse. He said, "Yes. I forgot about us."

"Do you miss me when I'm gone?"

"Uhm—"

"Do you think I'm pretty?"

"Ava—"

"I'm not your type, am I, Danny?"

He hesitated long enough to formulate an answer and consider how best to express it. He said slowly, "I do miss you, Ava. I do think you're pretty." The two little white lies filled him with a mixture of guilt and relief. He didn't think about her enough to miss her. Her prettiness was only something he recognized on an intellectual level. Thankfully, however, he doubted there'd be any more interminable candlelight dinners or awkward fumbling under a blanket in front of the television. He suspected they were having their final conversation. He forged ahead because he was a man who got things done, who didn't shirk his responsibilities, no matter how uncomfortable they made him. He said, "I'm sorry, Ava. You're not what I'm looking for."

She'd be a distinct catch for the right man, someone who'd be proud of her when they walked into a room together and heads turned in her direction. But whoever that man was, he wasn't Daniel White. Even now, with Ava's disappointment thick on the other end of the phone—when he was supposed to be thinking about them—a new thought had pushed its way to the forefront of White's mind.

He transferred the telephone handset to the opposite ear. Holding it in place with his shoulder tucked against his cheek, he picked up his pen and found a clean sheet of paper. When the incinerator project arrived in America (assuming the prototype proved successful in Haiti), it would provoke public enthusiasm and resistance in equal measure; ideas were only as good as a taxpayer's willingness to fund them. The public would need to know who'd pay to build, operate, and maintain the incinerator. An infuriating and unreasonable grassroots group would spring up as a matter of course, claiming the incinerator was unsafe, for no other reason than not wanting it built in their backyard.

He heard Ava say, "Don't be sorry, Danny. You are who you are. It'll be our secret. If it got out, it would be as embarrassing for me as it would be for you. If anyone asks, we can say work got in the way."

Intuitive, as well as smart, personable, and attractive.

Relieved that they were finished without drama or hysterics, White said, "Thank you, Ava. If you need anything, anything at all, just ask." As always, White meant what he said…

… but before the handset had settled in the cradle, he was already making notes. Taxpayers' concerns aside, politics would play a crucial role in the incinerator's construction. When the time came, the first one couldn't be built in any random northern state. Blowhard senators would insist on being consulted. The pretty-boy governor from Wisconsin, the one with good hair and the groundless belief that he was the smartest person in the room, would refuse for partisan reasons. He'd claim "unproven" technology, despite reams of contrary evidence. Someone would insist on a subsidy. Someone else would quietly demand a kickback.

White had a great deal to consider.

May, 2028

CHAPTER 16

WHEN STEVE'S HAND landed on CompuTech's door handle, a crazily preposterous thought occurred to him: what if he wasn't the only Steve Quinn? Would he pull open the door and come face to face with himself? Was that possible? At one time, Tamara had lived wherever he had been yesterday. By all indications, she lived here, too. Logically, that meant there were two Steve Quinns. By extension, that suggested he'd find an identical set of friends and colleagues toiling away in the building he was about to enter. The tequila headache had eased off in the afternoon's fresh air. This new, unimaginable mindfuck brought it surging back, making him wince and suck a sharp breath in through his teeth.

When the hammering bass line behind his eyes eased, he pulled the office door open and walked into a lobby that reminded him of an art gallery. Hidden spotlights shone on framed prints of aircraft in flight and ships on placid oceans. One wall was adorned with artistic versions of fluid management schematics. Designed to make an impactful first impression, a granite desk with a gently curving base rested on a midnight blue carpet. "CompuTech" was spelled out along the base of the desk in large shining gold letters. A receptionist behind the desk wore a telephone headset with a thin felt-tipped mouthpiece pushed up beside her ear. She looked up when the door opened, and then her eyes returned to the monitor in front of her. Yesterday, her hair was blonde with streaked highlights, combed back and secured it in a rigid ponytail. Today, it was a wave of warm chestnut, styled to break on top of her shoulders.

Without taking her gaze away from the computer screen, she raised an insulated shaker bottle to her mouth.

Steve said softly, “Hello, Erica.”

Her head came up. A moment later, her eyes widened and she recoiled with a scream, pushing away from the granite desk on her wheeled office chair. The shaker bottle slipped from her grip, dropped, and hit the desktop. The lid popped off, bounced onto the carpet and disappeared. Green liquid splashed onto the desk and splattered the front of her blouse. With her eyes pinned on him, she planted her hands on the armrests of her chair and pushed herself to her feet. She whispered, “Mr. Quinn? Steve? Oh my God. How are you here?” The shock on her face changed quickly to anger. “What is this? Some kind of sick joke?” Then she said something Steve didn’t think he’d ever heard outside of a movie. “I’m calling security.”

Remembering how ferociously efficient Erica was—an office could either sprint or shuffle on the proficiency of the receptionist, and CompuTech was the Usain Bolt of fluid management companies—Steve took two urgent steps toward the desk. Erica took two steps backward, maintaining the gap and the gigantic granite desk between them. He held his palms open, up near his shoulders, showing that he wasn’t a threat. “Don’t call security, Erica. I know I’ve been gone for a while.” He didn’t know any such thing, but it felt right. “I’m as confused as you are.”

“I doubt it,” she said, repositioning the headset mouthpiece near her lips. Her fingers worked the keyboard on her desk, and then she was murmuring into the microphone.

Steve wasn’t sure what to do. Run and hope for the best? Approach and beg her to listen? Gaping stupidly, frozen with indecision, he did the worst possible thing. He remained rooted in place and did nothing until the elevator doors split down the middle.

A solidly built man strode out. Five-foot-ten in highly polished Rockports, he wore blue jeans and a plaid shirt in various shades of green. His precisely trimmed goatee was speckled with gray. Up close, it was apparent he shaved his head to camouflage male pattern baldness, which always made Steve wonder: if someone deliberately shaved his head, was he truly bald?

When the man spoke, Steve knew that he'd have a Bostonian accent.

He was a compulsive hand shaker.

Steve had seen a version of him yesterday, wearing cheaper clothing. He was a friend and a colleague.

"I've been waiting for you," Ethan Turner said with a friendly smile. He glanced at his watch, a swanky gold affair with blue accents and more hands than required to tell time. "Erica," he said, "Steve and I are stepping out for coffee. Can I bring you anything?"

Her suspicious eyes were still pinned on Steve. Silently, she shook her head.

Ethan said, "No calls for sixty… make it thirty minutes, all right?" Without waiting for her to answer, he said, "Walk with me, Steve."

CHAPTER 17

CLINT ATKINS RETURNED to the US and did exactly as he'd planned after his Diablo crashed in the Congo Rainforest. He took a leave-of-absence and rode the Honda Supersport west out of Denver. He cleaned his apartment first and made sure there was nothing in the refrigerator that might spoil. He asked the old guy across the hall to check his mail and ensure pizza and real-estate flyers didn't stick out from beneath his door while he was gone.

The old guy said, "I find out who's letting those damned pizza people into the building, there'll be hell to pay." Beneath a fluffy fringe of white hair that stuck out haphazardly and matching white eyebrows as thick and furry as caterpillars, his suspicious eyes scanned the hallway in both directions, as if at any moment he'd catch the indifferent tenant who kept buzzing unauthorized people into the building. He took Atkins' key with a nod and dropped it into the breast pocket of his half-untucked shirt. He grabbed Atkins' forearm with a veiny, liver-spotted hand. Holding on tightly, he pulled Atkins toward him. "What about your parking spot?"

"It's yours until I get back."

Atkins prepaid his utility bills and next month's rent. That sort of thing. He canceled his television subscriptions. It might be a month before he returned, maybe two, and he wasn't getting much use out of the services, what with the constant reruns and his work schedule.

He considered taking the stairs up two flights and saying hello and goodbye to a lady who lived there. She worked as a dietician at the hospital, an attractive divorcee with whom he shared a vibe they hadn't yet gotten around to exploring, after crossing paths several times at the mailboxes and in the elevator. Instead, he just left. She probably wasn't all that interesting, anyway. This wasn't something he could possibly know, but over the preceding two or three weeks, a haze of numb apathy had shrouded everything life had to offer, perhaps understandably after becoming the vector of so much death. The idea of turning the vibe into something deeper left him indifferent, especially after she told him that she didn't travel, didn't read, didn't enjoy Thai food (this after a conversation about the take-away flyers piling up in the lobby), and explained how her ideal weekend started Friday after work with couch time and a reality program called Paradise Island, followed by a ten A.M. sleep-in on Saturday morning.

How was that living? How was that a list of interests? He needed something to work with. A starting place.

The ride into the mountains was cold—at heights above 10,000 feet, the May sunshine didn't carry much heat—but the chill air was clean and calming, at least until the Bruce Blainey Memorial Tunnel, which turned out to be unexpectedly spooky, what with the Supersport's tuned exhaust echoing off the walls around him. Not an individual who fell prey to silly heebie-jeebies, Atkins couldn't get the tunnel scenes from *The Stand* out of his mind. The parallels between the plague killing millions in Africa and the fictional plague in Stephen King's tour de force were far too obvious.

He put the tunnel behind him. The air warmed as the highway dropped from eleven thousand feet to two thousand. The anxious emotions stilled the closer he got to never-judgmental Las Vegas. When he rode into the city, he did so with a mind temporarily free of turmoil.

A couple of days later, he left Sin City the same way everyone leaves, with less money in his pocket than when he arrived. Unlike most, however, he'd won at the baccarat table. Not a fortune or anything, but enough to pay for a New York strip loin he could have cut with a butter knife, a bottle of Mount Gay Masters Select, and several hours with an escort named Brandi.

Or Candi.

Or Sandi.

Her name didn't matter much.

Afterward, strapped for cash and leaning on his credit card, he sprang for a Fendi handbag that Brandi said would be an amazing way of thanking her for such a memorable time. She left him at the Forum Shops at Caesars Palace with a goodbye kiss and a wink. He went in the opposite direction, back to his hotel room, where he finished what was left of the rum without an ounce of regret. It was as smooth and warm as a Barbadian beach in the gloaming. It did an excellent job counteracting the acidic guilt he was trying to ride away from.

When he woke up the next morning, he decided there was something to the notion that high-priced alcohol didn't give a person a hangover. He felt surprisingly good and, if not happy, then at least content. Making a promise that early in the day, feeling as good as he did, wasn't difficult. He vowed to stop drinking. By the time his leave of absence ended, Delta Air Line's medical department could insist that he piss in a cup all day long, and he wouldn't need to worry about the results. He also thought that if he were to do Vegas again, he'd exchange the escort and the rum for another steak. Hy's Gastro Pub had it figured out: some token greens with half a cherry tomato for color, limitless French fries, and the steak. Aside from a small selection of desserts, that was the entire menu. One sheet of heavy stock paper with the words "When you only do one thing, you do it well!" printed across the top. Atkins had overheard a patron at a neighboring table ask if he could have his steak cooked medium well. The waiter replied flatly, "It'll be medium-rare, sir. They all come off the grill at the same time."

Ninety minutes after he woke up, Atkins was heading south on I40 out of Las Vegas, rolling on the throttle and watching the tachometer sweep toward the red line. The Supersport accelerated with almost gravity-defying force. He worked up from third gear into fourth, and then fifth. The landscape on either side of the interstate became a blue-brown blur. The twin lanes in front of him unrolled like endless gray welcoming mats. The hot desert air funneled through the open vents of his leathers, not so much cooling his body as taking away the sticky heat of the day.

He was still feeling content when an aging minivan signaled left and deked abruptly sideways. One moment it was in the right lane, the next moment it was in the left, directly in front of him. The van's factory paint was denim-blue, the new-car gloss washed out long ago under a persistent southwest sun. The quarter panel above the left rear wheel was crumpled. The right taillight was missing a lens. A soccer mom trying to be ironic or remain relevant had stuck a sticker on the back bumper that read, "If you're gonna ride my ass, the least you could do is pull my hair."

A second before the battered minivan swerved in front of him, Atkins was smiling behind his helmet's smoked visor…

They all come off the grill at the same time.

Fucking priceless.

He'd given the waiter a huge tip for that politely delivered response. What kind of sacrilegious fuck-tard orders a New York strip loin grilled medium well?

In front of him, the minivan's brake lights inexplicably flashed bright red.

Atkins had time to think, *why's he slowing?*

Everything after that was physics: stopping distance based on the Supersport's weight, braking capability, and velocity versus the speed and mass of the minivan. As a former Air Force captain, Atkins knew the formulas. He also knew none of them mattered. There wasn't enough space between himself and the van. Instinctively, he grabbed all the front brake he could, mashed the toe-operated back brake, banged down through the gears, all with the knowledge that his reactions wouldn't make the least bit of difference.

The Honda's superb ABS system kept him out of an uncontrollable slide, kept him lined up in the center of the van's hatch-back, the bumper sticker like a bullseye to the motorcycle's front tire. He was traveling almost forty miles per hour faster than the van when the two vehicles collided with the force of a surface-to-surface missile. The Supersport disintegrated, throwing plastic and metal shrapnel in ten thousand different directions. The impact caved in the back of the van, all the way to the third-row seat. It lifted the vehicle off its rear wheels momentarily before gravity slammed it back on the asphalt. It slewed from side to side, tires squealing and smoking in protest. Then they grabbed and stuck, throwing the van into a violent roll that left a trail of safety glass and orange sparks behind. The muffler tore off and tumbled down the highway, igniting a smoky fire in the dry grass between the east and west-bound lanes. The rear axle on the driver's side broke free. The drive shaft, still attached to the transmission, bounced off the road like a demented ping-pong ball until the van slid to a final grinding stop, lying on its side.

Atkins corkscrewed up and over the van. In the time between the initial flood of adrenaline and the moment he struck the surface of I40, some twenty yards from where the impact with the van had occurred, he murmured the briefest of apologies.

"Forgive me," he said. "I didn't know."

Intended for nobody at all, and everybody in the universe, his admission of guilt was no less sincere for its lack of a defined recipient. Oddly, he remembered Martina Donato, the one time they rounded second base, Martina with her skirt bunched around her waist and his first peek of her magnificent lacy red thong...

Paul Moore was driving, his left hand drooping lazily on top of the Camaro's steering wheel. He lifted his right hand off the stick-shift, reached out, and tweaked the stereo volume *way* up. He kept his eyes pinned on the road. When Martina's screams had settled to gasps, when her hand came out of her hair and she relaxed her grip on the back of the seat, Paul turned down Loverboy or Streetheart, whatever was playing on the mixed tape at the time, and handed her the Palm Breeze and Coke. Martina took the bottle, tilted her head back, and swallowed deeply. The light strobing into the car from the street lights they were driving beneath made her whip-tangled hair shine and her black eyes glow. For a long time afterward, Atkins remembered her that way—the most beautiful thing he'd ever seen.

She passed the bottle back to Paul and said, "Holy shit, that was good. That hit the spot."

Paul answered as cool as Jack Frost, "No problem, girl," like nothing unusual had happened in the backseat. Later, he asked Atkins what he thought Martina meant. What was good? What spot was she referencing?

With a shading of eighteen-year-old pride, Atkins said, "Isn't it obvious?"

"The rum and Coke," Paul answered, with a nod. "What I thought, too."

Paul. Still his best friend, after all these years.

Simpler fucking times.

Clint Atkins was surprisingly serene when he died.

Had the highway patrol or the first responders asked the person driving the minivan what had happened, they would have heard a familiar story. "I didn't see him." They would have frowned, nodded, and said, "That's common with motorcycle accidents." Strangely, there was nobody to whom they could pose the question. The minivan driver had disappeared by the time they arrived. The van had been reported stolen three days before. Its license plate was no help. It belonged to a Dodge Ram out of Boulder City. The only two witnesses who bothered to stop hadn't seen the actual accident, only the resulting carnage.

CHAPTER 18

STEVE SHOOK THE hand that Ethan offered. "You've been waiting for me?"

"Not in here." Ethan strode forward and pushed open the heavy glass entrance door. He held it in place with an outstretched arm and waited for Steve to walk through. Outside on the sidewalk, he looked at his cell phone and his watch in turn, and then said, "Yes, Steve. I've been waiting for you."

Steve dropped his chin to his chest. With his eyes closed, he pressed the heel of his hand onto the bridge of his nose. "This isn't real," he muttered. "I'm not hung over. I'm still hammered."

Ethan laughed. "You're a student of metaphysics now?"

"I don't know what that means." Steve didn't look up. Speaking more to himself than to Ethan, he mumbled. "A tequila drunk isn't a normal drunk. That's the problem. Dreams are more vivid—"

"Come on. Last night you were in Dak's–"

"Zak's," Steve corrected.

"—you met a girl and drank too much. That's all."

"She ordered poppers. You ever hear of a tequila popper? They're lethal." As dreadfully hung over as he was, Steve didn't think to ask how Ethan knew where, or with whom, he'd spent the previous evening.

Ethan said, "What kind of tequila?"

"I don't know. I just drank them."

"Tequilas aren't all created equal, is all I'm saying."

Steve ticked a finger up and down at him. "That could be it. You might be right. Maybe it was some obscure brand from a hidden valley nobody knows about. Maybe the agave has a mystery ingredient because of the soil or the air. Terroir is the word, I think."

"That seems doubtful."

"Whatever she gave me for the hangover didn't help," Steve said, and then in an excited rush, as if vocalizing the words out loud would make them real, he added, "That's got to be it! She drugged me with the red pill. That's why I'm hallucinating, or whatever."

Ethan gave him a tolerant smile, and the smallest of shrugs, like, *I'll play along.* "She sounds like a freak. What did she look like?"

"Attractive. A little plump. She's Indian. From the continent, not the Great Plains. She has a nose ring. She's traveled all over the world, but get this: she's never been to India. She has an accent. A sexy Indian British blend. She went to LSE."

"Impressive," Ethan said. "Does this freaky girl have a freaky friend? I might be interested." His cell phone rang. As if to spotlight how incredibly busy its owner was, the screen brightened. He held up a finger. "Give me a minute, Steve," and then into the phone, "Ethan Turner."

Steve watched Ethan's lips tighten. His features darkened, and his eyes blazed. For an instant, Steve saw an apex predator encapsulated in the rigid set of Ethan's body and the savage expression on his face. He forced himself to dismiss his impression as quickly as it had arrived. The Ethan Turner he knew, the lighthearted friend who drank beer at Ballers after a day's work, didn't have a killer's instinct when it came to finishing a game of digital trivia, never mind anything more predatory.

"How bad's he hurt?" Turner said grimly, and then, "Okay. Don't call again unless he's dead." He disconnected and slid the phone into his back pocket. In a more moderate tone of voice, he said, "Sorry about that. I'm dealing with a crisis. I've got a few minutes to sketch out the basics. Answer your questions. Explain what comes next. By the way, the bar is called Dak's. In this world, it's called Dak's."

In this world.

Relief and fear stormed back in equal measure. Steve wasn't tripping on some toxic blend of tequila and whatever Paige's red pill contained. Yesterday and today's similarities and differences could be explained. *He was in a different world.* Beneath that revelation, the morning's terrible confusion seemed distant and insignificant because…

… two different worlds.

An infinite universe in which a singular planet Earth existed was no longer an incontrovertible fact. The multiverse was real. How was that possible? How did nobody know about it? How was he here, in this world? And where was the world from which he came?

The onslaught of fresh bewilderment must have shown on his face, because Ethan gave him a knowing smile. He spread his arms and rotated through his waist, expansive body language encompassing their surroundings. "It's nice here, isn't it? Not like the communal shithouse you came from."

An unexpected spike of defensiveness stabbed Steve in the heart. He didn't live in a dystopian septic tank. People met for coffee, found love, raised children… As grimy as things were, it was home until a few hours ago. He clamped his back teeth together, looked across the street, and said nothing. High-rise windows reflected a jetliner's twin contrails tracking east, white racing stripes across a bright blue sky. Sun diamonds twinkled off squeaky-clean cars. Disconcertingly silent traffic streamed past. At a circular concrete table outside a coffee shop called Java-Nice-Day, a young lady in a lemon-yellow sundress sipped a beverage topped with whipped cream. The hipster sitting beside her, white earbuds stabbing out from beneath a knitted Carhart hat on sixty-two-degree day, worked his phone with blurring thumbs.

Steve had to silently admit that with the possible exception of Turner's condescending tone, everything he'd seen here was better. When was the last time he'd enjoyed a beverage at a picnic table, while the mid-day sunshine bounced springtime's first tentative warmth off the windows surrounding him? Any objection he made to Turner's "shithouse" comment would have been hypocritical, made out of an unwarranted sense of protectiveness for a place he was already thinking of as "Over-there."

Turner said, "The question isn't whether or not this is real. I assure you it is. Everything you see is as real as a brain tumor. The question is 'how.' *How is it real? How am I here?* Ask me that, and I'll give you an answer."

"How" he was here, in this shiny new world, was indeed Steve's biggest question. His upper cerebral mind *wanted* to believe that he was lying unconscious on the hand-me-down sofa in his scabby apartment, drooling and snoring and experiencing an incredibly vibrant tequila dream. His lower primal mind (the part that didn't *think* because it already *knew*) told him otherwise. He was conscious and breathing the unsoiled air of a world he hadn't known existed twenty-four hours earlier. He had other questions, but "How?" superseded them all.

"Okay," he said, playing along. "How? How am I here?"

Turner said, "You know about the nuclear testing America did in the fifties?"

Confused by the non sequitur, Steve hiked his shoulders. "Vaguely, sure."

"Most people are. What they're unaware of is the magnitude of the testing." In the clipped manner of a manager with information to disseminate and a schedule that didn't allow for irrelevancies, he continued. "The testing between the mid-forties and the late-fifties amounted to the rough equivalent of 1.6 Hiroshima bombs detonating every day for twelve years. Not including the other countries that were testing at the same time. Forget about them. Forget about the Nevada tests. The Oceania tests are all that matter. Do you know where Oceania is?"

Growing weary of Turner's supercilious tone, Steve answered flatly, "Yes. I know where Oceania is." If a person flew five hours southwest from California, he'd find himself over the top of the Hawaiian Islands. If he flew a further five hours, he'd be over the top of Oceania, in close proximity to the Marshall Islands, an area where people willingly paid eight hundred dollars a night to sleep in a bungalow perched on stilts over the top of the bottle-green Pacific Ocean.

Turner said, "Between 1946 and 1954, the US conducted multiple tests in the Marshall Islands, including a couple of real doozies. One was called Mike. The other was known as Castle Bravo. Mike vaporized the island of Elugelab. It created a crater on the ocean floor 164 feet deep and over 6200 feet wide where Elugelab used to be. Castle Bravo was bigger. Seventy-four years later, America still maintains a military presence in the Marshall Islands, thanks to Castle Bravo."

Turner paused, giving Steve time to ask the next inevitable question, which he obligingly did. "What does this have to do with me?"

Drawing out the moment, Turner traced his goatee with thumb and forefinger and then said, "The combined release of that much energy in a short period of time, concentrated in a small geographical area, blew a hole in the universe."

Steve stared without comprehension, assuming Turner had switched to hyperbole.

Turner nodded. "It created a wormhole into a different world."

Incapable of saying anything intelligent, Steve parroted, "A wormhole?"

"Wormhole is the technical term. Basically, a tunnel connecting this world and the world in which you lived yesterday. In '54, shortly after this tunnel was created, it was named 'the Passage.' Not much imagination back then, I suppose." Turner continued with barely a pause. "The Passage travels through an area of nothingness called the Space Between. Some scientists believe the Space Between is what remains of the primordial soup. Cosmic embryonic fluid, if you will. Others with more transcendental leanings believe it's a kind of septic tank where fragments of the world's negative energy gather. Lost souls and so on, and so forth. A storage facility for the sorrow a suicide victim leaves behind. Like that."

"Where is it, this tunnel? Through the Earth? In the ocean, like at SeaWorld?"

Turner shook his head. "Neither. Physically, the entrance is near the town of Majuro. You know how an earthquake changes the terrain and occasionally opens up a cave mouth? A cave never existed before. Suddenly, there it is? That's basically what happened. An American marine found a fissure in the Earth, where no fissure had a right to be. A few feet down, there's a pool of black, shimmery scum. Looks like water skinned with oil. We do some exploration, discover this 'pond,' doesn't bottom out. It doesn't turn into an underground river. It doesn't drain into the ocean. It's a tunnel. We didn't know where it went. However, after several cautious months of exploration, we found out. We built a Quonset over it. Surrounded it in chain-link, razor wire, and heavily armed marines. Named it 'the Passage.' It's the only *direct* link between the worlds." He shrugged. "There are thin spots."

Steve mumbled, "Thin spots between worlds." Everything Turner said sounded like science fiction, right out of Lucas Films.

"It's a lot to absorb. Here's an easy-to-understand comparison: ozone molecules are naturally formed and destroyed in the Earth's stratosphere. Therefore, total ozone should remain relatively stable. However, sustained nuclear testing destroyed ozone faster than it could reform. Now, the ozone layer is thinner in some areas than it is in others. Apply that example, and you get an idea how thin spots between the worlds were formed. That's what scientists speculate happened with all those explosions."

Turner's phone chimed, indicating an incoming text. He ignored it. "Last night, you came to this world through a thin spot. Your journey was facilitated."

Steve said slowly, "There are two worlds. This one and the one I was in yesterday."

"Maybe more than two."

"They are separated by the Space Between and connected by a tunnel called the Passage."

"As well as thin spots," Turner said. "Correct."

"You facilitated a way for me to, what, slip into this world through a thin spot?"

"Slip. Interesting choice of word. But accurate, yes."

"Why?" Steve couldn't connect the dots.

"We need your special skills. Dark Sky needs your skills."

"Dark Sky?"

"Unimportant at this juncture." With a wave, Turner brushed the question away. "Your CompuTech expertise is why you're here."

Steve said nothing. His mind, already a storm of avid confusion, couldn't envision anything that he could do that someone else with similar training couldn't also accomplish. He worked in a specialized field, but much like an airline pilot, he wasn't one among millions. Literally, tens of thousands of people did what he did every day. Clearly, Turner wasn't being entirely forthcoming. He said, "Why not use this world's version of me?"

The expression on Turner's face turned somber. "I'm guessing you know the answer to that one."

A chill shivered up Steve's spine. His arms broke out in gooseflesh. Any lingering questions he may have had about his existence in this world, about Tamara, about who he might meet on the third floor of the CompuTech building, disappeared. He said, "I'm dead. In this world, I'm dead. Right?"

CHAPTER 19

"CORRECT. YOU'RE A corpse," Turner responded with a nod. "You and Tamara went on vacation over Christmas. Pool time, beach volleyball, so on, and so forth. Resort shit. After a week of umbrella drinks and drunk fucking, you flew home."

Steve smiled thinly. He didn't care for Turner's tone. In the past, if his friend Ethan had said something like that, he'd have done so with a wink in his voice. This Turner said it without the fun, and if a guy was going to say something like that, he sure as shit had to keep it light. That was a guy rule he should have known.

Turner said, "Your flight home crashed on landing. I don't know why you and Tamara weren't sitting together. You were in the half that burned."

Steve knew the story. He'd lived a version of it. He and Tamara weren't sitting together because the two free passes she won at the San Juan Airways Christmas party afforded them two seats on the airplane. The tickets did not include privileges. When a family of three was separated, Steve volunteered to swap seats, so a father could sit beside his wife and son. Steve said, "See you later," to Tamara, the last words he'd ever speak to her as it turned out, and then moved several rows forward. In the smoggy Over-there world, the seat-change saved his life. Without knowing, or having a way of finding out for sure, Steve assumed Tamara had traded seats in this world, rather than him. It plausibly explained why she survived here, and he did not. It further meant…

"Tamara's alive, then?"

"She was last time I saw her." Turner's tone rang with flat disapproval.

"What's wrong?" Steve asked. "What am I missing?"

"I've only seen her once since the accident." Now, his voice was laced with dislike. "She came with a box. Emptied your desk."

"What aren't you telling me? Quit dancing around."

Turner's disapproving expression became an unmistakable frown. Instead of meeting Steve's eyes, he watched the girl in the yellow sundress and her boyfriend in the Carhart hat walk away from the concrete table. It took him a long time to answer. "Everyone at CompuTech tolerated her, for your sake, Steve. Truth is, tolerating her wasn't difficult. We only saw her when there was no choice. A company event or a party. That sort of thing."

Steve was thoroughly confused. "What are you talking about? Tamara fits in at Ballers better than half the geeks." He waved a vague hand toward the CompuTech building and all the programmers who were, in all probability, toiling away on the third floor, as they would have been Over-there. "They love her. They love her friends."

"Nope," Turner said. "Ballers isn't fancy enough for her."

Stupidly, Steve repeated, "What?"

"I asked her about it at the Christmas party, before you went to Cancun. I was buzzed, otherwise, I wouldn't have bothered. I wanted to know why she never joined us on Friday afternoon. I said it was a pretty good time. Casual and relaxed. Trivia and beer. Everybody decompressing after a long week. She said, 'A sports bar? NASCAR and MMA on the televisions? Are you kidding me? My friends and I go to Gabriel's. I'm here for Steve's sake. I can't wait to leave.'"

Steve gaped.

"Sorry."

"Gabriel's?"

Turner nodded.

"She backtracks all the way into the city? To go to that self-impressed place?"

"Twenty-two dollar cocktails. Eighteen dollar pints. Chairs so deep you can't stand up after you sit down." Turner looked at his watch. "That's all I have time for. Let's head back."

Every time he spoke, the commanding edge in his voice diminished the Ethan Turner Steve knew from Over-there. For an instant, he missed the familiarity of the old world. After the months of lonely ambivalence in which nothing seemed to matter, the unexpected sense of loss caught him off guard. He said, "Does everybody have a twin here?"

Turner said, "Think it through. Mothers miscarry. Children drown in backyard pools. Teens drive stoned. There are murders, natural disasters—"

Steve held up both hands, palms out. "Okay. I get it. Not everybody has a twin. But, in general, they do. I need to see Tamara. That has to make sense to you."

Turner sighed. He looked to the side and then returned Steve's gaze. He said, "This eventuality was not unexpected. But, no. It doesn't make sense. People in this world are reflections of those in yours. Nothing more. It's important you come to terms with that fact."

Steve shrugged. "What can I tell you?"

Turner dipped a hand into his pocket and pulled out a cylinder the size of his pinkie. He opened it and shook out what appeared to be three aspirin tablets. He gestured toward Java-Nice-Day. "Wash these down with a coffee. Fortification. You're not going to like what you find. Don't expect a happy reunion." He freed several bills from a money clip and handed them over along with a hotel business card on which he'd scrawled a phone number. "A reservation in your name. My contact info."

Steve studied the bills curiously. Unsurprisingly, they looked different from what he was used to seeing. A mix of twenties and fifties, as well as a single one-hundred-dollar bill, the notes were of different physical sizes, the hundred being the largest, the twenty the smallest. The faces on the bills were unrecognizable, which, other than the cleanliness of this world, seemed like an excellent way of proving that he was *way* down the rabbit hole.

Possibly misinterpreting Steve's curiosity for gratitude, Turner said, "It's a loan. An advance. You don't expect me to give you three hundred bucks, do you?"

With nothing but the loose change he'd emptied out of the polished wooden bowl, the meager stack of cash was a small fortune. Steve gratefully folded it in half and slid it, along with the business card, into his pocket. He said nothing. Maybe after a good night's sleep, when he was less hungover, he'd have more tolerance for this world's irascible version of Ethan Turner. There'd been no need for him to mention that the cash was a loan. Instead of saying, "Thanks," and exacerbating the supervisor-subordinate dynamic Steve sensed was developing, he said, "You normally fill your pockets with aspirin?"

"I'm just in from Vegas. A meeting this morning. Baccarat at Plutus last night. I'll reschedule your appointment with HR. I won't be available until tomorrow afternoon. They'll get you up to speed." He was already several steps away, raising his phone to his ear.

With his hands stuffed into his pockets, his head tilted to the side with curiosity, Steve watched him go. After all the trouble that Turner had gone through to get him here, why wasn't he making an effort to keep him here? Why wasn't he locked away in a secure facility? He didn't want to be locked away—exploring this clean new city on a splendidly sunny day was a much better option—but the question required an answer. Steve didn't believe in healing crystals or chakra stones. The whoo-whoo shit sold to people too lazy to learn the actual truth of the universe's mysteries struck him as a blatant scam. However, if his arrival in this world had been "engineered," shouldn't he have been detained, supervised, and monitored until the task he was supposed to accomplish was complete?

He shrugged the question away. At the moment, his bigger worry was Tamara. If she was as different as Turner described, if she was a reflection, who would he find when he met her?

December, 1965
Daniel (Danny) White

CHAPTER 20

A MAN SLIGHT of frame and dark of complexion stood in the shadow of a large snow-draped pine tree, effectively invisible in a black wool coat and knitted watch cap. A light wind carried away every foggy exhalation. The tip of his nose tingled with cold, as did his toes. His gloved hands were jammed deep in his pockets, his right wrapped around the hilt of a wicked double-edged knife with a six-inch blade. He'd bought it in a sporting goods store a week before. He'd abandon it before dawn's first milky light brushed the horizon. He'd watched the Wisconsin governor's front door from his hidden position for three nights in a row. If the politician followed routine, he'd arrive home within the hour, after which the knife would have served its purpose.

The man in the shadows stamped his feet, told himself to ignore the temperature. He'd been cold before. He'd be warm soon enough. Action got the blood pumping. He glanced skyward, wondering when the snow the weatherman predicted would begin falling. Hopefully soon. It would muffle the sound of his presence. On the other hand, snow slowed down traffic, and he wanted to be miles away, preferably in another state, when aides and colleagues started asking why the governor hadn't shown up for work.

Ten days before, the shadow man had been eating lunch in a Bethesda diner when a tall, well-dressed, well-groomed individual walked in, accompanied by a jet of frosty air. Uninvited, he sat down at shadow man's table. He unraveled a green scarf covered in red-and-white candy canes from around his neck. In way of greeting, he said, "It's been a long time, Carl."

Carl Hill put a half-eaten Rueben sandwich down beside a serving of French fries, two Dill pickle spears, and a puddle of ketchup that appeared alarmingly red on the white porcelain plate. He finished chewing. Swallowed. Said without expression, "Not since basic training."

"Thirteen years," the tall man said. "Where does the time go?"

Hill picked up his coffee cup and took a long drink. He stared across the table out of dead-flat eyes. In a tone that matched his gaze, he said, "I'm here almost every day. I order a Reuben. In the winter, I drink a coffee. In the summer, a Coca-Cola. I've never seen you. And now you're here. Out of the blue. All the diners in DC, Danny? You come into this one?"

Daniel White pulled his leather gloves off, one slender finger at a time. He rubbed his hands together vigorously, getting the blood circulating into the tips of his fingers. He understood Hill's wariness. You do countless push-ups in the rain and mud beside a small group of men, you go as a unit to a ball game on a rare day off, you drink gallons of beer with them whenever possible... It doesn't take long to learn who your people are. You learn who'll push through adversity in silence and who'll push through complaining the entire time. You learn who's having fun and who's acting. You learn who'll extend a helping hand because he wants to versus the guy who helps because it's expected of him. In short, Danny White *knew* Carl Hill. Thirteen years and thousands of DC diners to choose from? White would have been surprised if Hill hadn't been wary.

White hadn't cared for Hill during basic—those sinister eyes—but a cultural expectation existed that required every soldier stand shoulder-to-shoulder with his brother-in-arms, whether he liked the man beside him or not, at least until they were deployed and went their separate ways. After deployment, guys often kept in touch. But not White and Hill...

... which didn't mean White wasn't aware of Hill's activities after the war. He worked for a spy organization, after all. He had contacts. He said, "It's cold. I need a coffee. Can I buy you a refill?"

Hill answered with a slight shrug, body language that said *you're driving the bus.*

White waved in the waitress's direction. When he had her attention, he pointed at Hill's empty mug, ordered a coffee of his own, and, after a second's consideration, a warmed-up wedge of pecan pie. Maybe not the wisest dietary choice, but oh-man, no other flavor of pie compared. Not only that, the sweet smell of caramel and nuts, of sugar and pastry hot out of the oven reminded him of home and the kind of comfortable innocence that existed inside a well-lived-in kitchen. White needed that kind of pleasant memory now, a minute before he deliberately sheared off another slice of his soul.

Starting as far back as childhood, when a person crosses paths with his first schoolyard bully, innocence begins to erode. Once started, the interminable process never ends. It can never be reversed. It does, however, occasionally accelerate, such as when a person goes to war or is a victim of violent crime. That's when the trauma breaks off a large fragment of a person's soul all at once. White knew the upcoming conversation with Hill would be one of those accelerated moments. He wasn't happy about it. He hadn't decided to recruit Hill lightly, but he couldn't come up with a better option. Unfortunately, sacrificing a shard of his humanity in exchange for the greater good was a necessary part of the job.

The waitress placed a fragrant triangle of pie and a steaming mug of coffee in front of him. He nodded his thanks. After she walked away, he asked, "How've you been, Carl?"

"Getting by." Hill looked to the side, as if to hide an expression that contradicted his spoken words. The truth was, he was bored. He joined the marines in 1952 when the American government needed warm bodies who'd follow orders. If his morals and motivations were dubious... well, the Korean Peninsula was several thousand miles away from the home country, a long way from the judgmental eyes of people who used words like "fair" and "humane." After basic training, he was given a Springfield M1 rifle, shipped to Korea, and told to kill North Koreans and, later, Chinese soldiers. He spent the remainder of '52 dirty and hungry. He spent the first few months of 1953 cold—frost-bite, teeth-chattering, gotta-piss-every-twenty minutes—cold. He didn't mind. Shooting Zipperheads went a long way toward alleviating his suffering. When the weather started warming up and getting more tolerable, the UN, North Koreans, and Chinese ended it all, signing the Korean Armistice Agreement in July. He went home to America and spent the next decade hoping the fragile truce would shatter. Failing that, he prayed another war would flare up so he could start living again, shooting whoever the government told him to shoot instead of clocking time barely getting by. He watched optimistically as the situation in Vietnam fell apart. If the US got involved, maybe he'd end up back in Asia with an M16. He'd heard talk of soldiers-for-hire. Mercenaries, they were called. He was seriously thinking about investigating that option if there wasn't too much rah-rah bullshit training involved. He needed something, anything to turn the tedium around…

… which included listening to Danny do-gooder because… well, the man worked for the government. Presumably, the spook had sought him out for a reason.

"Getting by?" White asked. "Construction, I think? Installing aluminum siding? Not much like Korea, is it?"

Hill's slim frame stiffened. His sinister eyes flickered with angry fire. "Why'd you ask, you already know?"

"Sorry about the police force entrance exam." White tipped his head toward Hill's Reuben. "Finish your sandwich. Don't hold off on my account. I'm going to…" He forked off a piece of warm pecan pie. His mouth watered in glorious anticipation. The first bite was always the best bite. He raised the pie to his mouth…

The delectable explosion of flavors was everything he expected. He shut his eyes for half a second and tried unsuccessfully to suppress a moan of pleasure.

Glorious.

When he opened his eyes, Hill was staring at him. "Get a room," he said, and then, "What do you know about my exam?"

"Not much," White said with a shrug. "I know it didn't happen for you." This was only partially true. Hill had written the exam a few years after returning from Asia. With the passing of time and the shortening of distance, dubious morals and motivations were given less leeway. He'd been deemed an unacceptable police force candidate. Hadn't come close, if the truth were known. White figured (correctly) that Hill's failure might have ratcheted up the man's tightly controlled psychosis. Ironically, that made him more suitable for the ask that was coming.

They sat in silence, White pretending it was companionable, Hill on the edge of a knife, knowing that something significant was about to happen. White ate his pie. Hill ate his sandwich. When they were finished and there was no valid reason for them to remain together any longer, White put his fork down, parallel to the side of his crumb-littered plate, and patted his lips with a napkin. The pie had been a fleeting diversion, an enjoyable delaying tactic. The good mood it brought him was already fading. The purpose of the lunchtime meeting was no longer avoidable. His belly did a slow, disgusted roll. His mind shoved away the imagined judgment of moralistic friends and family. They didn't know what had to be done to make the world a better place. They weren't aware of the sacrifices that occurred in pursuit of the greater good. Not even President Birch would know precisely what took place in order to turn his goals into reality.

White leaned in, closing the space between himself and Hill. Voice low, he said, "Carl, you're right. There's a great number of diners in DC. This meeting wasn't happenstance." With the president's tacit approval in mind, he reluctantly reached into his coat pocket and pulled out a folded slip of paper. He placed it on the table. Slid it in Hill's direction with the tips of his long fingers. In doing so, he unknowingly planted a seed that would grow into the highly illegal, extremely efficient covert branch of Global Solutions.

Hill picked it up, unfolded it, scanned the two separate lines of letters and digits, and said, "What's this?"

"That's a Swiss bank account containing fifteen thousand dollars, along with the password you'll need to access it. When we're done here, I suggest you transfer the money into your own account. As a way of determining the legitimacy of the conversation we're about to have."

Hill refolded the paper and tucked it into the pocket of his coat. "You went to Hong Kong," he said. "What I heard, you got recruited. You're a spook. You have resources at your disposal."

White nodded. "That's the truth of the matter."

"You want me to do something outside the agency's purview."

"Do you know the name, Jordon Jameson?"

"The Wisconsin Governor? That Jordon Jameson?"

"The very same."

"Self-impressed prick," Hill said.

White nodded. The governor liked to be seen wearing a white shirt with the sleeves rolled up, a loosened tie around his neck. His dark hair was usually tussled, as if he'd pulled an all-nighter working hard for the American people. He enjoyed spouting clichéd inanities, like, "I used to box. In the ring, I fought for myself. In Washington, I'll fight for you!" His carefully cultivated image was a complete fabrication. DC insiders knew the man's hair was cut and styled to look as it did. He was a fierce Democrat. He therefore opposed everything President Birch wanted on principal, whether it was a good idea or not, especially if he thought loud and active resistance would further his career, make him look good, or bulk up his bank account. White found it incredible that Jameson had turned down a sizable bribe to accept the incinerator project. Presumably, the governor thought he could make more political hay (and ultimately more money), opposing the project.

White said, "His pretentiousness isn't my concern. It's actions detrimental to the country with which I have an issue."

Hill said, "Uh-huh," like he didn't care one way or another about the man's purported "detrimental actions."

White appreciated the response. You're paying someone to carry out wet work, you don't want to worry about emotions, biases, and opinions clouding your operator's judgment and affecting his performance.

Hill said, "Detrimental to the state, and there's nothing the agency can do, huh?"

White said nothing.

"You want him gone. Unofficially."

White remained silent.

"Any criteria?"

"Inside two weeks."

Hill nodded.

White stood. He fastened his coat buttons, pulled on his gloves, looped the cheerfully colorful scarf around his neck once, and flipped the tail over his shoulder. He said, "The fifteen is yours, just for having the conversation. In two weeks, maybe the Post will run an article about something tragic happening to the governor. If I see that article, another fifteen will land in that Swiss bank account. If I don't," he shrugged. "Good seeing you, Carl. We won't speak again."

White had misspoken twice in ten seconds. His relationship with Carl Hill was only just beginning, and seeing the man again hadn't been good at all. But there was no negotiating with Governor Jordan Jameson.

Most politicians suffer from arrogance and hypocrisy. Most are smart enough to make deals, to compromise, to go along to get along if the situation warranted. Not Jameson. He took a politician's usual afflictions to the top shelf. He set the gold medal standard. Not only had he refused the bribe, but he fought the incinerator project with a zeal disproportionate to the plan. He used it as a jumping-off point to attack the president and the administration on a myriad of unrelated issues. He did it with a condescending, smarmy smirk on his face, the subtext of which read, "I'm the smartest person in the room."

Unfortunately for the "smartest person in the room," blind narcissism prevented him from realizing that he'd bumped into an immovable object in the form of Danny White's presidential orders. There'd be no more committees, debates, or hearings. No more consultations. No more studies. White had the information he needed. He was on a tight timeline, and he'd run out of patience. He walked out the diner's front door, while chills that had nothing to do with DC's December weather rippled up and down his spine. As unpleasant as they were, moralistic shivers wouldn't prevent him from fulfilling the president's wishes.

In Wisconsin, ten days later, the first lazy flakes of snow that Carl Hill had predicted started to fall. A four-door Chevrolet Bel Air pulled to a stop in front of the governor's home, tires crunching on the hard-packed snow covering the driveway. Hill's hand tightened on the handle of the knife in his pocket. The car door opened. The dome light blinked to life, casting weak light into a dark front yard. Governor Jameson gathered his belongings from the passenger's seat and climbed out of his car. The door slammed shut with a heavy chunk. The yard fell back into its previous darkness. For a final time, Hill mentally rehearsed the sequence of events that would follow…

… how he'd move out from the beneath the shadow of the pine tree when the governor's foot landed on the first step up to his front door, how he'd move with whisper-quiet stealth on the fresh snow beside the driveway and reach the bottom of the staircase when the governor reached the top, how he'd bypass the creaky second riser he had discovered earlier when he rehearsed his route and smashed the porch light, leaving the stoop in darkness, how he'd be directly behind the governor when the man opened his front door, how he'd shove him inside, trip him, land on top of him and pin him in place with a knee between his shoulders, how he'd drive the double-edged blade into the side of the governor's neck five times in rapid succession, how he'd drop the knife, push himself to his feet, and walk out of the house, closing the door gently behind him, all of it, from start to finish, fast and methodical. Clinical. The element of surprise was important. The governor used to box. He was familiar with defending himself.

Hill had never done anyone up close. It wouldn't be a problem. Putting an end to several years of tedium was incentive enough. Thirty thousand tax-free dollars didn't hurt, either. And although he hid his opinion from Danny White, the fact that his first up-close-and-personal was a self-impressed politician made the hit much, much easier than it otherwise might have been.

The governor's foot landed on the lower step.

Hill was already in motion.

May, 2028

CHAPTER 21

STEVE USED SOME of Turner's cash to buy a raspberry lemonade with too much ice from Java-Nice-Day. The barista, sporting perky pigtails and acne-dappled cheeks, surprised him with a genuine smile and a level of interest uncharacteristic for a teenaged female. He sipped the juice she served him through a paper straw, lightly scratched his cheek, and considered his next move. Did he head to the airport and catch Tamara at work? Shoot a solo game of pool in the lobby of her building while he waited for her to return home? Backtrack into the CBD, and hopefully find her at Gabriel's?

This late in the afternoon, he wasn't sure he'd find her at the airport.

If she was as unfriendly as Turner described, if she became overwhelmed with the sudden appearance of someone she thought was dead, meeting her at home would almost certainly provoke an extreme reaction, possibly a 911 call. He momentarily imagined trying to explain himself to the police—who he was, where he came from, why the only thing in his pocket was the key to Tamara's home—and gave up when he realized there was no scenario in which the cops didn't throw him in a windowless room with soft padding on the walls.

Gabriel's made the most sense. Neutral ground, distracting surroundings, witnesses in the event their meeting went badly. Based on Turner's comments and judging from Tamara's luxury apartment, she might not be the congenial customer service agent he used to know.

She might not be the same the person who kicked everyone's butt at digital trivia on Friday night and gently teased the geeks with whom he worked for playing *Call of Duty* in their parents' basements on Saturday, instead of asking out one of the ladies who occasionally accompanied her into Ballers.

He slurped the last of the juice out of the cardboard cup through the soggy end of the cardboard straw, and then removed the lid and ate what little ice remained. The cold made his back teeth hurt, but the slurry of sugary ice tasted incredible. His parched body sucked up the moisture like a cactus on the first day of the rainy season.

With his decision made, Turner's loan in his pocket, and the warning about Tamara in his ears, Steve headed back into the city toward Gabriel's, carrying the cup, straw, and chicken burger he'd stowed in his pocket for the yellow dog. Between the lemonade and Turner's aspirin, he felt good. Sleep deprived, but good, aside from nerves that pushed him with an insistence he couldn't resist, toward an overpriced cocktail lounge he normally would have made every effort to avoid.

CHAPTER 22

STEVE RODE A city bus several blocks and then walked several more, all without seeing a garbage can. He entered Gabriel's still carrying the cup, straw, and plastic-wrapped chicken burger. At the bar, he ordered a sparkling water and a glass of ice, doubtful his tequila-poisoned constitution could handle anything stronger. In return (along with his water and ice), he received an unimpressed frown from the bartender. Presumably, the man had calculated his tip based on water, compared it to what he would have received on an eighteen-dollar pint, and deemed Steve a low-value customer. Steve didn't care. The bartender's showy appearance did not impress him. Gabriel's management may have insisted their bar staff wear leather aprons, white shirts, and black armbands to hold up their sleeves—it was that kind of a pretentious place—but they probably didn't insist on twisted-at-the-end mustaches and oiled beards. It seemed Gabriel's was the same in both worlds, and wasn't that a steel-toed kick in the crotch? The one thing that would have benefitted from a significant change was the one thing that remained exactly the same.

Steve chose a half-circle-shaped booth that gave him an unobstructed view of the front door. While he waited for a dead woman to walk into the lounge, he nursed the sparkling water and pushed the empty Java-Nice-Day cup around the table in useless circles. His stomach was twisted into such nervous anticipation that he could barely swallow. He imagined how it might happen when he saw her, how he'd wrap her tightly in his arms and bury his face in her neck so he could smell her lingering perfume and the underlying scent that was hers alone, how he'd drop a hand to her rear and give it a couple of gentle slaps so he could hear her familiar giggle and listen to her say, "Stop that," without meaning it.

After he had waited an eternal thirty or forty minutes, the front door opened, and a group of three walked into the dimly lit lounge, bright daylight behind them making it impossible to see anything but silhouettes. The door swung closed. Steve heard a laugh that he instantly recognized. His eyes adjusted, and for the first time in five months, he saw her.

Tamara wore a businesswoman's blouse, dress slacks, and high heels. Flanked by similarly dressed companions, she looked like a one hundred thousand dollar executive, not a minimum wage passenger service agent. The confidence he'd felt—the certainty that meeting her was the right thing to do—suddenly felt questionable.

Legs shaking, he stood. Steadying himself with his fingers splayed on the table top, he said tentatively, "Tamara?"

She came to a complete stop. She tilted her head and looked at him through wide, shocked eyes. A hand flew to her mouth. "Steve?"

"Yes."

"That's not possible," she mumbled, and then at normal volume she said, "Who are you?"

"It's me." He nodded. "Steve." His tongue was thick; nervousness had dried out his mouth… despite reassuring himself there was no reason to be nervous. This was Tamara, after all. Except it wasn't, not exactly, and as much as he wanted to prove Turner wrong and enjoy a "happy reunion," he didn't know what to expect from the woman standing in front of him. In a dehydrated croak, he said, "I'm here. I just came from CompuTech. I was at our apartment this morning."

One of the women who'd followed Tamara into Gabriel's put a protective hand on her shoulder. She looked as startled as Tamara.

Tamara's second companion leaned in and asked in a perplexed whisper, "Who's he?"

"He looks exactly like Tamara's old boyfriend."

Sounding bemused, Tamara said, "You were in my apartment?"

"I wasn't there last night. This morning, I was."

"I was up at four-thirty. I didn't see you."

"I don't know what time I got there. You go to work at four-thirty A.M.?"

"I'm in the gym at five. I get up, grab a pre-mixed protein shake and do my workout. Then I go to the office. How were you in my apartment and I didn't know?"

She'd asked a question he couldn't answer. He said, "I was in no condition… I wouldn't have heard you. I didn't expect to see you. I thought I was somewhere else. You're supposed to be…" His voice failed. He wondered, were there time zones between worlds? How late did he leave Zak's? Midnight maybe? One A.M.? Assuming an hour walk from the bar to the apartment, he would have been sound asleep long before Tamara got up for the gym. If she was already gone when he arrived, then he'd somehow jumped ahead several hours when he crossed over. He shrugged. "I don't know. Maybe your alarm goes off. You get up. Jump into your routine. You're in a rush. I was buried under a blanket on the sofa. You don't expect someone to be there… so nobody is there."

Tamara's bewilderment melted away. Two vertical lines appeared between her eyes. Over-there he'd named them her "livid-lines." "I can't believe you *broke* into my apartment!" She hit the word "broke" with a steely edge.

"I didn't break in," he assured her. "In a way, it's my home, too. I have a key. A bunch of my things are there." He knew this was an extreme exaggeration—the scabby apartment and her opulent building shared nothing more than an address—but in his eagerness to see her, he hadn't thought about his approach. He hadn't figured out what to say. The need to explain falling asleep in one place and waking up in another hadn't crossed his mind. His existence in this world was supposed to be the impossible-to-explain part. Now he was on his back foot, desperately searching for common ground, and judging by the crossed arms and flinty glare, failing miserably. "I can explain," he lied as reassuringly as possible. "It will take a few minutes."

"They aren't *your* things. They're mine. They're reminders of a time before the accident." She pulled her cell phone out of her purse. "I don't know who you are. I'm one step away from calling the cops. Another word, you creep stalker, and I will."

"Give me five minutes, Tamara. Please." He held up his arms, showing her open palms, a placating gesture. "Right here. Right now. Your friends will be watching. Nice and safe. You've got nothing to lose." He tried a smile. "You've got to admit, you're curious. Right?"

She stared at him for a long time. In the background, unrecognizable music played. People murmured, and glasses clinked. For an instant, he saw a flicker of interest behind her shock and anger. She slowly lowered her phone. She looked back and forth between her hovering companions. "Ladies," she said. "I'll be five minutes."

Steve returned to the cushy bench seat on which he'd waited for her. Tamara sat down opposite him, her handbag on the bench beside her, phone on the table near her fingertips. Her companions found a table a few feet away and did a poor job of pretending they weren't paying attention to everything happening beside them. He ignored them. His attention was on Tamara. He'd expected shock and grief. They were the same emotions he'd grappled with over the preceding five months. He hadn't expected anger, although he probably should have, after ambushing her and telling her he'd been inside her apartment. Now, though, sitting across from her in silence, he decided his unexpected appearance was not the entire reason for her anger. Beneath her expertly applied makeup, he recognized a rigidity in her features and a heaviness under her eyes, sure signs of persistent stress and fatigue. An undercurrent of seriousness had replaced the light-heartedness he was used to seeing. She reinforced this assessment a second later, when she fixed the bartender with an intense stare.

In the strange telepathic way that people have of picking up stares, the man looked up from the counter on which he was preparing cocktails.

She widened her eyes and gave her head a slight wobble.

The bartender, lips knife-blade thin below his twisted mustache, walked out from behind the bar carrying a cocktail glass in each hand, clear liquid and wedges of lime. His face was blank as a white-washed wall.

Tamara said, "Less ice today, right?"

"Yes, ma'am." His noncommittal voice made the honorific sound disrespectful. He set the drinks on the table, did a one-eighty, and started for the bar.

"Two checks," she called after him, and in a mumbled voice, "in case that wasn't obvious."

Steve watched the interaction with unhappy curiosity. His immediate conclusion was that she and the bartender had a history that ended unpleasantly. For an instant, he felt a stab of irrational jealousy. It disappeared as quickly as it arrived, leaving behind a fresh feeling of loss. He'd come in search of a lady whose favorite day at work was Casual Friday, who enjoyed starting the weekend with digital trivia in a crowded sports bar, who tied her hair back on Saturday, and wore sweat pants on Sunday. He'd found a self-assured professional in an upscale lounge with her equals, resplendent in clothing reminiscent of Gucci or Dior. Not a hair out of place. Turner's statement echoed in his mind: people are reflections. They're not the same between worlds. Steve recognized Tamara, but he didn't know her. Her history was irrelevant.

She plucked the straw out of one glass, dropped it on the table, and took a long swallow. Some of the tension left her body. She set the glass down. Folding her arms, she said, "Well?"

Hoping to thwart her eavesdropping companions, Steve answered in a lowered voice, "First, I'll tell you what happened. Then I'll tell you how I ended up here." He wanted to split the story into separate parts. Establishing who he was, erasing doubt in her mind, would lend credibility to the more implausible part of the story—the part he doubted she'd believe. The part he scarcely believed himself. "We went to Cancun on vacation. Our return flight—"

"Don't say 'we' and 'our.' I went to Cancun with Steve Quinn. He died in the crash."

"The way I remember it, *you* died in the crash."

"Oh, Jesus."

"Hey!" Steve said more forcefully than he intended. "You sat down. I assumed you were going to listen. Stop interrupting. You might learn something."

She stiffened. The livid-lines deepened. "I'm VP of Operations at the largest regional airline in the northwest. I don't appreciate being spoken to in that tone." She sounded simultaneously defensive and aggrieved, as if explaining who she was and what she did happened so frequently that it had become an unwelcome chore.

"I know you as a passenger service agent at an insignificant connector," he said. "Not that it makes any difference to me." He continued in a hurry in case she took his comment as an insult and decided to leave. "Either way, you won two free standby tickets at your company Christmas party. We went to Cancun…"

He recounted their struggles with inoperative air conditioners and how they'd switched rooms twice in an effort to find an appliance that blew *cold* air on an eighty-six-degree day. Her features softened and a smile brushed her lips when he spoke about a beach bar that became a favorite, a place that served generous portions of Pico de Gallo and tortilla chips and signaled the beginning of happy-hour each day by playing "Hotel California" on a dock situated between bottles of tequila and rum. When he explained how he survived the crash in which she died because of a simple seat swap, she wept silently, using a napkin to blot the corners of her eyes.

She finished the first gin and tonic and sipped the second one.

He expected a caustic reaction when he described his arrival in this world, but including details only he could have known regarding their relationship helped lessen her skepticism. Undoubtably, two gin and tonics also helped take some of the sting from her nettles. She left her phone alone; she didn't call the police as she'd threatened earlier, nor did she stand up and leave. When there was nothing left to tell, she sat back and exhaled heavily, like she was trying to blow away all the emotions of their meeting. Staring at the ceiling, she muttered, "Give me a break. Please?"

Without a clue as to what might happen next, Steve waited for her to regroup while, inside, his heart galloped, and the rose-colored reunion fantasy slipped farther away.

It took twenty or thirty seconds for her assertive manner to reappear. In the politely non-negotiable voice of the executive she was, she said, "It seems like you're Steve—"

"I am."

"—but unfortunately, you're not the Steve I knew."

He nodded, unsurprised. As each minute ticked past, it had become clear that this version of Tamara wasn't the person he'd known for nine fulfilling years, no matter how much she looked like her.

Tamara said, "I don't understand what's happening. I don't know how you're *almost* him. I don't buy this different world nonsense." She glanced at her companions, held up an index finger, and mouthed, "One second." Her gaze returned to Steve. "I'm leaving. I've had a really long day. I'm exhausted. And now, I have *something else* to think about all night. Thanks for that." She stood. Spring-loaded, her friends bounced to their feet and rushed toward her. She said, "Ladies. I'm sorry. I have to cut this short. I'm going home."

A chorus of "Are you okay?" and "What can we do?" ensued, followed by a chaotic bustle of air kisses and hugs. One of the women said she'd pay for Tamara's drinks, and Tamara thanked her and replied, "I'll see you at Pilates in the morning. After that, lunch. My treat. To make up for… whatever this was."

Steve picked up the Java-Nice-Day cup. With his eyes on Tamara striding toward the front door, he hurriedly asked one of the companions, "Where are the garbage cans in this city?"

She answered with a confused look.

"On the street?" He jiggled the cardboard cup. "I couldn't find a garbage can."

"Most people are morons," she said. "Give them two cans, one for trash, one for recycling, you'd think they'd throw the right thing in the right can, wouldn't you? But they don't. So the city removed all the cans. How do you not know this? Leave it on the table." She paused. "By the way..."

He glanced at her expectantly.

"... Tamara's been through a lot. You should leave her alone."

"If that's what she wants," Steve said, and started for the front door.

"That *is* what she wants. She didn't ask you to leave with her."

The comment put a hitch in his step, but he kept moving.

Out on the sidewalk, Tamara was waving at an oncoming taxi. She cut him a sideways look. In response to the surprise that must have shown on his face—taxis were a lavish expense they didn't spend money on Over-there—she said, "I'm not walking fifty miles in high heels." In a less severe tone, she said, "Where will you spend the night?"

Steve's mouth flapped open and closed. Without hope, he said, "I stayed at the apartment last night."

"You stayed in my apartment without permission. I'm asking about tonight." She did not rationalize the un-invite with comments about the small size of her apartment, how there was nothing in the fridge, or that it was difficult to keep clean with only one inhabitant, never mind two... She left no room for negotiation. He was not welcome.

Steve sighed and dropped his gaze to his shoes. He wondered how she'd react if she knew he'd peeked in her underwear drawer earlier in the day. He said, "Ethan Turner booked me a hotel."

A look of surprise crossed her face, followed quickly by an unmistakable expression of dislike. It appeared as though she liked Turner as much as he liked her. Belatedly, Steve thought he should have mentioned Turner's name earlier. It would have been a good way of adding supportive evidence to the story he'd told her. He said, "We still need to talk, Tamara."

"I'm not sure about that," she said. A taxi that reminded him of a Toyota Prius rolled to a noiseless stop. Double parked, the driver ducked down and peered through the passenger's window. Tamara stepped between two parked cars. As she opened the cab's door, she said, "I'll need time."

He started to ask, "How much time," but she slammed the door shut, cutting off the question. He watched the car drive away, losing sight of it in traffic a few seconds later.

He swore under his breath.

When he learned that Tamara was alive, he imagined his second night in this shiny new world would begin when she came home from work, and he tore her undies off with his teeth. Seven minutes later, they'd start again, setting a more leisurely pace. Ridiculous, maybe. Unrealistic. Not an expectation grounded in reality. On the flip side, could he have reasonably expected the day to go as poorly as it had? Unlikely. And, with orders to meet human resources from a man who was acting more like a boss than a friend, Steve didn't expect tomorrow to be much better.

Morosely, he fished the hotel business card that Turner had given him out of his pocket.

CHAPTER 23

AFTER THE CALAMITOUS meeting with Tamara at Gabriel's, Steve checked into the hotel Turner had booked for him. Comfortable and impersonal, the room had a queen-sized bed and a large television standing on a mass-produced credenza. In the three-piece bathroom, a facecloth, hand towel, and bath towel were stacked in a tidy pyramid on a laminated counter designed to resemble marble. For some reason, there were four rolls of toilet paper on the counter, arranged like a four-leaf clover. Four! Like the maids had witnessed something intestinally catastrophic in the past and didn't want to deal with it again.

Surveying the room took less than a minute, after which Steve sat on the foot of the bed and stared at an unremarkable print in a generic frame, hanging at a crazy angle on the wall. He asked the empty room, "Now what?" and realized that he'd discovered the answer to the question he'd asked himself earlier. He wasn't locked in a secure facility because he had no place to go and very little money to get there. Turner wasn't worried about Steve running away because he didn't need to be. If Turner harbored any concerns, he only had to station someone outside the hotel in one of this world's freakily quiet cars.

The moment that paranoid idea entered Steve's mind, it lodged there. Without evidence or proof, he *knew* Turner was monitoring him.

He turned on the television and used the remote control to thumb through a long list of channels. The programs he saw resembled those from Over-there—news, sports, dramas—although none were exactly the same. He turned it off. On a different night, he felt sure that what he saw on television would have captured his attention. Comparing the differences would be fun and interesting. Educational. Tonight, he was having a difficult time concentrating; too many strange and unexplainable changes in the last twenty-four hours, on top of which the visit with Tamara had shaken him. Even making allowances for the surprise of seeing him, she'd acted badly. He wasn't sure how to reconcile losing her twice, once through cataclysmic death and, five months later, through disinterest on her part and dislike on his. Alone in a run-of-the-mill hotel room, with nobody to text or meet for a beer, a wholly unexpected longing for the scabby apartment and the mindlessness of a familiar sitcom filled him with lonely depression.

Fifteen minutes after he entered the hotel, with the room's stubbornly silent walls pressing in on him and the unpleasant emptiness enveloping him, he straightened the crooked print on the wall and headed for Zak's or, if Turner was to be believed, Dak's in this world. He didn't expect to find answers or fulfillment in a bar—that was too much of a cliché—but that's where all the craziness began, so who knew? If nothing else, he'd no longer be alone with his thoughts.

He exited the revolving front door to the hotel and jigged sideways into the shadows at the side of the entrance. He gave the street an uneasy scan and immediately felt foolish. Who did he expect to see? Some guy in a ball cap slouched down behind the steering wheel of a parked car, trying not to look in his direction? Someone with his collar turned up, pretending to tie his shoelace?

Steve saw nothing suspicious or worrisome. He started walking.

Happily, Dak's wasn't significantly different from Over-there. The entire atmosphere was a little less worn out, or, for the perpetually optimistic, it had a little less personality. If asked, Steve would have likened it to a new car versus an identical model a couple of months old. Maybe the leather seats had creases. Maybe the carpet under the gas pedal had a heel-shaped wear pattern. Maybe the door panels had scuffs where a person's foot scraped when he climbed in and out. Other than that, the place was the same, right down to the stage along the back wall, sixteen inches off the floor, so every patron had a good view of the band.

Tonight, a DJ was making the music happen. According to a faux leather folio bound with a wide red ribbon—easier to clean greasy chicken-wing fingerprints off fake leather than the real thing—the DJ played different styles of music on different days of the week. Yesterday, it was blues, the day before techno. Tomorrow jazz was scheduled, the good kind that made a person move his feet, rather than the Michael Bolton kind, Steve guessed. Tonight was classic rock, according to the folio.

As in the Over-there world, thirsty patrons bellied up to a cube-shaped bar dominating the middle of the room. Low tables with candles and comfortable chairs with cushions lined the perimeters of the space. For no other reason than his own nostalgic amusement, Steve sat in the same place as he had the night he crossed over, which already felt like several months ago. His stool wobbled when he sat down. He snagged two circular coasters and leveled out the short leg. He flipped through the folio, past two pages of fancy cocktails and several pages of whiskey choices until he found an extensive beer list all the way in the back. He ordered an IPA and listened to "Dream On," a bona fide rock classic going back to 1973, if he remembered correctly—weird thing to remember, but when you're talking about one of the greatest rock anthems ever, maybe not *too* weird—and he wondered how Aerosmith had crossed between the worlds. How did any music cross over? For that matter, how did *anything* cross? Why this particular thing, but not that one? Why Estee Lauder, but not the cologne he wore? That was a head-scratcher, something Steve could have spent a great deal of time thinking about… or no time at all because the answer was probably unsolvable.

He shook his head and mentally said, *Who cares?* "Dream On" was a masterpiece in any world. That was all that mattered.

Someone sat down several stools to his left. He flicked a glance in that direction, scarcely registering the individual's presence.

Now that he was stuck in this world, what was he supposed to do for money? Turner's loan wouldn't last long. What about a job? A place to live? The answers depended on Turner, the meeting with HR, and the plans that Dark Sky—whatever that was—had in store for him. A flood of anger joined the mixing bowl of confusion and disappointment. He didn't like being a passenger, completely under Turner's control. The situation couldn't last. He had to take charge in some way. Push back. Force a change—which all sounded good in theory, but was impossible to put into action without more information.

A woman's accented voice said from his left, "Come here often?"

Steve smiled, remembering the look Paige gave him when he asked her the same question. Same bar, same stool, same question. Vastly different circumstances. He said, "That line should be put out of my misery." He swiveled, grinning to take the sting out of his words…

…and recoiled in shock.

CHAPTER 24

THE SMALLEST OF innocent smiles brushed the woman's lips. Her shoulders were down, her back as straight as a telephone pole. The nose ring still dangled from her left nostril, looking as silly and pointless as it had twenty-four hours before. In contrast, the Meghan Markle messy bun looked just as good. Her clothes were different. Tonight, Paige Patel was dressed like a day at the office: a long voluminous skirt in random shades of blue and green, a solid white blouse, a light gray alpaca sweater with the top button fastened, and the sleeves pushed up her forearms.

Steve whispered, "What the fuck?"

She crossed one leg over top of the other, flashing him a pointy-toed, high-heeled boot from beneath the skirt. In her quiet voice, that engaging mix of Indian and British, she said, "Staring is impolite, Sweet Pea."

He said, "Someone was watching the hotel. Was it you?"

"It wasn't me."

"Last night, you drugged me with the red pill."

She paged slowly through the folio. "I *facilitated* with the red pill."

Any way you do the math, Steve thought, *four quarters add up to a dollar.* He said, "You told me you were in HR. With a tech company." His voice sounded feeble. "Did Ethan Turner send you?"

"Smarter than the average bear, aren't you? I'm going to try a Deep

Dark Whiskey. And a wee snack. Maybe jalapeno poppers? Do you like those?"

"Jalapeno poppers? Peppers filled with cheese and deep fried in scalding hot oil?" He shook his head and made a disbelieving face. "What's not to love?"

Paige blew past his mild sarcasm. "I wonder if they have them here?"

"What's with you and poppers?"

She laughed and waved over the bartender. "What's your name, sweetheart?"

The bartender said, "Lynn."

A wave of vertigo washed through Steve's body.

Lynn.

Not Linda, like Over-there, but close enough.

Paige said, "You look tired, Lynn. Like it's been a long week. Kiddies at home?"

"Two. They run me ragged."

"You've got a lot on your plate. I'm going to add a little more. Sorry about that." She ordered her Deep Dark Whiskey and then asked, "Have you got jalapeno poppers?"

"Six to an order."

"Great." Paige showed Lynn the two-fingered peace sign. "Two orders, please."

"And an Old-Fashioned," Steve added. Not the best choice on his limited budget, but Turner's money spent pretty well, and the IPA he'd been nursing didn't have the snap, crackle, or pop he needed to settle his jangling nerves. After the rush of sadness he experienced watching Paige walk away a mere twenty-four hours before, the blissful warmth that filled his heart now was intoxicating. Unfortunately, the abrupt mental cartwheel made the confidence and rapport he'd built with her feel murky. He couldn't decide what to feel.

While they waited for the jalapeno poppers, Lynn returned with a metal cocktail shaker, a butane torch, and a cedar plank. She lit the plank on fire and then promptly extinguished it with an upside-down tumbler, effectively filling the tumbler with smoke. She let the smoke twist inside it for several seconds before removing the cedar plank. With smoke curling out of the tumbler, she dropped in an ice cube the size of a golf ball and poured the contents of the shaker on top of it.

Paige watched the elaborate procedure, ooh-ing and awe-ing with clear enjoyment.

Steve nodded. Now, he understood why Paige had apologized for adding to Lynn's workload: a Deep Dark Whiskey was a complicated cocktail.

When Lynn finished, Paige took a sip and moaned with appreciation. Steve took a deeper, quieter mouthful of his Old-Fashioned. On Dak's sound system, Fleetwood Mac's unparalleled "Go Your Own Way" began to play. It occurred to him that the song was twice his age, and it still ended up on everybody's classic rock playlist. He said, "This is such—"

"A great song?"

"What I was going to say."

"Forty years old. It hasn't lost a thing."

"Forty?" He laughed. "Closer to sixty. *Rumors* was released in 1977. It still ranks as one of the best albums of all time. It was selected for preservation in the National Recording Registry."

"Which means?"

"It is culturally, historically, or aesthetically important and informs or reflects life in the United States," he quoted.

"Look at you going all Jeopardy on me."

"I remember weird things," he said. "Why won't Ethan tell me what's happening? Why delegate the task to you?"

"He's busy. He's got something happening in Las Vegas tonight. Also, it's my job, isn't it? Upper-level managers aren't good at one-on-one interactions. With handing out compliments or delivering bad news. I am." She flashed him a huge grin. "He explained the basics, I assume? A nuclear explosion created a physical link between our two worlds?"

Steve said, "The Passage." He didn't have time to think about the "bad news" part of Paige's statement. She'd already moved on.

"That was the most significant result of the testing. However, to this day, scientists are discovering consequences beyond what was obvious in 1954. Initially, the Castle Bravo fallout spread over 7000 square miles. Radioactive ash found its way into every living thing. This created immediate problems. Everything from lesions and hair loss to cancer and radioactive cow's milk. As fallout circled the globe, more problems became apparent. Thyroid tumors, birth deformities, severe growth retardation—"

"To name a few."

On a roll, Paige ignored the interruption. "The energy and the fallout combined in ways we don't understand. This confluence thinned select areas between the worlds. Thin spots can be found as far away as Japan, Australia, and Florida. They're common on the west coast of North America, probably because that's the first significant land mass the fallout reached."

Lynn carried over two plates with the jalapeno poppers, accompanied by a gooey-looking dipping sauce and random sprigs of limp parsley, to help give the impression that poppers weren't as bad for a person's waistline as they were. Paige picked one up by the stem. She tilted her head back. The tip of her tongue touched her bottom lip. She took a bite, closed her eyes, and sighed with pleasure. "Yummy. A wee bit hot." She fanned a hand in front of her mouth and gestured at the plate. "Eat."

Steve found the whole performance disturbingly erotic, considering they were only jalapeno poppers. He did a palms-up. "In a minute." He could live without cheese on most days. He disliked burning hot food every day. He sipped his Old-Fashioned. "How do you know about thin spots?"

"People show up in strange places without reasonable explanations. They're vagrants who come from nowhere. They have unrecognizable currency in their pockets. Everything they consider important is in a backpack. They say demented things, leading people to believe they're psychologically unstable. Some of them certainly are. But, analyze what they say and the similarities are...compelling." She waved a dismissive hand, brushing the subject aside. "You're not one of those people. The red pill allowed you to tolerate the thin spot."

"I knew there was something wrong with that alley. When I got near it," he hesitated, searching for the right words, "it pushed me away." In a cascade of frustration, he downed all of the remaining Old-Fashioned and chased it with a mouthful of beer. "What does any of this have to do with me?"

She gently touched his hand. "Go easy. Otherwise, you're no good to me."

"Pardon me?"

"We have unfinished business."

He looked into her dark eyes, which were full of wry humor. Was that an invitation? Lord help him, he couldn't tell. It sounded like an invitation. He'd heard guys a decade older than him say they'd reached a point when women no longer saw them. They became invisible. Steve couldn't remember the last time an unknown woman had shown an interest in him, although he hadn't been paying attention. He thought he was a little young to be wearing the invisibility cloak the old guys spoke about. His uncertainty must have showed.

"You're hopeless, aren't you?" Her quiet voice dropped a tick. He turned his head slightly to hear her better. She said, "Do you still want to do bad things with me?"

In a dry voice, he said, "I have no idea what's going on."

"Do you?"

"Do I ever."

"You've got a nice, anonymous hotel room, I think?"

That settled the uncertainty, even for a guy who'd lost the ability to tell if he was being propositioned. He flicked a glance at her legs and the boot-clad feet peeking out from beneath her skirt. "Will you wear those kick-ass boots?"

"Absolutely." She tilted forward. With her lips brushing his ear, she whispered, "Indian women tend to have too much body hair. I don't have that problem." She paused, giving him time to catch her implication. "You understand, Sweet Pea?"

He swallowed dryly and gave her a single dumb nod.

She straightened. "Do you like it here in this world? Not your personal circumstances. I understand that's an irritation. Change is difficult. I'm talking about the greater environment." She waved a hand around in vague circles, meaning, he guessed, everything in the world.

He thought about the clean air, the aggressive recycling programs, the preponderance of hydrogen-powered vehicles, the lack of pollution... He couldn't get over how much cleaner the outside air smelled. He'd never considered the smell Over-there as bad. The "greater environment," as Paige called it, was indisputably better than Over-there. He said, "It's way nicer."

With a nod and a smile, Paige said, "Yes. It is. Thanks to a 1964 hurricane that flattened Haiti and President Birch's foresight. Your world and this world are diverging, Steve. Remarkably similar in 1954, they are now vastly different. The divergence began with Castle Bravo. Decades of little changes and experiments have accelerated the divergence. The result of those cumulative choices is the beautiful world you see today. It's all in jeopardy. You're here to help prevent that."

She drained her glass and smacked her lips theatrically. "The secret ingredient to the perfect Deep Dark Whiskey is definitely the cedar-smoked tumbler." She opened her purse, fished out her wallet, and put a fifty on the bar. "You're not a cuddler, are you? I don't like sharing my side of the bed."

"I don't take up much space."

An hour later, on top of a thick layer of blankets (so as not to hole-punch the mattress with a spiky boot heel), Paige straddled him with one hand in her hair and the other on his chest for balance. Lying on his back, the view was... bewitching. She hadn't lied when she said she didn't have excessive body hair. Her breath came in rapid, tiny moans as she lifted and dropped her hips. When he tried to match her rhythm, she told him to lie still and let her do the work. At one point, her cell phone chimed. Her eyes snapped open, and she gasped out a curse. She reached for the phone on the bedside table.

"What?" he said incredulously. "Now?"

"That's the sound of something important, my friend. Work never stops." She started grinding her hips again. "I don't expect you to stop, either." Panting shallowly, nibbling her lower lip, she thumbed in a reply and then tossed the phone at the clothing littering the floor beside the bed.

Some unknowable time later, the sound of running water awakened Steve. He lay on his back with his fingers linked beneath his head, his eyelids drooping sleepily. When he no longer heard the shower, he called, "Do you want to order—"

"I'm going home," she interrupted.

"Really? You don't have to."

She poked her head out of the bathroom. Wrapped in a thick towel and raking wet hair behind her ears with her fingers, she made a gentle, shushing sound. "We'll both sleep better in our own beds."

Too drowsy and content to object, and unable to disagree with her logic, Steve lay back with a yawn. A few minutes later, she walked out of the bathroom, fully dressed. She leaned over and kissed him on the temple. Cold, wet hair tickled his face. She murmured, "Don't rush tomorrow. Two is early enough. I have some arrangements to make."

"Arrangements?"

She pulled back. Stood. A second later, the door to the hallway opened. Standing in the slash of light filling the entrance to the hotel room, she said, "That text? You're flying to Africa tomorrow night." She winked. The door clicked shut behind her. The bright, warm light in which she was haloed, vanished.

CHAPTER 25

ETHAN TURNER BOUGHT a ten-foot length of rope off a spool in a hardware store, after which he headed to a twenty-four-hour Walmart. His attention was split between the mouth breathers in the store and the decidedly un-Paige-like response she'd answered with after he texted her earlier in the evening. He'd told her to advise Steve Quinn that he'd be flying to Africa. She responded with a bright yellow thumbs-up emoji and a misspelled statement saying she'd let him know.

Baffling.

Where was her typical request for details? Her usual short, concise plan of action? And, a spelling mistake? Auto-correct never got the better of Paige Patel.

Turner could have told Quinn about the Africa trip himself, except Paige was a people person, skilled at breaking contentious news. Not that he cared about Quinn's feelings—the man was going to the Congo one way or another—but he did care about minimizing resistance. You'll never get the best out of a man if you lock him in a cage and tell him he has no choice. Ordering someone who'd recently survived a plane crash to climb aboard another airplane and fly to a dangerous part of the world with people he didn't know, in order to help with a task about which he had no knowledge, was like locking him in a cage.

On the other hand, give him the perception of freedom—let him visit a girlfriend, encourage him to enjoy a cold beverage on a grand spring day, insist that he explore his polished new world—he's bound to help more willingly. Helping is less of an obligation now, and more of a "thank you." He's responding to the privilege he's been given by providing a favor in return. If he's extra impressed with what he sees and experiences—Turner thought this part was a long shot but remained cautiously hopeful—maybe he becomes an asset. An inside man involved in design and construction at CompuTech? Not simply an employee, but an individual whom Turner knew, and with whom he'd worked? Quinn's future value could be incalculable.

Much of that was up to Paige Patel, the sugar-coating expert. Turner had instructed her to be vague about the details. *Wait until you're high above the Atlantic to fully explain the purpose of the trip*, he said. If Quinn objected at seventy-eight thousand feet, how explosive could his reaction be?

A second reason Turner couldn't brief Quinn himself was his uncertainty about when he'd be back on the coast. He'd convinced himself that Sean Caulder, Global Solutions' Texas representative, had reached his best-before date…

… hence Turner's return to Vegas and an evening co-mingling with the human slugs in Wally World, like the woman in the fitness section trying on workout gloves. She wore low-rise exercise pants with "Juicy" written in pink across her wide-as-a-wheelbarrow ass. In what had to be a wonderfully deliberate attempt at coordination, she also wore a matching pink thong, the straps of which rose well above the waistband of her pants. Then there was the clown in the grocery section, scuffing his shabby bedroom slippers back and forth on the floor, as he compared different brands of low-calorie microwavable dinners. His *Dark Side of the Moon* T-shirt was a size too small, exposing a crescent of hairy, white flesh that sagged over the waistband of his sweat pants.

Funny how these were things Turner didn't want to see, but from which he couldn't look away. He didn't much like Wally World, although that didn't prevent him from enjoying the irony: among the sweatpants brigade, he was the only out-of-place person in the store, what with his overpriced jeans and tailored dress shirt.

It didn't take him long to find what he needed—Walmart had almost everything—and an hour and a half later, on the other side of town, he knocked on a door to a *way* off the Strip motel room. In a city known for security cameras, you couldn't be a high-profile Texas senator and enjoy your Thai hooker threesome unless you went to an area that was deliberately dark and purposely discreet. Dressed in black, with his jacket collar turned up and a ball cap pulled down low, Turner blended in perfectly.

Sean Caulder answered the knock, cracking the door open without delay. He said politely, "Mr. Turner? This is an unexpected surprise." In a comical act of contradiction, he immediately slammed the door shut in Turner's face.

Turner was ready. He'd given himself space. He rocked back on one foot for momentum, raised the other foot, and kicked the door violently above the knob. It burst open. He heard a grunt of surprise. He exploded into the room, the small backpack of supplies he wore bouncing on his shoulders. As fast as he kicked open the door, he slammed it shut behind him.

Hairy and round, his middle-aged paunch still wet from the shower, Caulder staggered backward, one arm twirling the air for balance. The other hand clutched the towel around his waist in a useless attempt to hold it in place. Eyes wide with indignant anger, he shouted, "What the hell is this?"

Turner responded with a smile lacking friendliness or joviality. He pushed an open palm slowly toward the floor and said, "Shhh," drawing out the sound into a long sibilant hiss. Caulder fell silent. Turner said, "All you had to do was hide your money in the Turks. Avoid behavior that might draw unwelcome attention. Be discreet."

He gave the room a quick left-to-right appraisal. Beneath a heavy layer of shower steam, it stunk of cigarette smoke and stale beer. The bathroom fan made an unbalanced squealing sound that rose and fell like a distant police siren. The blankets on the king-sized bed were a tangled mess, the tangerine-colored lamp shades tilted at unnatural angles. He said, "This is not discreet."

"Of course, it is. That's why I'm here." Caulder sounded confused. "I'd rather be at Mandalay Bay or Plutus."

"In life, Sean. Day to day," Turner said. "You put in long hours at the office. Drive the kids to dance lessons. Baseball. So on, and so forth. You take the wife out for dinner once a month; call it 'date night.' You forget about sex, like every other married man on the planet. Time goes by, kids move out, you get divorced. You follow the natural order of things, in other words. You retire and move to the islands. That's when you start burning up the cash Global Solutions paid you. That's when you hire all the Thai escorts your Viagra prescription can handle. What you don't do is rent a room in Vegas and hope the pros don't recognize you. That is not discretion."

Turner paused, took a breath, and scanned the room. He pointed at the television. "Grab the TV, would you? Shift it so it faces the closet. And put the chair in front of the closet door."

The problem with what Turner had in mind lay in the manner in which the average hotel room was constructed, specifically the low ceilings. He'd spent time thinking about the problem on the flight from the coast and couldn't come up with an answer. He considered his mystification indicative of a stable mind. People who committed suicide in hotel rooms had the mechanics figured out because they, of course, did not have stable minds. He ended up resorting to Google, in conjunction with a hazy memory of Chester Bennington's sad passing, Linkin Park's talented young vocalist, and before him, Michael Hutchence's untimely death in Sydney, before he understood how suicide by hanging was possible in a hotel, despite the limitations of the room. Vaguely queasy after his research, Turner deleted his browser history. He didn't want to inadvertently stumble on that heartbreaking shit ever again.

Caulder didn't move. He said, "What?"

"I'm losing patience, Sean."

With a sigh that was probably designed to sound like exasperation, Caulder did as he was asked, rotating the television on its stand, carrying the desk chair to the closet, and sitting down with the towel draped modestly on his lap. "What are we doing?"

Turner shrugged the backpack off his shoulders, caught it as it fell, and lobbed it at Caulder's feet. "You watch a movie while the ladies were here?"

Caulder dropped his chin to his chest. He said nothing.

"Boot it up again. Put it on mute." A few seconds later, the movie was running. Lots of closeups of naked flesh that Turner couldn't see very well with the TV angled the way it was, but Caulder could see easily from his position on the chair. Turner said, "Open the backpack."

Caulder picked it up, unzipped it, pulled out a pair of white underpants with a lacy waistband and a T-shirt with a brightly colored graphic of a unicorn standing beneath a rainbow. The catchlights in the unicorn's oversized anime eyes were as big and shiny as five-carat diamonds. Colored sequins were sewn into the rainbow. It had taken Turner longer than he had expected to find adult-sized clothing that looked like something a child might wear, but Walmart had almost everything.

Caulder repeated, "What are we doing?"

"Put them on," Turner ordered, making a show of pulling out his cell phone and bringing up the camera app.

"Pictures? Blackmail?" Caulder shook his head. "Nope. Not going to happen. We can figure this out. But not with photos."

"There's nothing to figure out. The figuring-out part is done." Turner pulled the stun gun out of his jacket pocket, stepped forward, and pressed the device against the Texan's upper hip. Manufactured to produce electricity in the same phase as a human's nervous system, but at a much higher voltage, the weapon disrupted the tiny neurological impulses that allowed Caulder to move his muscles voluntarily.

Basically, all the extra voltage "confused" and overwhelmed his neuromuscular system. Turner knew that it caused intense pain, as well as a complete loss of muscle control and physical balance. He held the device in place until it stopped its distinctive rattling; for five long seconds, it dumped 100,000 volts into Caulder's body.

Every muscle in the man's body contracted uncontrollably. He stiffened, lost his balance, and tumbled off the chair. His teeth snapped together with a loud clack. He lay spasming on the stained hotel carpet, eyelids fluttering, eyes showing only the whites. A line of silver drool leaked from one corner of his mouth.

While he waited for Caulder to recover, Turner sat on the foot of the bed and read a particularly good article about virologists' struggles to understand why the infection ravaging Africa was initially so lethal and then so rapidly benign. As tragic as the death toll was in the African slums, most people agreed the world was fortunate that the virus did not survive long outside the human body. Had it survived longer, a mass extinction event would have been entirely possible. He had to Google "mass extinction event." The phrase sounded like something with an official definition. He learned it had to do with magnitude and rate: typically, at least seventy-five percent of a species go extinct in a relatively short period of time. That was a goddamned lot of humans. Turner thought he'd prefer the thinned-out world when it was all said and done, assuming he was among the fortunate twenty-five percent. There was a great deal more information he didn't have time to read...

... Thirteen minutes after he'd been stunned, Caulder struggled to a seated position. Turner was impressed. Thirteen minutes was a decent recovery time for a man so clearly out of shape. The average was fifteen minutes. A few seconds later, after a certain amount of awareness had returned to Caulder's eyes, Turner held up the stun gun and said, "The little bastard smarts, doesn't it?"

Caulder slurred, "I'm dizzy. I feel sick."

"Yeah. It had the same effect on me, back when I did my training. Don't worry about it. In a few hours, the muscle pain goes away. No long-term effects." He nodded at the underwear and t-shirt. "Now, Sean? Remember what we were talking about? Put them on."

Caulder did so, in deliberately slow and sullen silence. When he was "dressed," Turner wobbled the phone camera at him. "Here comes the tricky part. You're not going to like it, but this only works if we sell the scene." He tossed Caulder the ten-foot section of rope. He'd previously tied several knots in it, such that each knot had tightened on top of the one below it, forming a single knot the size of a man's fist halfway down the rope's length. He'd also fashioned a slip-knot into one end of the rope. He told Caulder, "Stand on the chair."

He continued giving simple, one-sentence instructions: *put your head through the loop.*

Drape the rope over the top of the door, so the knot is dangling inside the closet on the opposite side of the door from which you're standing.

Kick the door shut.

"I won't forget this," Caulder said. His voice rose. "You don't have any idea who you're fucking with. I have powerful friends. I will hunt you down. You won't get away with this."

Turner, who'd heard this kind of thing before, was surprised it had taken Caulder as long as it did to start with the threats. He waited for the diatribe to peter out and then asked, "You done?"

"Fuck you," Caulder snapped.

"Okay, Sean. Smile like it's your birthday. It's picture time." Turner snapped several photos of the Texas senator standing on the chair with his back to the closet door. Tethered in place by a short length of rope, wearing a young girl's clothing, an adult movie playing on the television… nobody would question what had gone on in the hotel room. He said, "You don't want these pics getting into the media, do you?"

"They'll ruin me." Caulder's sudden rage had turned into desperate tears. Blubbering, he said, "Delete them. Please. You've made your point. I won't do anything like this again. I promise."

"I know you won't. I believe you. I think you understand the word 'discretion' better than you did an hour ago. But I'm not going to delete the photos. You'll have to trust me to keep them confidential. I trust you won't do anything that would necessitate me publishing them. If we both exercise our new understanding of discretion, neither of us has anything to worry about. Do we?"

Caulder shook his head.

We're almost done," Turner said. "Just one more thing."

He reached out and hit the Texan with the stun gun again, a full charge, a full five seconds.

As they had earlier, Caulder's muscles lost all control. He stiffened and kicked the chair out from beneath him, and his body weight yanked the rope across the top of the closet door until the fist-sized knot inside the closet jammed against the door frame, preventing the rope from sliding any farther, tightening the slip-knot around the man's neck for an impossibly long thirteen minutes.

It wasn't a perfect crime scene.

The burn marks the stun gun left on Caulder's hip were the biggest red flags. There was no way to rectify them, so Turner dismissed them. The question as to why Caulder had a chunk of rope with him was something with which the crime scene investigators would surely struggle. But men didn't normally wear unicorn shirts and lace-trimmed underwear either, so perhaps the rope wasn't much of a concern. As for trace evidence, investigators wouldn't know where to begin. In a hotel room like this, there would have been an abundance long before the senator's autoerotic asphyxiation frolic went horribly wrong. Eventually, if they were exceedingly diligent, they might backtrack Caulder's movements as far as the Global Solutions convention at Plutus, where they'd learn exactly nothing. There wouldn't be any way of determining who was in the room with him. If investigators somehow got that far, they'd have to travel to nine separate countries to speak with nine diplomats who didn't know anything about Caulder's personal life, his proclivities, or where he had gone after the Plutus gathering dispersed.

Turner made sure everything he'd entered the room with, aside from the rope, was stowed in his backpack. He tugged up his collar and pulled down the brim of his cap. It was time to go. The two men who had other business in Vegas were on their way to pick him up. He wondered how one-half of the duo, the individual who'd been in the automobile accident, was feeling. When he changed lanes in front of the motorcycle, he'd misjudged his timing, underestimating the speed the bike was traveling. It must have been moving at a goddamn good clip when it hit the minivan in order to lift the back end of the van off the road.

Even with airbags softening the impact, his man had taken a beating. Apparently, the bruise across his chest where the seatbelt grabbed him made breathing hurt. He had facial contusions from shattered safety glass, a raised bump on his head from the side window, and a mild whiplash from the violence of the rollover. He'd be wearing a thick white collar around his neck for a couple of weeks.

He assured Turner that his injuries wouldn't slow him down. Turner had shrugged. He expected no less out of Brian Messier. What else was a highly experienced mercenary going to say? The man was as indomitable as El Capitan or the Rock of Gibraltar. After a couple of Extra Strength Tylenol and a nap on the back seat during the long drive home to the west coast, he'd feel as good as new. Or, if the pain was unmanageable, Percocet instead of Tylenol, although the pain would have to be much, *much* worse than unmanageable. As well as that shit worked, it came with side effects that were often worse than the symptoms.

As for the guy riding the motorcycle? He was on an unknown astral plane, mulling over his decision to break the nondisclosure agreement he'd signed.

Turner scanned the room a final time: the thin carpet, the toppled chair, the adult film on the television, the man hanging from the rope. The bathroom fan squeaked indifferently. He sighed. The whole scene wore him out and left him dispirited. The tawdriness of it all. He wasn't much of a drinker—didn't care for the taste of alcohol and deeply disliked the loss of control it caused—but a shot of something that burned on its way down seemed like a good idea.

He turned off the light. He hung an overly quaint sign for the standard of the hotel on the exterior doorknob. "Shhh. I'm sleeping in today!" Then, sticking to the shadows, he started walking to the rendezvous point, already thinking about tomorrow's problem: talking Steve Quinn into going to Africa. Turner could have sent a CompuTech local, as he had intimated to the politicians in Las Vegas, but nobody would volunteer to go, what with the plague in Africa and all. He'd have to force the issue. He'd have to kidnap someone. That would attract attention. Afterward, he'd have to kill the individual because he couldn't have that person returning to the US knowing the truth. More attention. Also, why kill an asset? Diablo drone engineers weren't a dime a dozen.

No, using someone equally qualified, a person who didn't have a presence in this world and who therefore wouldn't be missed, made way more sense.

CHAPTER 26

STEVE THOUGHT HE'D put the worst of the crash behind him. Paige's statement as she left his hotel room proved him wrong. He slept fitfully, dreaming of oily orange smoke and the panicked screams of people unable to escape the burning airplane. At four A.M., he gave up and turned on the television. Lying under the covers and leaning against the headboard, he cycled through the channels, coming to a stop on what appeared to be a morning news program.

He assumed the news in this world would show similar content to what he would have seen in his own world. Wildfires burned near LA, a European country experienced a flood, famous Hollywood people were adopting causes as if they were authorities on the subjects... A politician would fake an apology. A VIP would say, "... thoughts and prayers..."

Instead, he saw the dramatically troubled faces of reporters in Africa.

Steve hadn't heard the word "pandemic" much in the years since Covid-19 had reached its absurd pinnacle. Over-there, it had nearly disappeared from reporters' lexicons. However, here, in this world, reporters spoke almost exclusively about a pandemic named Covid-28. By definition, Covid-28 wasn't a pandemic, but the media preferred alarmism to accuracy; they happily used the word whenever possible to describe the massive death toll wreaking havoc in Lusaka, Luanda, and

Harare. Scientists couldn't explain where the virus came from. They didn't know why it died as fast as it arrived. The reason it remained so localized was a mystery. Reporters speculated, in the same hyperactive fashion as 2020, what might happen if the virus did become more virulent. It wasn't spreading, but what if it did? They backstopped their fear-mongering with images of the cities' respective slums. Sad and unfathomable to a middle-class Westerner during "normal" times, the sprawling shanty towns were now made horrifying by the addition of teams clothed in fluorescent orange hazmat suits and protective breathing apparatuses, of hastily built Quonset huts for the storage of bodies, and, in the unfocused distance, of incinerators for disposal of the dead. Charity organizations—the Red Cross, UNICEF, and Global Solutions—were onsite helping in the manner they always did, administrating medical care (everything from toothaches to inoculations), and supplying food, shelter, and water.

Steve watched with rapt attention, his body tilted toward the television, the remote control frozen in his hand. He found himself breathing shallowly, a malignant knot of horror growing at the bottom of his stomach. Covid-19 had been a problem magnified by incompetent politicians and the overzealous media, both of whom turned the public's uncertain fear into hysterical panic. Worldwide, several million people had died. This was different. What he was watching on television was the death of more people *in one city than the entire global death count* of Covid-19.

As with the coverage of Covid-19, it wasn't long before reporters began repeating themselves for lack of new, incendiary details. That didn't stop Steve from scrolling through the channels in search of a story with a different angle until he glanced at the bedside clock and realized how late in the morning it had become. If he didn't get a hustle on, he wouldn't have time for a shower and brunch (or any other delaying tactics he could dream up), and still make it to CompuTech by two.

He did not want to go to CompuTech. The visit was going to result in a fight. There was no way on God's green Earth he was going to Africa. Not after what he'd just watched. The fact that Ethan Turner expected him to go, knowing Steve's recent history, was another clear indication that this wasn't his world. His friend Ethan from Over-there would never have suggested he climb on an airplane again.

Steve walked into the CompuTech foyer closer to three than two, and came face-to-face with an exhausted-appearing Ethan Turner.

Turner gave him a cursory smile. He said, "Good afternoon," and then made a show of checking his watch, a large chrome gadget with wristband links resembling dime-sized washers. "Didn't Paige say two? We'll talk in the conference room." He spun around and walked toward a small room off the lobby.

Gently chastised, Steve followed, thinking, *we're getting to it now*. The cordiality he'd seen from Turner the day before, had disappeared. The hard-edged individual Steve had seen glimpses of was on full display. He took a seat in a comfortable leather chair and then immediately stood and twisted the rod at the side of the window, closing the Venetian blinds, cutting off the glare that Erica was shooting him over the top of the monitor on her granite desk. Once back in the chair, he gave the room a studied look.

Decorated like the lobby, with framed prints, deep carpet, and a rectangular glass-topped table, the room was ideal for impromptu meetings or interviews. Steve suspected its main purpose was to keep casual visitors who didn't merit admittance into the inner sanctum away from the proprietary work taking place in other areas of the building.

On the other side of the table, Turner washed a hand down his thighs, smoothing away the wrinkles in his jeans. He adjusted his shirt cuffs. He looked at his watch and then his phone out of eyes underlined with dark crescents. Steve waited in determined silence, curious to see how this farcical power play would end. Finally, Turner glanced at his shoes. He inhaled. His shoulders and chest rose and his head came up and he opened his mouth...

... and Steve cut him off. "I'm not going to Africa."

Turner's lips thinned, and his eyes narrowed. "Paige filled you in?"

"No." Steve shook his head. "She told me about the past. How I got here, in other words. She did not discuss the future. *Why* I'm here."

"Africa is the future. That's why you're here. You're most definitely going."

"No. I'm not."

"Is that right? You're positive?"

"Yes."

"I'll give you one opportunity to change your mind—"

Steve started to object.

Turner held up an open palm. "Hear me out." He waited until Steve gave him a reluctant nod. "You have no money other than what I gave you. You have no identification that makes sense in this reality. As of tomorrow morning, when your hotel reservation runs out, you have no place to live. As far as I can see, the only thing you do have is a story that doesn't rationally explain who you are or your presence here. Does that sound right? Is that accurate, so far?"

The precariousness of his position suddenly loomed large. Steve said nothing.

"That's fine. The question was rhetorical," Turner said. "Worse than what I've outlined to this point is your presence in this office. CompuTech does private work in a secure facility. Anyone who gets past Erica needs an invitation or a visitor's pass. I know Erica didn't extend you an invitation. I don't recall giving you a pass." He waggled a plastic CompuTech tag dangling from a lanyard around his neck. "Minor problems, all of them easily managed."

Coming from a person who had money, identification, and a job, Steve thought that Turner was being disingenuous. He said nothing.

Turner kept talking, compounding the so-called minor problems. "The big question—you're not going to like this, Steve—but the big question that can't be swept under the rug is what you know. How would you explain your classified knowledge to the authorities without the ability to explain who you are or why you're here?" Turner answered his own question and made Steve's situation incalculably worse. "There's no way. There's no explanation. Especially if I weigh in. You see, I don't work for CompuTech. CompuTech works for me. And my office is situated in the Pentagon." He shook his head with feigned regret. "You'd be locked in bureaucratic limbo for years. The criminal justice system wouldn't know what to do with you."

Steve tried to ignore an outburst of uneasy butterflies. There was no reason for them, except...

... *The Pentagon?*

Was Turner attached to the CIA? The previous day, he'd said, "Dark Sky," without elaborating on what Dark Sky was or what it did. Steve assumed that Dark Sky was the name of a company. Maybe, though, it was an internal department, or a special program within the agency. The name sounded sufficiently nefarious. Like code words.

Turner said, "I answer to one person. One person only. He lives in a white house located on Pennsylvania Avenue. He's given me a great deal of latitude when it comes to getting things done. Now, where do you see yourself, if someone in this building phoned corporate security? Erica, for instance. People who don't know better might underestimate her. A pretty face. A marvelous ass. They'd be doing her a disservice. If she came at me, I'd take her down, no question. I outweigh her by at least seventy-five pounds. If I let my guard down, though? If she came at me from the side? She'd go Beatrix Kiddo on my butt. Odds would be closer to seventy-thirty. You see what I'm saying? Everyone from the American President, all the way down to CompuTech's receptionist, has a vested interest in preventing you from walking out the front door."

Steve stared at him for a long time without saying a word. The shading of nervousness had turned into bitter fear, rendering him incapable of speech. The situation was *way* out of his control. He was at Turner's complete mercy, on top of which no sane person wanted to draw the eyes of an immensely powerful spy organization. "Let me see if I understand," he finally managed. Swallowing dryly, trying to get his vocal cords working properly, he said, "Yesterday, you needed my 'special skills.' Today, you'll have me… what… thrown in jail if I don't follow orders?"

"Correct."

"Thanks for nothing. Buddy."

The fleeting smile that crossed Turner's haggard face was not friendly. "Why do you consider me a friend? Because you hung out with my twin in the other reality? I'm not him. People in this world are reflections of those in your world. I thought I made that clear."

Steve closed his eyes. He sagged in his chair. He sucked in a shallow breath and released it. "I don't get it. I don't even know what you want me to do."

Turner said, "Finally. Progress." He held up his hand, thumb, and index finger an inch apart. "Dark Sky was working on a project in Africa. It involved a drone. Unfortunately, it crashed. It didn't burn, probably because it was carrying hundreds of gallons of water that doused any fire before it had a chance to get started."

Steve had a sudden inkling as to where Turner was going. He said, "Let me guess. All this water was contained in a fluid management system that CompuTech built?"

"Correct."

"Why was it carrying water? Firefighting? Drought relief?"

"Unimportant at this juncture. Let's stay on point."

"Why me? What am I supposed to do? You act like I'm the same guy I was in this world. I'm not an engineer. Maybe my twin was before he…" Steve's voice trailed away. He was going to say, *before he died, but* the words were spooky and unreal. They caught in the back of his throat. "Maybe he was. I'm not."

"Am I wrong to assume you didn't work on the project? You don't have any knowledge regarding its construction? Its operation?" Turner shook his head. "If you weren't the right man for the job, Paige wouldn't have given you the red pill. Meeting her wasn't fate. You must know that."

Steve shook his head at his own naivety. A few drinks. A pretty face. He'd tripped on his dick trying to impress Paige with the work he did at CompuTech. Without knowing it, he'd aced a job interview. He should have known better. Nobody showed the kind of interest in his work that she had. Not his parents. Not his friends. Tamara didn't deign to pretend. "As long as you enjoy it," she'd say, giving him a gentle pat on the cheek before she stopped listening.

Turner said, "You'll go to the crash site as a consultant. Look at the debris. Identify anything related to CompuTech. Examine it. Try to determine if a malfunction within the CompuTech system was responsible for the crash. We don't want this kind of accident happening again."

Later, when the mission turned catastrophic, Steve would realize that Turner had deftly avoided answering the most fundamental of questions: why had he chosen Steve for this job? Why not a CompuTech employee from this world? He doubted Turner would have answered truthfully, but eventually Steve would wish he'd asked the question.

He said, "I don't have a choice, do I?"

"You're looking at it all wrong. This isn't a negative thing. Reframe your perception," Turner answered. "A man with ten dollars and a happy soul is a millionaire."

"What?"

"It's all upside, is what I'm saying. Help us with this Africa thing. Come back. Restart your day job. The only difference is, you'll be doing it here instead of the shithouse you came from. Get things cooking with Tamara again, if you want." He gave Steve an exaggerated look of fright, like, *why would you want that?* "If your chief concern is the flight to Africa, stop worrying. Dark Sky is sending you to Tanzania via London Heathrow. First class on a Boeing Soundwave. That's as safe as air travel gets."

Steve gave him a blank look. "What's a Boeing Soundwave?"

"Boeing's supersonic airliner. You didn't think you'd go that far subsonic, did you?" Turner chuckled and then added, "Of course, you did. Your world doesn't have supersonic air travel, does it?"

A flare of interest made ignoring Turner's condescension easier; the man had to know supersonic travel didn't exist Over-there. It ended in 2003, when Air France and British Airways permanently grounded the Concorde. At the time, Boeing knew the aging Concorde's life span was close to an end. They wanted to be the aerospace company that replaced it. "Time" had become a commodity, and Boeing was gambling on the public's growing demand for speed. But building a supersonic jet for the modern age had enveloped the company in years of development hell. The terror attacks in New York that decimated the airline industry in the early 2000s further slowed the airplane's development. Ultimately, Boeing shelved their supersonic plans.

In this world, however, they had apparently forged ahead with tenacity.

Steve knew most people didn't care about this techie stuff. He found it fascinating. Cruising at three times the speed of sound, making the journey from America's West Coast to the European continent in a quarter of the time it took flying subsonic, napping comfortably on lie-flat seats... It all piqued his curiosity.

Turner said, "You going to Africa, Steve? Have you changed your mind? Or am I calling corporate security?"

"Are you going, too?"

"No. The benefit of being CEO. I'm sending people. Corporate reps. Security types." He slapped his thighs with open palms. Stood with a tired, worn-out groan. Said, "Before you leave, you need to get with HR. They'll sort out your paperwork for the trip. Take a passport photograph. So on, and so forth."

Steve's surprise must have shown on his face.

"What?" Turner laughed. "Getting a passport is child's play. You forget who I work for?"

Steve wasn't thinking about a passport. Given his reluctance about traveling to Africa and Turner's insistence he go, he'd expected to be detained inside the CompuTech building under Turner's watchful eyes until the flight's departure. He said, "You're not afraid I'll run?"

“We’ve discussed your limited options, Steve. Get outside and enjoy the day. Clean air. Blue sky. Appreciate the opportunity you’ve been given. Be back by seven.” Turner paused and then added less magnanimously, “Keep in mind how fast Paige found you when you left the hotel last night.”

CHAPTER 27

STEVE LEFT COMPUTECH and walked directly to Tamara's building, the need to say "Goodbye" moving his feet with imperativeness. In a few short hours, he'd journey to a plague-ridden continent for reasons he didn't understand, on the same kind of vehicle that had nearly killed him five months before. The idea he might not see Tamara again felt entirely plausible. He wouldn't miss an opportunity to say something more heartfelt than, "See you later," twice in one lifetime.

But instead of riding the elevator up to the fourteenth floor, he stared at the polished brass numbers above the entrance doors, asking himself what he was doing and questioning his sudden unexpected reluctance. Where did this hesitation come from? What was he waiting for? He'd watched one tenant enter the gleaming glass edifice. He'd watched another leave. He had Tamara's spare key in his pocket. There was no reason to remain cemented to the sidewalk.

When another tenant left the building with long, purposeful strides, Steve shoved uncertainty aside. He rushed forward and caught the closing door before it clicked shut. He walked toward the elevator, slowing long enough to roll the cue ball at the triangular rack of balls at the far end of the pool table. A bright yellow fish in the gurgling aquarium watched him out of bulbous black eyes. Three minutes later, with the false confidence evaporating like morning mist, he knocked on Tamara's door.

She opened the width of the security chain and peered through the gap. Her lips thinned. The vertical livid-lines between her eyes appeared. "How'd you get into the building?"

"Someone left. I caught the door."

"We're supposed to wait until it closes. Management tells us every month in an email blast, 'Wait until the door locks behind you.' Why're you here?"

"I'm going to Africa tonight."

The displeased expression softened. "One second," she said and shut the door.

Steve felt a spike of excitement. She'd invite him in for coffee. He'd tell her how much he wanted to see her when he returned. She'd want more details about his life Over-there. In time, they'd smooth out the rough edges with increasingly pleasant conversation. They'd agree they weren't exactly the same people they lost in the crash, but the differences were small in comparison to everything they had in common, everything they'd gone through.

While he waited, he looked left and right, admiring the way the overhead lights shone on the unblemished walls. The stain-free carpet showed minimal wear. A compression track down the middle where everyone walked was the only indication it wasn't brand new. It was probably replaced quarterly, just for appearance purposes. The soft hum of the HVAC system filled the hallway with cool, lily-scented air.

Out of nowhere, Turner's word popped into Steve's mind—reflections—and the mental game of Jenga he was playing collapsed. All at once, he understood his doubts. This was not his world. He was standing in a building that shared nothing more than the scabby apartment's address, intent on saying farewell to a virtual stranger. Feeling suddenly foolish and self-conscious, he glanced at the elevators. If he rushed, could he escape before she opened her door? He muttered a frustrated curse, knowing there wasn't time, no matter how quickly he moved.

He crammed his hands into his pockets. Shifting his weight from side to side, he desperately hunted for something to say, now that his goodbye speech had become word salad.

The apartment door opened. Smelling like she'd just climbed out of the shower, Tamara stepped into the hallway. She held the chain across the jamb so the door she pulled closed behind her didn't automatically lock her out. Her hair was tied in a loose ponytail, reminding him of Tamara's casual Over-there style. She wore an oversized sweatshirt. Her gray cotton gym shorts had an aggressive-looking bird of prey—a seahawk, eagle, or falcon—embroidered on one leg. Her toenails were pink.

Nostalgia punched Steve in the heart. His breath caught. Her weekend appearance was so intimately familiar. Except for the bare feet. There was no way the Tamara he knew would have stepped barefoot into the hallway of the scabby apartment, although that was more about the cleanliness of the carpet Over-there than anything else.

She said, "You don't want to go to Africa. That's a terrible idea. Africa is unsafe."

"You're talking about Covid-28?"

"You know about it?"

"I saw it on TV. They say it's isolated. Contained."

"They say a lot of things."

"Ethan isn't giving me a choice."

She made a face. The livid-lines returned. "Tell him, 'No.' Tell him you're not going."

"I tried. He pointed out how few options I have."

"I'm sorry. Ethan is—" She paused, frowned, and seemed to consider what she'd say next. "When the other Steve invited me out for drinks with his friends, I'd only go for an event. Like the Christmas party. I wouldn't go day to day in case Ethan was there. He'd buy rounds. Everyone would say 'cheers' because the drinks weren't coming out of their pockets. Meanwhile, he's looking at his fancy watch like he can't wait to leave. Everyone else is wishing he'd get going, so they could have some real fun."

"That doesn't sound… terrible."

"You've met him. He was always showing off. He'd banter and laugh, but when he smiled, I never believed it. Why's he forcing you to go to Africa?"

"Something to do with what I was working on Over-there. He thinks I can help with it here. He says it has to be me, now that I'm—" Steve let the sentence trail off, once again unsure how to say, *now that I'm dead* without choking on the words. He continued. "He's vague. It's a Dark Sky project. That means it's classified. It sounds like John Le Carre or Robert Ludlum to me."

"What the hell is Dark Sky?"

"You don't know?"

"I've never heard of it."

"I think it's like the CIA or the FBI. Some government agency out of the Pentagon. Whatever it is, Ethan is the head of it. He said the president is his boss."

"If you believe him."

Steve said nothing.

Seconds stretched.

Tamara crossed her arms. She stared down the hallway and mumbled, "I acted badly yesterday. I'm sorry. It wasn't a good day. I was tired. Seeing you scared me."

He made a noncommittal mouth noise that she interpreted accurately. Her humility disappeared. She fixed him with sharp eyes. "I know. Everybody says, 'Oh, I'm so tired.' 'Oh, I had a bad day.' The difference is, I'm not making excuses. I took time off after the crash. Turned out, sitting at home with nothing to do was no help. I can't get the stink of burning plastic out of my nose." She tapped the side of her head several times with an index finger. "After three weeks, I went back to work. I go in exhausted because I don't sleep. I spend half the night having 'what-if' conversations with myself. During the day, I fight for my life. For my colleague's lives."

"What do you mean?"

"After the crash, bookings dropped way off. San Juan Airways can't fly around with half-empty airplanes. It's economic suicide. We can only compensate so much with a reduced schedule. We don't want to alienate the passengers we do have. I'm trying to get people on our planes. The regional press is telling them not to. Every day, there's a new article about our safety record. Our poor service. I'm a VP, so I get blamed, like it was my own personal negligence that caused the crash. People who don't know shit, talking shit. If it wasn't for news out of Africa, the national media would be all over us. That kind of negative attention? The company wouldn't survive. As it is now, I'm not sure we'll make it."

"You were pretty hard on the bartender."

Tamara snorted a derisive laugh. "That guy? He thinks he's so cool with his leather apron. His curled mustache. He's hitting on all the ladies. We're supposed to be impressed with a bartender's long spoon? I don't mind if he gives it a try," she hiked her shoulders, like, *that kind of behavior is expected,* "but when it didn't go his way with one of my married friends, he went from the world's most attentive bartender to the most useless. Twenty-two dollar cocktails? He doesn't get to act that way. I expect service. I'm not going to cut him any slack. Read the room. Know your audience. Act like a man. Take 'No' graciously."

Steve figured by the end of her little speech, she was no longer referring to the bartender. She was speaking directly to him. She had shifted emphasis as smoothly as a seasoned politician.

She glanced at her candy-colored toenails, raised her gaze, and stared down the hallway again, an infinitely sad expression on her face. She said, "Sometimes, when I wake up at three A.M., I'll reach for him. When I can't find him, I'll look at my phone and wonder why he hasn't texted. Not a single text, all day long? Why? Then, I remember why I'm awake in the middle of the night, staring at the ceiling. Sometimes I miss him so much, I lose my breath. I literally can't breathe."

"I know," Steve said.

Tamara touched his forearm. "I understand why you're here. But you're not the person I lost in December. No matter how much you look like him. Take care in Africa. When you get back? Don't come looking for me. I have to protect my heart. I'm not ready for a relationship. Especially with a replica of my last boyfriend."

She backstepped into the apartment. "Watch out for Ethan. He's not your friend. He has his own agenda. I think he's dangerous. Goodbye, Steve."

The door closed between them, with a finality that was as permanent as the plane crash in the other world. Steve wasn't as despondent as he might have been. She was a stranger in all but name, which made her opinion objective. Her use of the word "dangerous" matched a growing feeling he had about Turner, beginning with their first conversation in front of Java-Nice-Day. His thoughts, as he walked to the elevator, were on the Africa trip, and not on this world's version of Tamara.

October, 2005
Daniel (Danny) White

CHAPTER 28

DANIEL WHITE DECIDED to retire on a Tuesday.

Four years after making that decision, he had dotted every i and, aside from one uncrossed t, was ready to disengage from working life.

He stared out the window of his favorite coffee shop and thought hard about that solitary t. A book about the fall of the Roman Empire sat open on his leg. A pen lay on the table; he enjoyed underlining sentences and making notes in a book's margins. It was a habit he knew bibliophiles abhorred and something he couldn't explain. He seldom referenced his notes. A short double espresso was growing cold on the table beside an oversized bran muffin. He wore what his niece referred to as an "old-man-vest," a fleece she'd bought him because October mornings in DC were harbingers of the frigid winter lurking around the corner. Outside, every gentle gust of wind blew leaves off the trees lining the street, carpeting the sidewalk in orange and yellow. Photographers called this time of day the golden hour. Surely autumn, with its soft light and vivid color, was their favorite creative time. Unfortunately for White, the beauty of a crisp fall morning hadn't inspired him with fresh ideas regarding the uncrossed t.

On the fateful September day when he decided to leave public service behind, he didn't know what kind of world he'd retire into. For close to four decades, he'd worked in the shadows in an effort to make America a more habitable place. He felt like he'd succeeded within the mandate President Birch had given him in November 1964. Outside those finite parameters, he was less certain. Forty years after their meeting, as a patriotic surge of never-seen-before proportions began, and people from every corner of America rose up and said in one voice, "I have to do something," White was forced to admit that he'd already done everything he could. After repeatedly shaving away pieces of his soul in service to the nation, he didn't have anything left to give. He'd grown tired all the way down to the marrow of his bones. The fight had changed. He no longer had the energy to battle evils that had grown in size and scope. It wasn't just the planet that needed saving anymore. Now, vast swaths of mankind had become a pestilence that needed to be dealt with.

Globalization, a concept that didn't exist in 1964, had spawned multi-culturalism. Globalization's success—perhaps "inevitability" was a more accurate word—was predictable, what with high-speed internet and jet travel. Multi-culturalism, on the other hand, was an abject failure, the evidence as clear as the sky was blue, seconds before the Twin Towers collapsed. Only the terminally naive chose to believe that wildly different cultural groups could exist harmoniously in a single society, despite an abundance of evidence to the contrary. The liberal West could never meld civilly with a centuries-old culture that considered stoning a woman to death for adultery, or murdering thousands with an airliner was a just punishment or an appropriate protest. Not to mention all the other unbridgeable gaps: ethnicity, language, greed… Pollution, unfettered consumption, and overpopulation had become the problems of the twenty-first century. Solving them, if possible, would take new people with inherent optimism and innovative ideas. Finding one such person before he turned his office lights off for the final time was White's final, uncrossed t.

He didn't tell anyone about his decision to retire right away. In the days after September 11, there was a mountainous amount of work to be done. He was too much of a patriot to abandon his country in its hour of most desperate need. But the seed was planted that day.

It sprouted a few months later when Carl Hill said he, too, was retiring, a statement that gave White a quiet chuckle; "retire" assumed a legitimate job.

Hill had decided to leave his violent, clandestine life behind and move to Thailand. He'd bought an Irish bar in Chiang Mai with the money the US taxpayers would never know they paid him. Danny White wasn't sure how every city in every country he'd ever visited had a so-called Irish bar, but Hill found one with an attached apartment. He moved in with a Thai lady he met on a website called Asian Friend Finder. Their relationship was the very definition of symbiosis. She was half his age, an abysmal housekeeper, decent company, and an excellent cook. For her part, she liked Hill just fine and loved the perks that came from living with a wealthy American.

White and Hill had developed an association that White hadn't anticipated in the Bethesda diner when he told Hill they wouldn't talk again. Throughout the years, politicians of every stripe had threatened White's reign, either harboring a personal grudge, jealous of the quiet power he wielded, or disagreeing with his (and therefore the president's, agenda). Sometimes, he felt like the biggest impediment to his mandate was the people intent on tearing him down. Those people never presented a problem that was too large. If White couldn't find a solution, he fabricated one using his expansive network of contacts, political will, manipulation, and, as is always the case, philanthropists' money. Failing that, he added brute force to the formula and contacted Carl Hill. Hill was adept at finding an individual's pressure point, or creating them if someone was so squeaky clean he or she couldn't be diverted off a particular course. If White's request was complicated, if it appeared as though the job was too big for one person, he gave Hill more money and let him sort out the particulars. White needed results. The details were unimportant.

A small part of him envied Hill, this professional who had a full career and then chose to retire into a new experience with someone he cared for. White had continued seeing Ava when he needed someone on his arm at a social event, but he remained single, childless, and without hobbies. He told anyone who asked that work kept him too busy for a personal life. Despite his rare moments of envy, he wouldn't have exchanged Hill's life for the one he'd lived. He'd been instrumental in changing the world, starting in 1966 with Haiti's first high-efficiency incinerator, and a few years later with a specially developed vaccine designed for impoverished people in disaster zones.

The incinerator was an unqualified success, although—Haiti being Haiti, a country proficient at finding a problem for every solution—keeping it supplied with fuel was a constant struggle.

The first incinerators burned oil. Haiti's oil supply was continually compromised, usually because the country had to rely on someone else to pay its fuel bills and once because several million gallons went missing, along with a high-level Haitian bureaucrat. White guessed the man now lived in a villa with a stunning ocean view, spending the money that Nicaragua (the tanker's next port of call) paid him for arranging the shipment of the oil at a heavily discounted price. White couldn't help being impressed at the level of maneuvering the theft must have taken. The bureaucrat, the ship's load master, and probably the ship's captain, along with several low-level paper pushers, had conducted a master class in corruption.

The vaccine was also a success, albeit a highly confidential success.

Vaccinations were common after natural disasters, when water sources were contaminated, dietary needs weren't being met, and basic sanitation was nonexistent. In those situations, charities routinely administered thousands of inoculations, all of which contained the standard protections: cholera, hepatitis, yellow fever, and typhoid, among others. The new cocktail, however, contained something extra that rendered men close to sterile. As Birch said (in more sanitized terms), *when people can't look after themselves, when government can't accomplish its most fundamental job (taking care of its population), then pumping out more babies is not the answer.*

A decade after the vaccination and incinerator "experiments" were introduced, Haiti's birth rate had dropped significantly, and the environmental improvements around Port Au Prince were remarkable. White wasn't surprised. Absent of human intrusion, anyone with eyes could see how quickly nature reclaimed the landscape. Mother Earth's appreciation was unarguable, especially when enormous amounts of garbage were managed, rather than being left to contaminate the very environment in which people lived. Even that far back, the smoke out of the incinerator's chimney was less than one percent carbon. Debris that didn't burn, like porcelain, was crushed, mixed with gravel, and used to repair Haiti's subpar system of highways and roads. The ash was used to fill in old excavations, such as the empty pits where buildings once stood.

Killing the Wisconsin governor in 1965 was Hill's first political assassination. It wasn't his last. As it turned out, politicians were only a small part of the problem. Environmentalists became a growing irritant. As is typical with idealists, money wasn't enough to keep them from beating their drums. Hill discovered that if he went in hard and fast with that group before they had time to hamstring approval processes, they were an easy faction to subdue, unlike organized crime, who had a history of forcing solutions with violence. Mob bosses and their lieutenants, who mistakenly believed they were hard, who believed they owned politicians, had never before dealt with Hill's cadre of well-trained and enthusiastic mercenaries. Hill had likewise dealt heavy blows (literally) to union leaders, America's second-biggest obstruction (behind politics), to efficiently built infrastructure projects. Initially, he struggled to find common ground with these highly principled men. In time, he learned that if you smash a framing hammer into the soles of their feet and threaten to bury one of their children, even difficult people to dissuade come around.

When White and Hill talked the final time—when Hill announced his pending retirement—he'd suggested a couple of names, young go-getters, as he referred to them, whom he thought might make an ideal replacement. White took the names with thanks. In typical Daniel

White fashion, however, he had other plans. He was less interested in who'd take over from Hill than he was in finding his own replacement. He needed someone who'd become top dog at Dark Sky. He suspected that person might be hesitant to work with strangers, no matter how glowing their references. A worthy successor would have his own contacts, people he trusted implicitly, to carry out the unsavory work that Dark Sky required. In fact, if he didn't come with his own people, White wouldn't have considered him worthy.

White kept his antenna tuned. Eventually, he found, researched, and vetted his potential replacement, a young man who had joined the marines in December of 2001, as so many young Americans did. The man had gone to Afghanistan. Four years later, he was still there. At twenty-seven, after several promotions, he'd proven himself to be a more than capable manager. Unwaveringly patriotic, a staunch believer in Western values, he'd earned himself a reputation with the decisions he made and the lengths he'd go to promote and defend those values. There were unsettling whispers as to what those "lengths" entailed, whispers involving hallucinogenic injections that shattered men's minds. Daniel White ignored the whispers. After four decades, he'd learned that brute force was an ingredient as necessary as pecans in a pecan pie, and not something required in only the rarest of circumstances. His naivety in 1965, when he hired Hill, believing that he'd need the man's skills only once, made him smile today. He was aware of the strange irony: to build a cleaner, more wholesome world in which there was plenty for everyone, the people who wielded power had to abandon their personal, moralistic inclinations.

White's list of successors dropped to one.

Danny White had beaten the Washington odds, remaining head of Dark Sky behind the Global Solutions curtain. He'd outlasted ten different presidents. He'd taken Birch's charity a long, long way. Every major city in the United States was burning garbage in high-efficiency incinerators. Only a small number of coastal cities continued irresponsibly pumping sewage into the ocean. It was just a matter of time before they joined the cities using technology that converted human waste into clean water. Currently, he had a team working on the growing problem of plastic. They'd figured out how to turn it into building materials, 2 × 4s and such. Suitable for interior walls, away from the sun's degrading UV rays, it would save forests and repurpose what had become an unexpected problem. At seventy-nine, White was proud of his record. He was simultaneously discouraged at the worsening state of the world.

Outside his favorite coffee shop, the sun was higher in the sky, promising a stellar fall day. His book remained forgotten on the table, as did his pen. He swallowed the stone-cold espresso and absently began peeling the wrapper off his bran muffin. He should have been out there enjoying a morning run, but a nagging calf injury had curtailed his mileage. In truth, he logged fewer miles than he had a decade ago. That total was down from a decade before that. He'd get the mileage back up once he retired. First, though, the uncrossed t and the question it raised…

… who would succeed him if Ethan Turner turned down the job?

May, 2028

CHAPTER 29

AERODYNAMICS CHANGE WHEN an aircraft breaks the sound barrier, which necessarily makes a supersonic airliner a small aircraft compared to a typical passenger jet. In practical terms, that meant a Boeing Soundwave didn't have the physical space for suites, bars, or showers like some airlines offered in their much slower, much larger jumbo jets. United Airlines compensated with comfort, sophistication, and branding, labeling their Soundwaves "Ultra by United."

Steve knew the Soundwave would be ultra-fast. He was unprepared for how ultra-luxurious it was. The wide leather seats, with the Ultra logo embossed into the headrests, appeared as comfortable as La-Z-Boy recliners. Drink holders in the armrests held bottles of Evian. The pillows were large, the fleece blankets thick. Brushed-steel and wood-grain high-lights gave the interior a refined aesthetic. Soft music played in the background. He was looking with wide-eyed wonder at the difference between a car and a Porsche, a boat and a Beneteau, a shotgun and a Benelli…

One of four impossibly gorgeous flight attendants (Ultra contracted a modeling agency to handle in-flight staffing, a trick that wouldn't have sneaked past the unions in his world) said in a voice as warm and rich as twenty-year-old Port, "Welcome aboard, sir. My name is Elsa." She tapped the nametag pinned on her uniform with a long finger. The tag was made from the same brushed-steel as the trim-work, her fingernail painted the same delicate red as her lipstick. "May I show you to your seat?"

Awed by the plane and intimidated by Elsa's beauty, Steve nodded dumbly and followed her down the aisle in silence. When they reached his seat, she asked, "What can I get you to drink?"

He looked at her vacantly. He wanted to comb her straw-blonde hair after she stepped out of a shower. He wanted to fasten the clasp of her necklace, while she held her hair out of the way. He wanted to buy her a drink.

Or a house.

"Sir? Your pre-take-off cocktail?"

"Oh. Right. What do you have?" His voice sounded cracked and unnatural. He winced and told himself to quit acting like a seventeen-year-old just off the farm. He was on board an airplane talking to a lady. That was all. To prevent himself from imagining her lying on a beach wearing nothing but suntan oil and Ray Bans, he reminded himself that she wasn't a rare orchid that only blossomed for six days high in an obscure Andean mountain valley. She was a person, a woman who doubtlessly issued instructions to her boyfriend on the "correct" way to load a dishwasher, and who "helpfully" pointed out obviously green traffic lights from the passenger seat of their car when they went for a drive.

Behind him, he heard low giggles. He looked over his shoulder. Two male flight attendants (combined body fat less than ten percent) were escorting a couple of female passengers to their seats. Both ladies had flushed cheeks and dreamy, distracted expressions. Steve felt a small measure of relief. He wasn't the only wonder-struck person on the airplane.

Elsa smiled, like I've *seen this reaction before*. Her ice-blue eyes sparkled. With pride in her voice, she said, "First time with Ultra? It's nice, isn't it?"

"A little overwhelming."

With an agreeing nod, Elsa said, "We have all the standards.

Beer. Wine. Gin and tonic. Rum and Coke. Vodka and seven. Dealer's choice."

Steve said, "Gin and tonic. Please and thanks," relieved that his natural-sounding voice had returned.

"Coming up," she answered.

From the comfort of his La-Z-Boy, he watched her walk away, every step a beautiful symphony, and for a moment he was on a beach with a bottle of coconut suntan oil in his hand. He blinked, shook his head, and took stock of his surroundings. He was on a Boeing Soundwave, a technological marvel that didn't exist Over-there. He'd arrive in London well rested in a fraction of the time it would have taken him a day ago. He wondered what kind of fuel the plane burned in this shiny world of plastic building materials and hydrogen-powered automobiles. The San Juan Airways crash was a distant memory. He couldn't guess how much Dark Sky had paid for his fare, but he vowed never to travel by air again, unless it was on Ultra by United. Thoroughly comfortable in his La-Z-Boy, he never wanted to return to the dirty, worn-out world from which he'd come.

Unlike on most airplanes, there was no need to avoid eye contact and guiltily pretend to read a novel or search for a seatbelt, while less fortunate passengers walked through first-class to their cattle-class seats. Every seat on a Soundwave was first-class. Most of the passengers filing past were grinning, their eyes everywhere, apparently as impressed as Steve. Notably unimpressed, either blind to the opulence or determined to be indifferent, were four beefy men in suits, all of whom gave Steve expressionless nods as they made their way to their seats. One of the men was black. Another one wore a wide white collar, as if he'd been in a recent automobile accident. There were fresh cuts on his face. The slash running from his temple to his ear was held together with two flesh-toned butterfly bandages; both looked bright and healthy compared to the gray pallor of his face. The differences between the quartet ended there. All of the men were tie-less. Each had hands as large as pie plates and knuckles as hard as bolt-heads.

Their chests, shoulders, and backs were as thick and bulky as oaken whiskey casks. Steve assumed they were the Dark Sky security types Turner had mentioned. Their presence gave him a momentary chill…

… and then a warm breath fluffed across his ear and a whispered voice said in a posh accent, "I could eat that one with a spoon."

Steve swiveled in his seat. "Paige?"

She was staring across the aisle at a male flight attendant who was busy stowing a passenger's carry-on bag into an overhead bin. She dragged her gaze away from the FA and looked at Steve with a grin. "Don't be jealous," and "Close your mouth. You're acting like you've never traveled on a Soundwave."

"You know I haven't, right?"

Her grin widened. "It's something, isn't it? Slide over."

"Oh, for… You've got your own La-Z-Boy, right?"

As usual, when Paige had something in mind, she ignored him. He squirmed over, and she sat down, partly on his lap, partly in the wedge of space he created. The enormous seat was almost wide enough to accommodate two people. They were cozy, not crowded. To prevent his right arm from being trapped between them, he lay it across her shoulders. Her left hand rested on his right thigh because there was nowhere else for it to go. She wore the same kind of billowy skirt she'd worn before, a fitted tank top, and Blundstones, a more comfortable choice of footwear on a long flight, compared to a professional's high heels. The messy bun was in place, as was the nose ring. She smelled sweet, cinnamomic. Only a meager layer of cotton and a flimsy scrap of silk separated him from the memory of the previous night and that slippery, velvet-smooth skin. He was nowhere near as uncomfortable as he might have been.

He complained anyway, felt it was expected, and hoped it might distract her from his growing arousal. "The flight attendant is going to make you go back to your seat."

"We've got a few minutes." She wriggled her butt, snuggling in a little tighter. "It doesn't feel like you mind."

The truth was, he didn't mind. Not at all. He was unreasonably pleased to see her again. Outside of fiction, love doesn't happen overnight, but it only takes an instant for a spark to ignite, turning a sepia-toned existence into a world of saturated color. The storm of excited butterflies in his stomach surprised him.

A male flight attendant arrived, carrying his gin and tonic and a flute of Champagne for Paige. Elsa was a step behind with two small platters, each decorated with bite-sized pieces of cheese, assorted crackers, and oysters on half-shells. Paige pulled a table top out of somewhere. With a contented smile and a murmured thanks, she efficiently transferred all the cheese and crackers to one plate and all the oysters to the other. She was comfortable and unintimidated. This wasn't her first trip on a Soundwave. She nudged the oysters in Steve's direction. "Eat them all, Sweet Pea. I insist. You need to keep the tank full. Have a wee bit of cheese too."

When he shook his head at the cheese, she said, "Yummy. More for me." Then she called him a freak for not liking cheese. He reciprocated, saying only a freak would eat coagulated blobs of protein and fat.

He asked, "Why are you here?"

Serious, executive Paige replaced playful, casual Paige. "I speak for Global Solutions, don't I? If we run into issues in Africa, I'll handle them. It's my job. Like I said before, Ethan isn't good at delivering bad news."

Steve didn't have time to think about that cryptic, rather foreboding answer before she said, "Even in a Soundwave, London is a long flight. Plenty of time for a history lesson. You might say, 'Boring.' You might become distracted and drift away," she shot Elsa a pointed glance, "but stick with me. I won't take long. What comes next speaks directly to why you're going to Africa."

Her eyes narrowed, and her forehead creased in thought. She said, "Here, in this universe, you've seen one city, so making comparisons is impossible. But know this: in what you'd refer to as 'the Western world,' or 'the first world,' many cities are as squeaky clean as this one. The reasons are wide ranging. The two most impactful reasons are connected. First, this world did not bow down to the altar of Climate Change as your world has. Second, President Birch decided Haiti was irredeemable."

She paused, seemed to gather her thoughts, and began, "In the wake of Hurricane Cleo, Birch recruited a very smart man named Daniel White. He told White to create a charity that would help people in their time of need and concurrently benefit the United States going forward. Essentially, he wanted compensation of a sort from a county that he believed was taking advantage of our good will. White named the charity Global Solutions. He collaborated with the Swedes—lots of money helped facilitate the partnership—and together, they built the first high-efficiency incinerator.

"I'm using the incinerator project as an example, by the way. GS initiated numerous similar strategies. Clean water, agricultural advancements, sewage treatment. A myriad of others. Although nobody knew it, Birch successfully started the first Green Revolution. He was ahead of his time."

Steve sipped his drink. He figured he'd just learned the reason Paige hadn't reacted with interest when he bragged about building sewage treatment plants on the night they met. They were old news to her.

"Birch was also a product of the time," Paige said. "1964 marked the end of the Baby Boom. The planet had never seen a population explosion, like it did between 1946 and 1964. Overpopulation became an overwhelming concern. The planet *couldn't possibly* provide enough. Not at the pace with which the populace devoured resources. Deep thinkers believed that by the year 2000, the price of commodities would spike dramatically, causing a multitude of problems, including mass starvation."

"That didn't happen," Steve said unnecessarily. He popped an oyster and cracker into his mouth. The pepper-cracker was a crunchy complement to the salty oyster. Normally, he would have passed on the oysters—slimy and wet, they weren't his favorite food—but Paige's comment about keeping the tank full hadn't gone unnoticed. A gentleman didn't intentionally disappoint a lady, after all.

Paige said, "You know why?"

He shook his head.

"The huge population increase meant that proportionally there were a larger number of smart people. They figured out more efficient, more effective ways to produce the necessities humans require to thrive. However, in '64, this concept wasn't understood. Overpopulation was the accepted peril. Hive-mind ruled the day… just like in your world today, Steve.

"Over-there, radicals who get their 'facts' off social media have indulged themselves in climate alarmism. The end is nigh! Reduce carbon at all costs otherwise, the icecaps will melt, the seas will rise, there'll be mass starvation, dogs and cats living together… 'Pollution' is a huge word. It encompasses every byproduct of human evolution. 'Carbon' is a small part of the definition, but it caught the public's attention. It was popularized by an ignorant Hollywood elite and promoted by a left-leaning media." Paige flicked the air dismissively and made an annoyed hissing sound. "Lunacy. One country builds two coal-fired power plants a week. Its neighbor suffers brownouts because wind turbines and solar panels are not reliable or green."

Steve opened his mouth to object. Paige held up an open palm, cutting him off.

"I'm not a so-called 'denier.' Solar panels sacrifice vast amounts of farmable land, have a finite lifespan, and can't be recycled. They produce ten watts of power per square meter. Wind power is worse. As an energy source, it's *far* from green. Don't kid yourself. A wind farm is enormously expensive to build and maintain. They're noisy. They're a blight on the landscape. They're ridiculously inefficient: one watt of electrical power per square meter. At the end of their seventeen-year lifespan, a turbine is garbage. It ends up in the same landfill as the solar panels. That's pollution. Tell me I'm wrong."

He said, "That's a lot of numbers."

"I'll put this whole conversation into perspective. The average refrigerator uses two hundred and thirty watts *per hour*. If the population of the United States relies on wind, they might as well say goodbye to ice cubes in their mojitos. In comparison, nuclear produces two thousand watts per square meter. These are the facts, Steve. Not even the most fervent greenie can dispute them."

"They'll try."

"You have to admire their conviction; state your opinion loud enough, as many times as possible, and maybe it will change the facts." Paige laughed and slapped her forehead with her palm in an exaggerated show of frustration. Then, she became serious again.

"Over-there, pseudo-scientists conceived 'Climate Change' as a brand. They couldn't make a compelling case for the more specific 'Global Warming.' It's become a multibillion-dollar industry invented by dooms-day extremists. You want proof? Here it is: despite limitless amounts of money, the first world isn't getting cleaner. The standard of living is dropping. As for people in the second and third worlds, they don't care about the environment. They don't care about the standard of living. They have one priority: their next meal. Their farms are inefficient. They burn dung for fuel. They cut forests down with no regard to loss of habitat, driving away the animal life they need to survive. Existence is all that matters."

Paige paused for a quick sip of Champagne before continuing. "The irony is, the third biggest carbon polluter in the world, behind China and India, is food waste. In a world in which one hundred million people are facing food insecurity, food rots in landfills because it looks funny."

The usual airline announcements started on the PA system. "Boarding complete" was followed by a flurry of flight attendant action. Elsa and her colleagues collected empty plates, transferred unfinished drinks from crystal glasses to plastic cups, and instructed people to fasten their seatbelts "… in preparation for an on-time departure." Passengers not intelligent enough to use the restrooms before boarding the Soundwave left their seats and rushed to the lavatories at the front and back of the airplane.

Paige kept talking. “In an effort to ‘Save the Planet,’ vote-pandering politicians spend colossal amounts of money on a problem that barely exists, creating more pollution and contributing to a lower standard of living. Imagine if a small percentage of the billions spent to pacify the Climate Change fanatics was directed toward programs that would cost less, elevate people’s lives in real ways, and, as a happy benefit, reduce carbon?”

“I doubt that’s possible.”

“Of course, it’s possible. I could name ten projects that would do exactly that. They’ll never happen. Politicians prefer virtue signaling over fixing government corruption or eradicating chronic diseases. Climate Change is the money shot. Creating land tenure agreements in third-world countries isn’t exciting enough.”

Steve didn’t know what a land tenure agreement was or how it could help an impoverished African farmer reduce pollution. He didn’t ask. Paige spoke with such authority that her answer was irrelevant. She’d be fully committed to whatever she said. She’d have facts and figures to back it up.

Elsa walked down the aisle, closing overhead bins on the right side of the cabin. A male FA followed her, closing the bins on the left-hand side. More announcements that nobody listened to aired on the PA—put mobile phones into airplane mode, fasten seatbelts, adjust seatbacks into the upright position.

Paige said, “Today, countries larger than Haiti are exhausting all manner of resources with complete disregard for the environment. India’s answer to garbage disposal is to back a dump truck up to a river bank and, bombs away. Slums the size of Spokane and Toledo litter Africa and South America. The occupants pump out umpteen babies a year. They’re afraid of infant mortality. Human population will peak at around 10 billion, according to current thinking. At the rate the planet is being populated, subsequently razed, and irrevocably contaminated, will Mother Nature continue to provide the necessities? Mark Twain said, 'They aren't making more land.'"

"That isn't the quote," Steve said.

"Don't nit-pick."

"You just told me there'll be proportionally more innovators to figure out these problems."

"I did. But we'll never know who they are. When existence is your only goal, you can't rise above the slum and attend university. Sadly, these people are not a priority. 'Moral' politicians have chosen Climate Change instead. Their hypocrisy is outrageous." She hiked her shoulders. "President Birch considered Haiti a microcosm. Could a small population of takers be contained? Could a small land mass be cleaned up after a natural disaster? Could this combined strategy save resources that could be redirected and better utilized? The answer was a resounding 'Yes.' The incinerators worked. The population of Haiti dropped. Fewer people, less pollution, less squandering of everything from money to farmland."

A second chill, colder than what he experienced when the Dark Sky heavies walked by, surfed Steve's spine. It was one thing to discuss global difficulties and suggest theoretical solutions. It was quite another to assert that the problems were so intertwined and enormous that they had to be considered an overwhelming existential threat to the planet.

The door at the front of the airplane closed with a heavy, reassuring thunk. Elsa and another FA walked down the aisle, doing a final table-tray, chair-back, and seatbelt check.

Steve said, "You have to go back to your seat now."

Paige stood. "Until the day he retired, Danny White kept Global Solutions' mandate in mind. Thanks to the Passage, we know what this world would look like if he, and the people he worked with, hadn't taken aggressive action. It would look like yours. That's not going to happen here. After we get to altitude, I'll come back. We'll get comfortable." She looked down the length of the Soundwave's aisle.

When she looked back, she'd drawn into herself. Her eyes were distant, her face overwritten with strain. He hadn't seen that expression from her before. He didn't understand it.

She said flatly, "There's another… element… I have to explain. I assume you've heard about Covid-28 in Africa?"

Steve nodded.

"I'll be back," she said.

He watched her return to her seat, watched her sit down, settle in, and buckle up. It may have been a simple fluke or an unhappy accident, but their eyes never met. It made the truths as she told them, and her final somber question feel far more consequential.

He propped his chin in his hand and slowly scratched his cheek with four fingers, trying to understand the fresh surge of apprehension. From the moment he and Paige met in Zak's on classic rock night to now, about to cross a continent at three times the speed of sound, everything he'd gone through had been engineered. Why, then, would a seemingly out-of-the-blue question about Covid-28 be any different? Maybe he was being overly jaded, but her question didn't strike him as random. It didn't *feel* random. He couldn't dismiss it. How did it factor into Paige's extreme version of the truth and Turner's insistence that he, Steve, was the only person who could examine a crashed drone in the African jungle?

CHAPTER 30

FORTY MINUTES PASSED between the time the flight attendant closed the door and the seatbelt sign blinked off. The digital altimeter on the monitor in front of Steve showed the Soundwave climbing quickly toward their initial cruise altitude. More and more of the continental United States disappeared behind them as, incredibly, the airplane accelerated toward Mach three. Tech geek that he was, Steve should have been enthralled. Instead, he constructed a mental diagram of Paige's lecture. Using different-colored lines, he connected the various elements and points she'd made. He layered that diagram on top of everything Ethan Turner had told him. Finally, he added a third layer: his own extraordinary arrival in this world. All the various elements were related somehow, so they all belonged on the same diagram.

He studied the layered picture as a whole, rather than one picture separate from the other.

Understanding grew.

A schematic diagram doesn't make sense until a person knows what it represents and can conceptualize it in three dimensions. The conceptualization turns a mish-mash of seemingly unrelated lines into conduits, as real as the pipes integral to the fluid management systems that CompuTech built. Until Paige asked about Covid-28, Steve couldn't visualize the diagram in 3D. Her question was the component that forced the pieces to mesh. His mental schematic became a fully rendered 3D blueprint. Complete comprehension hit him like a baseball bat to the solar plexus.

Covid-28 was manmade.

Like a mosquito infected with malaria, the fluid the Dark Sky drone carried had been laced with the Covid-28 virus. It had been dispersed with a system this world's version of him had built, the purpose of which was the murder of millions of people deemed not only worthless but parasitical, as determined by a select group of people.

Hyperventilating, Steve gripped the armrests hard enough that his knuckles turned white. He wanted to stand up and throw something, smash something, kick, and scream, swear and somehow unload the horrific knowledge he'd been given. Carrying on in that manner was impossible, of course. He'd be dragged off the plane in handcuffs and dumped inside a criminal justice system that didn't know what to do with him, a scenario Turner had made a point of describing earlier in the day. He was trapped, constrained without options until the Soundwave landed in London, after which he was still trapped. Turner had given him the illusion of freedom, but there'd never been a moment when he'd been unmonitored. Undoubtedly, one of the jobs the Dark Sky heavies had been given was to keep sharp eyes on him all the way to Africa.

Now, Paige's and Turner's evasiveness made sense. She had spoken about controlling problems associated with overpopulation, while avoiding explanations as to how that goal was attained. Turner had talked about a drone plumbed with a fluid management system that CompuTech had built. When Steve asked why the drone was carrying water, Turner had answered, "… unimportant at this juncture…" The two of them had doled out the information in bite-sized pieces until this moment, on board an airliner at seventy-eight thousand feet, where he had no choice but to contain his reaction and wait for the tsunami of repulsion and rage to settle.

He gulped his G and T, emptying the plastic cup.

He wasn't ready for Paige's return.

She sat down and nestled in, as she did earlier. She tried a weak smile on him, which Steve didn't acknowledge. Without blinking, she studied him over the rim of her plastic Champagne cup. Finally, she said, "Did the shoe drop, Sweet Pea?"

"Dark Sky is committing genocide."

"Genocide is the slaughter of people from a particular ethnic group or nation."

With tight control, Steve said, "Who's nit-picking now? Should we ask the Africans?"

Her face flushed a darker shade of mocha. She was suddenly very interested in the video highlighting Big Ben and Westminster Abbey and various other famous London attractions playing on the seatback monitor in front of them.

He said, "How is this atrocity possible? The mechanics of it? Global Solutions is huge. The infrastructure alone should make it impossible."

"That's the secret. Global Solutions is huge. Dark Sky is tiny. It's buried deep."

"It's buried because it's morally reprehensible."

Paige squirmed. She refused to meet his eye. In the same dead monotone as earlier, she said, "It's buried because its methods are unorthodox."

"Unorthodox is a fancy word for illegal."

"We're preventing a problem. One failure is more than humanity can afford."

"My world isn't a failure," he said automatically. Right now, his so-called failure of a world was looking good. Right now, all he wanted was a one-way ticket back to the scabby apartment. He wanted to return to Over-there's version of Ethan Turner, who was his friend, to his over-done Romanian property manager who wanted to be his friend, to the yellow labrador, the pollution, and the Toughs, to a place where the cost of living didn't number in the millions.

He said, "Size doesn't explain how nobody knows about it."

"Dark Sky's mission is so extreme, so impossible, most people can't imagine its existence. If someone could imagine it outside of a fictional setting, what could he do about it? What would he say? Who'd he tell? It's so farfetched he'd come across as an unhinged nut. Who'd believe him?"

Mulishly, he said, "Someone would pay attention."

"Okay," she conceded. "Let's pretend you have more than vague assertions. Maybe you have proof of some kind. You speak up, and someone pays attention. Then what? In all likelihood, Dark Sky would be shut down inside the US before your claim gained momentum. It would continue operating in other parts of the world." She paused, took a breath, and doggedly picked up her earlier thread. "The size of the American government makes Dark Sky undetectable. It's one of only four governmental agencies operating without congressional oversight. Look at it this way: how many agencies make up the US government? You know, like DEA, CIA, Homeland Security, etcetera? How many?"

"I don't know."

"You don't know. It wouldn't be hard to figure out, but already you don't know. Let's break it down. Let's look at the Department of Transportation as an example. How many internal departments exist inside the Department of Transportation?"

"I don't know."

"Off the top of your head. How many?"

"Airline, rail, marine." Steve shrugged. "Roads. Maybe others. Probably others."

"Good. So, let's take airlines as an example. How many departments would shelter under the FAA's umbrella?"

"Licensing. Certification. Accident investigation. I don't know. Lots."

"Exactly. Lots. And contained within each of those departments, how many people? Dozens? Hundreds? Can you honestly say it would be impossible to hide a handful of people inside the entire US government? What about a couple of hundred spread across several countries? Or in an inherently secret place, like China?

"Global Solutions employs hundreds of people. A select few of them work for Dark Sky as well. The others aren't aware that occasionally their day-to-day duties intersect with Dark Sky. Let's say a Dark Sky rep needs to attend a meeting in Las Vegas. This individual asks Global Solutions' internal travel agency to arrange flights and accommodations. As far as the travel agency knows, Dark Sky doesn't exist. Therefore, the request could only have come from a fellow GS employee. Someone who's attending a verifiable symposium."

Steve had no response; her explanation made too much sense. They sat in severe silence for several long minutes until he broke it and asked, "What happens if I don't do what Turner wants? Will I be disappeared?" He hit the word hard and felt her flinch.

"No." She looked stricken.

"Will I be eliminated with extreme prejudice?"

"No! Turner considers you an asset. He wants your knowledge."

"Isn't that the term these CIA guys use? Extreme prejudice?"

"That's enough!" Her voice wavered. "That never occurred to me."

Steve nodded skeptically, too distracted to notice the way her eyes cut to the side for a small piece of a second. Another wholly undesirable thought popped into his head. As Global Solutions' human resource expert, Paige had eased him into this awfulness with slow mastery. Was sleeping with him part of her strategy? Before he could stop himself, he blurted out, "Did you sleep with me to soften the blow? Some misguided attempt to get to me accept mass murder?" He hated the insecurity in his voice and immediately wished he could pull the question back. Masochistically, he hoped she'd answer.

Staring at some invisible spot at the front of the cabin, Paige said, "I slept with you because we have a connection. If that helped, 'soften the blow…'" she shrugged. "I'm not going to apologize for it. Last night was as much for me as it was for you."

"I guess that's something."

"I'd hoped to make that clear before—"

"Before I realized I was going to Africa to cover up a problem?

That's why I'm going, right? Not to prevent another accident, but to cover one up?"

"You're not supposed to like it, Sweet Pea. That's not possible." Paige leaned in and, very softly and very tenderly, kissed his temple. "That's not possible," she repeated, lessening the doubt in his mind about her view on Dark Sky's Covid-28 program: she enthusiastically supported some of the organization's projects—maybe most of them—but Covid-28 wasn't one of them.

CHAPTER 31

THE REMAINDER OF the flight went by faster and slower than Steve would have liked. Faster, because he was in no rush to begin helping Dark Sky, and slower, because the knowledge that Dark Sky was murdering millions kept whirling around in his head. At one point, angry at his untenable position, blaming the messenger, and confused that he was still attracted to her, he looked toward Paige's seat. The Dark Sky heavy with the white neck collar and butterfly bandages stood near her, looking down, apparently listening. As Steve watched, the man raised his head. Out of expressionless eyes, he returned Steve's gaze. He gave Paige a quick nod and then walked in Steve's direction. Up close, towering over Steve, the man was the size of a refrigerator. His well-tailored coat did nothing to diminish the size of his chest, back, and arms. His bandaged face shone with a film of sweat. The air the Soundwave was flying through was glass-smooth, but he swayed and clutched the back of the seat as if the airplane was transiting an area of turbulence.

He said, "My name is Messier. Ms. Patel has indicated—"

Steve interrupted. "Is that your first name or your last?"

"Last. It doesn't matter. Ms. Patel has indicated that you're not pleased with your involvement in this assignment." He paused, possibly to emphasize the next thing he said. "I don't care. Mr. Turner told me to extend you a certain amount of latitude. He likes happy employees. He believes happy employees are motivated employees."

"What happened to your neck?"

"We're not sharing," Messier replied. "I'm explaining the way it is."

"Does it hurt? I bet the collar is itchy."

Stone faced, Messier said nothing.

"It's going to feel extra hot in Africa. That's a shame."

Messier's face hardened. The sheen of sweat on his forehead took on a warmish glow. His jaw worked from side to side, but he maintained his composure. He, too, was constrained at seventy-eight thousand feet with limited options. "We've got some time in London before our connecting flight. Enjoy it. Eat a Pret a Manger sandwich. They make good sandwiches. I like them. Wash it down with an overpriced beer. Or not. Like I said, I don't care. Whatever you decide, don't try and run away with your discontent. Do that, and my latitude goes away." He dropped a hand the size of a pie plate onto Steve's shoulder and squeezed.

Steve stiffened and sucked in a painful breath through clenched teeth.

Messier said, "Remember, there's four of us. We have eyes on you. And Mr. Quinn? Word to the wise. I don't like smart mouths."

Steve hadn't planned on being a "smart mouth." If he'd thought about it, he would have kept his lips tightly zipped. But he hadn't thought about it. The soft-ball taunts he'd thrown at Messier had come from down deep, where instinct and reaction overruled analytics and planning. Somewhere over the Atlantic Ocean, he'd decided there was no circumstance under which he'd help Dark Sky. He hadn't yet figured out how he'd resist and his lower primal mind had grown impatient. It had aggressively asserted itself, said, "Enough," and started pushing back, without apprehension or regard for a guy as huge, and dedicated to Dark Sky, as Messier.

The four-hour connection time in London gave Steve plenty of time for a sandwich and an orange juice, seven A.M. being too early for warm, overpriced beer. He ate slowly, his eyes clocking Messier and the other Dark Sky heavies, one of whom was always nearby. Outside, aircraft from countries around the world taxied to and from the terminal building. Inside, the terminal was a noisy crowd of constantly changing nationalities, inadequate seating, and indistinct announcements. London, it appeared, was a nexus of global aviation. As busy as the terminal was, however, it had an insular feeling. Everybody was mindlessly scrolling, checking messages, or loudly carrying on cell phone conversations nobody else wanted to hear. He was alone, isolated in a crowd of hundreds.

Paige sat down opposite him and asked, "How are you, Sweet Pea?"

He held out a hand, palm down. It vibrated with sick, jangly nerves. Knowing about the atrocities in Africa and accepting them were two different things. Travel fatigue was also setting in. He was lightheaded, almost dizzy. Prior to the five-hour red eye across the Atlantic, he'd been awake all day. The Heathrow stopover was stretching out, and he still had a nine-hour subsonic flight to Tanzania in front of him; unfortunately, not every airline operated Boeing Soundwaves. He'd be a zombie by the time he checked into the hotel, as would the rest of the GS group.

How was he doing?

Not great.

Paige covered her mouth with the back of her hand, hiding a yawn. Her eyes were bloodshot. Steve looked at her and felt a strange mixture of pure affection and terrible sadness. He hadn't known her long and would have enjoyed getting to know her better, but how sustainable was the spark between them? Within days, they'd be back in America. She'd return to whatever she routinely did at Global Solutions, presumably without a second thought as to the reason they'd traveled to Africa in the first place. He'd be left struggling to reconcile the intelligent, attractive woman sitting opposite him with the executive indirectly connected to the annihilation of millions. It wasn't something he could do. That being the case, his only choice was to lock the memory of their personal time in a box, and bury it in the back of a mental closet, or risk seeing it over and over again, and reliving the joy of the moment and the sad knowledge that it would never happen again.

He said wearily, "What happens now, Paige?"

"We'll spend the night in Moshi, Tanzania. In the morning—"

"There's not much point flying Mach three, when the connecting flight is four hours later, is there?"

She hiked her shoulders. The fatigue on her face and the way she slumped in her chair told him she agreed. She continued. "In the morning, we fly to the Democratic Republic of Congo. To a town as close to the downed drone as possible. After that, we motor up the Congo River with locals who know the tributaries into the rainforest."

The longer Paige talked, the murkier the details became. The jungle spanned 264 million acres; there was no way to predict how long they'd be in the country. Dispirited and drained, Steve stopped paying attention after she told him their journey wouldn't yet be halfway complete when they landed in Tanzania. He tuned her out. The Heathrow pandemonium surrounding him (which had recognizable patterns inside it) overwhelmed the sickening internal monologue playing on a loop inside his head. In the external din, he found a strange tranquility.

CHAPTER 32

AFTER AN INTERMINABLE four-hour stopover, the party of six Dark Sky employees departed London Heathrow on a Boeing 787 Dreamliner, bound for Moshi, Tanzania.

Nine hours later, Steve caught a glimpse of Kilimanjaro's snowy crown as the plane descended into Moshi, landing as the setting sun splashed the sky in bright hues of red and orange. After touchdown and a short taxi, the Dreamliner came to a stop. Trucks with built-in staircases drove across the ramp and nudged up against the side of the jet. The airplane's doors opened, and a blast of dry equatorial heat reminded him that he was no longer in the northern hemisphere. He grinned, thinking of Messier's thick white collar.

He joined the rest of the passengers as they descended the stairs and walked across the tarmac toward the terminal building. In the distance, at the far end of the airport, he spotted the husk of an unidentifiable aircraft burned to blackened ruin… hopefully, a derelict used for training purposes. On the other side of the runway opposite the terminal, a row of sun-bleached, sand-blasted hangars stood side by side, fronted by several small aircraft. Too distant to identify positively, Steve thought one was a Cessna Caravan and another a Beech 200.

A crowd of three hundred crew and passengers formed at the entrance to the arrivals hall, splintering into ragged lines as they crept closer to a row of customs officers. He noticed two of the Dark Sky heavies ahead of him in line. Messier and the other heavy remained behind, possibly because of the dynamics of the crowd, but in all likelihood, because they wanted to keep eyes on him.

Customs was quick and organized. After a few of the usual, *why are you here? How long are you staying?* questions, asked first in French and then in English, Steve, Paige, and the rest of the Dark Sky people exited the secure area of the airport and immediately spotted an individual holding a hand-lettered sign reading, "Global Solutions."

Messier spoke with the man holding the welcome sign and then looked at Steve and the others out of dull, exhausted eyes. "Ms. Patel, Mr. Quinn, and myself will proceed to the hotel in one truck." He swiped the edge of his hand across his forehead, mopping away the sweat. He took a pill bottle out of a pocket, shook a tablet into his hand, and dry swallowed it. Nodding at the other heavies, he said, "You three will follow in the second vehicle. Tomorrow morning we'll meet in the lobby at oh-eight-hundred. Let's roll."

They exited the building into full darkness—the sun sets quickly in the mid-latitudes—and as they drove away from the airport, Steve felt a sense of place begin to grow despite not being able to see where they were going. The air conditioning in the Toyota Land Cruiser didn't work. He was soon filmed in a layer of sweat but remained reluctant to lower his window in an effort to catch a cooling breeze; the air was filled with the nauseating reek of burning garbage. Frequent yellow and orange barrel fires flickered on both sides of the road alongside the occasional small, well-lit convenience store selling everything from potato chips to hardware.

The AC wasn't the only part of the Land Cruiser in need of maintenance. Steve asked the driver why the steering wheel was misaligned at least thirty degrees. The driver, who didn't act concerned, said in heavily accented but perfectly understandable English, "Truck needs a front-end alignment." A disconcerting rhythm developed: as the Toyota accelerated, the front suspension began to shake violently and pull the truck sideways toward the shoulder. The shake went away after about forty miles an hour, but typically, before the truck reached that speed, the driver spiked the brakes and slowed to a virtual crawl. With kidney-rattling force—the cushioning in the seats had long since worn out—they'd thump over a speedbump built across the highway before beginning the entire process again. With each violent bump, Messier groaned unhappily and exhaled a quiet expletive. The man was suffering. The medication he swallowed at the airport was clearly not as effective as he needed it to be.

After forty minutes of this uncomfortable carnival ride, they arrived at the hotel. The second truck was nowhere in sight. Steve didn't know at what point it had taken a different road and gone its own way. He didn't have time to give it much thought. When he climbed out of the Toyota, a welcoming committee of two rushed out of the hotel with happy smiles, fist-bumps, and hugs. They greeted Paige with, "Welcome, little sister," and him and Messier with, "Welcome, my brother." Their infectious good cheer lifted his spirits a degree or two.

The hotel was a modest three-story building with five front-facing windows per floor, most of which were dark. The lobby was similarly dark. The television was off, as were the spotlights inside cabinets that held carvings of elephants and giraffes and artwork depicting Kilimanjaro. Either the hotel wasn't filled to capacity, or the two employees who greeted them, and who were now handing out room keys, were almost finished for the day and in a rush to go home. All in all, it had a comfortable, old-fashioned feeling. In Europe, it would have been called a "boutique hotel," serving people who preferred local establishments over global chains. Maybe that's what it was called in Africa, too. In Steve's mind, it was more of a guest house than a hotel.

He accepted his key with gratitude. After napping sporadically for only a handful of the twenty hours he'd been traveling, his eyes felt like they had fine sand in them. He thought he might be hungry, but the idea of food was unappetizing, and anyway, the dining room was empty and dark. Every muscle in his body felt limp and insubstantial. He couldn't wait to lock himself in his room, away from people and noise. He turned to the wide staircase leading up to the second floor, the comfort of his room, and the bliss of welcome sleep.

Paige's hand landed on his forearm. She said quietly, "Stay with me. In my room. I'm way too tired for… you know." She gave him a shy sideways smile. "I'd still enjoy the company."

On the other side of the hotel's shadowy lobby, Messier said into his cell phone, "Hang on." He pulled the device away from his ear and barked, "You two. This isn't a holiday. You're not on a couple's retreat." He winced, apparently at the sound of his own voice, because when he continued, he'd dialed down the volume. "Your key, Mr. Smart Mouth. Hand it over. You'll bunk with me. I'm not taking my eyes off you." He snapped his fingers a couple of times and held out an enormous hand in Steve's direction.

Paige made an exasperated noise. "Oh for…" She turned toward the staircase and walked away, mumbling, "Asshole."

"What was that?" Messier called after her.

Without looking back or slowing, she said, "Don't pretend you didn't hear me, Brian."

Messier watched her go with an angry scowl on his face, which Steve quite enjoyed. She didn't work for Brian Messier. She wasn't about to be subservient to him. Messier didn't like it and wasn't sure how to handle it.

He turned his glare in Steve's direction. He nodded at the opposite sofa. "Sit. I'll be done shortly." His eyes remained fastened on Steve as he raised his phone and said, "I'm here. I have to say, your man has a smart fucking mouth."

CHAPTER 33

NINETY-THREE HUNDRED MILES away from Moshi, on the west coast of America, Ethan Turner sat in his leather office chair and considered the muffled conversation he'd just overheard. If he'd been another man, he might have had a whiskey in his free hand, a Cuban smoldering in an ashtray, or a pretty young thing with talented hands massaging away the sudden tension that tightened his shoulders and neck. But he was Ethan Turner. Aside from lavish wristwatches, his vices included the clear sky and clean streets that he saw out the floor-to-ceiling window, a stunning view he'd helped create, and a snapshot of a world he would protect at all costs. "Saving the Planet," to hijack a wildly inaccurate phrase when applied to Steve Quinn's world, was actually working here. It was not something he'd jeopardize.

He asked Messier, "Can Quinn overhear me?"

"Probably. Hang on."

Muffled once again, Turner heard Messier say, "Wait for me over there," followed by Quinn's quick response, "Those pain pills make it hard to concentrate? You just told me to sit here."

"I'm losing patience. Now, fuck off." A second later, no longer muffled, Messier was back on the line. "I'm here."

Turner smiled faintly. He could almost see the flecks of angry white foam gathering at the corners of Messier's mouth. He wasn't generally so irritable, but when he went too long without adequate food or sleep, he turned into an ornery grizzly bear with a three-inch thorn jammed in its paw. If Quinn wasn't careful, he was going to experience Messier's intolerant side at close range.

Turner asked, "Couple's retreat, Brian? What's going on? Why're you playing camp counselor?"

"They're bumping uglies. She asked him to stay in her room. I want to keep an eye on him."

"Really?" Turner exhaled heavily. "That surprises me. I didn't see that coming." He liked Paige. She was a dedicated member of the Dark Sky team, fully committed to *most* of the world-improving projects they'd initiated. He wouldn't have sent her to Africa without having confidence in her ability to untie tangles at borders, to organize the logistics required to get them to the downed Diablo, and yes, to unveil Dark Sky's African mission to Quinn—this, despite her disapproval of the Covid-28 program. She was no less valuable if they were emotionally involved, but Turner had a healthy paranoia about couples who worked together. When matters of the heart were involved, people became unpredictable. The question as to whether Paige was an asset or liability was suddenly in play. He said, "Is Quinn with us? Has he gotten with the program?"

"No."

"You're sure? It hasn't been long. Is it possible he'll come around?"

"Hard no," Messier replied with finality.

Disappointed, Turner nodded. Hoping Quinn might become an asset had always been an optimistic moonshot. A secondary goal. The primary reason he'd been chosen for the African job was the fact that he wouldn't be missed, should the mission capsize. Turner wiped a hand down his face, tracing the edges of his goatee with his thumb and forefinger. What did the faceless "they" of the world say? *Hope in one hand, hand grenade in the other?* Something like that.

He might have made a different decision if Messier hadn't spoken with such assurance. But after all the preceding years in which they'd worked together, from the Afghan desert to areas around the globe where Dark Sky had a covert presence, Turner had learned to trust his man implicitly. He asked Messier to do something, Messier did it. He was as reliable as the tides.

Turner said, "All right. Quinn doesn't make it home. Maybe he falls out of the boat. Gets eaten by piranhas—"

"There're piranhas here? I didn't know that. Those little bastards—"

"Goddamn, Brian. I wasn't speaking literally. Keep him on a short leash until you're done at the crash site. Then, take care of him. Make it look accidental. I don't care if African wildlife is involved or not." Turner hesitated, not happy with what he was about to say next, but believing it necessary. "It's important Ms. Patel doesn't suspect a thing. If she's aware you had a hand in his death. If she gives any sign—"

"The piranhas?"

"Correct. Use your best judgment. Ms. Patel is not our enemy. I'd prefer she makes it home. We clear?"

"We're clear. Anything else?"

"Give me a sec," Turner replied. He rose, circled his desk, and came to a stop in front of the window. Temporarily blind to the view, he thought the situation through. He hadn't become head of Dark Sky without the ability to look into the future and think around corners. It struck him that when a private in the trenches wants something, he says, "Give me A, or I'll do B," believing the ultimatum puts him in the driver's seat. The thing is, a private is nothing more than a worker bee. Inexperienced. Ignorant. Tasked with one job, he's incapable of looking at his demand from a wider point of view. He can't understand that C, D, and E are possibilities.

Turner was no private, no worker bee. He knew there was usually more than one outcome for any given situation. He thought hard, trying to imagine scenarios in which Quinn survived the African continent. He couldn't see them. His faith in Brian Messier was absolute. When it came to tactical shit, this pseudo black-ops stuff, Messier outmatched Quinn in every way. The one exception was tech, and computer acumen didn't apply deep in the African jungle. This was an umbrella drink and lounge chair kind of job for Messier. As easy as they came. On top of which, judging from Messier's surly tone, he didn't much like Quinn. Drilling one into the back of the geek's head and leaving him to decompose in the jungle would be a pleasure for the soldier, not a problem.

Turner couldn't visualize scenarios C, D, or E from any angle. As far as he was concerned, the time had come to discuss other matters.

He said, "Brian? You there? How're you feeling? Earlier, what pain pills was Quinn chirping about?"

CHAPTER 34

MESSIER DIDN'T ANSWER immediately; he couldn't remember a time he'd felt worse.

The bruise across his chest was a spectacular sunset purple. He sipped every breath. Anything deeper and searing pain lanced from his collarbone to his sternum. His neck muscles shrieked in protest every time he moved his head. He had to rotate his entire body in order to see something off to the side. The neck collar was supposed to help with that, but Quinn, the smart-assed son-of-a-bitch, nailed it when he suggested it would be extra uncomfortable in the Tanzanian heat. Even the cut on the side of his face itched like sizzling fire, and he couldn't scratch it for fear of peeling off the butterfly bandages and re-opening the wound.

All of that paled in comparison to the riot inside his skull. His headache was monstrous. Everything he looked at wobbled in and out of focus like ghostly, living-dead salsa dancers. He knew he was suffering from whiplash. Hence, the white collar. He had little doubt he was also suffering from a concussion, even though the CT scan and the MRI he'd undergone before leaving the States hadn't indicated anything abnormal. Resting on two back-to-back, long-haul flights should have helped ease the symptoms. Instead, they were getting worse. He couldn't remember getting on the airplane in Heathrow.

He'd taken a Percocet in London. Quinn watched him swallow

one more. The drugs managed the pain, but they also backed him up, so now his lower abdomen was sore and bloated. As hungry as he was, the thought of food made him nauseous. Or maybe it was the drugs that made him nauseous. Or the concussion. Messier didn't know. Didn't fucking care. If there'd been a way to kill the son-of-a-bitch on the motorbike all over again, he would have happily done it. Slowly. Just to ensure the man hurt as much as he was suffering right now.

None of this was information with which he'd enlighten Ethan Turner.

They'd watched each other's backs since 2005. More than once, they'd almost died together. Afterward, they celebrated the miracle of life together. When Turner stumbled into this Dark Sky opportunity—however that came to be—and was told to assemble a team, his first call was to Brian Messier.

Messier had been Turner's frontman for over two decades. He'd never, not once, given Turner a reason to question that choice. In retrospect, Messier knew he should have begged off this mission, but he hadn't felt terrible when he climbed on the airplane in the States. Now that he was here, there wasn't a chance in hell he'd let his boss down, or give him the slimmest reason to believe this assignment—babysitting a tech geek—would be the mission he failed to complete.

In response to Turner's question, Messier said, "I'm fine. He saw me swallow some Tylenol is all." With that mildly deceitful answer, he inadvertently created a massive black hole separating his loyalty and Turner's faith.

Turner accepted the answer, but he was no private, no worker bee. The Covid-28 program was far too sensitive not to have a contingency in place. He sent a just-in-case text to another trusted asset and told her to keep her schedule clear; she might need to go live in three or four days. Had he known the informational vacuum between him and Messier would have profound global consequences, his text would have been more than perfunctory.

November, 2005
Daniel (Danny) White

CHAPTER 35

ETHAN TURNER WAS in no way a racist. He simply didn't like anyone from the Arab world. He didn't like the men because they were the ones who flew airplanes into buildings, killing thousands. He didn't like the women because they gave birth to babies who A: became men who flew airplanes into buildings, or B: became women who gave birth to babies who eventually flew airplanes into buildings. This thought process was not open to interpretation or subtlety. In Turner's mind, these were facts, as indubitable as time, gravity, Kurt Cobain's genius, and the exquisite perkiness of silicone boobs. It all became "fact" for him on September 11, 2001, at an age when all young people are figuring out who they'll be, when the opinions and attitudes they're forming are free from the influences of parents and guardians and are, therefore, something foundational that can't be changed. When he went to Afghanistan three months after the terror attacks, he did so with the utmost conviction. Four years later, his belief in the inherent righteousness of America's goal hadn't wavered, so when a tall, elderly gentleman wearing a loose-fitting linen suit, Ray Ban Clubmaster sunglasses, and a wide-brimmed straw hat asked him if he wanted a greater role in serving America's interests, Turner's answer was a fast and easy, "Yes."

This was in an office attached to a hangar at Kandahar Airfield, which erroneously reinforced Turner's assumption that the old guy wanted him to do something more important in Afghanistan. Something more significant. The shithouse of a country was, after all, the epicenter of America's biggest threat. The conversation that followed proved his assumption incorrect. In fact, it went in an unexpected direction, in no small part, because the immediate impression the old guy gave Turner became insignificant so quickly. He'd come across as a limp-wrist in his crème-colored outfit, especially the Panama hat. With his precise speech, thin gray hair brushed carefully back, and the delicate vintage Longines on his wrist, he reminded Turner of a grandfather, a long-since retired administrator trying to maintain his grip on the glory of the position he once held.

Turner followed the old guy into the office, closed the door, sat down, and took a few seconds to enjoy the air conditioning before asking, "Who are you? What's your name?"

"We'll get to that. Not knowing is better. It makes for a more unbiased decision." The old guy nodded, as if he approved of his response. "I'm going to tell you as much as I can. By the time I'm done, I guarantee you'll have more questions than I have answers. At that point, I'll ask again, 'Do you want to play a greater role in serving America's interests?' If you're still interested, I'll present you with a nondisclosure agreement. After you sign, I'll formally introduce myself and welcome you into a world bigger than you ever imagined." He waved an uncalloused hand at the colorless horizon and scorching heat on the other side of the window. "A world far greater than the confines of this place."

Turner waited impassively, showing the old guy none of the interest he felt, holding a flurry of anticipatory excitement in check.

"If you don't sign," the old guy shrugged, "I'll fly home. You'll go online. Within a few minutes, you'll know who I am, and you'll have an inkling as to what you passed on. Only a hint, mind you. The smallest fraction of what you missed, and the good you could have done." As he spoke, he placed his leather briefcase on the table. With long, slender fingers, he unsnapped the catches. Withdrew a sheaf of papers. "You need to know... The ramifications of breaking the NDA are permanent. Worse than a life sentence in Leavenworth. Do you understand what that means?"

Turner nodded slowly. He'd always considered "life sentence" a misnomer. You go to prison until you die? That's a death sentence, not a life sentence. And, in this case, the way the old guy was laying it out, "death sentence" was a far more accurate description. The only thing more permanent than life in Leavenworth was a bullet in the back of the head.

Shit had just become real.

He suddenly wished he'd spent a little more time with CNN, Fox, the New York Times. Maybe then he'd have more than an "inkling" as to who the old guy was and what he might ask. But Turner didn't consume the news. Why would he? Here in the desert, he *was* the news. The reporters stateside didn't know what was real in Afghanistan and what wasn't. Everything they said had an ungodly Nolan Ryan-type spin on it. You're looking for accuracy you might as well watch "reality" shows, *Survivor* or *Big Brother*, bilge like that, before cable news. When Turner had free time for television, reading, or recreation, he was watching a movie, flipping through a magazine, or working out in the gym.

He said, "I'm listening."

The old guy gave him an approving nod. He said, "Very good," and then told him as much as he could. Or was willing. It didn't take long. It didn't amount to much. He finished with, "That's all." From within the briefcase, he withdrew a slim gold pen. He placed it on top of the papers. "Last time," the old guy said. "Do you want a greater role in serving America's interests?"

Turner said nothing. He stared out the window, squinting through the heat waves radiating off the tarmac, distorting the shape of the tan-colored mountains on the distant horizon. As promised, the old guy had raised more questions than answers. But, set aside the effeminate mannerisms and listen to what he said, and it was evident he was a goddamn heavy hitter, which wasn't much of a surprise. He was the only passenger on a Gulfstream G5 that had arrived in Kandahar for the sole purpose of speaking to Turner.

It took Turner less than two seconds to decide. He didn't need to know anything else. The power the old guy was talking about bestowing on him in service to America was all the information he required. He picked up the pen and scrawled his signature on the NDA.

The old guy said, "My name is Daniel White. I'm head of an organization known as Dark Sky. Only a select few at the highest levels of government know what that means. Welcome aboard."

Turner's eyes went wide as realization hit. Snatches of articles and programs he'd read or seen came back in a rush. Daniel White. Upper echelons of the White House. Close to the president. Seldom seen, seldom heard, frequent rumors about the power and influence he wielded, but no hard truths as to his role. Turner smiled. He was delighted he'd signed the NDA. He was going to work for Danny White.

White smiled, too, as if he knew what Turner was thinking. He gathered the signed papers and tapped the horizontal and vertical edges, tidying the sheaf. He locked them, along with his fancy gold pen, inside his briefcase. "Get packed," he said. "The Gulfstream is fueled. The pilots are ready. We're going to Washington. I'd like to be airborne within ninety minutes. We have a great deal to discuss."

May, 2028

CHAPTER 36

IN MOSHI, MESSIER thumbed off his cell phone and rose unsteadily to his feet. He wobbled the way a person does when he stands up too quickly and experiences a momentary bout of dizziness. Holding the sofa, he recovered, pocketed his phone and then said, "Let's go." He pointed to the wide staircase.

Steve led the way across the dimly lit lobby. He took the stairs two at a time, ten to the switchback, ten more to the second floor. At the top he shot a glance over his shoulder and saw Messier on the landing, bent at the waist and swaying, his large body heaving for every loud, ragged breath. Steve watched without sympathy for two or three impatient seconds, thinking about how much he wanted sleep, how he didn't care whose room his bed was in, as long as sleep happened soon...and wouldn't it be nice if his warden hurried the hell up?

As if in answer to Steve's silent plea, Messier raised his foot to the next riser and climbed. On the seventh step, he staggered. He teetered backward, the wrong direction when a person is climbing stairs. His left arm shot out, searching for the banister, missing it.

In sudden revelation, Steve realized the three Dark Sky heavies were nowhere in sight, Paige had disappeared and Messier was vulnerable. His best, possibly only opportunity to turn his fortunes around, was happening in front of him. Right now. Before the thought had fully coalesced—his primal mind was driving again, unconcerned and indifferent to the future—he swiveled on his heels, leapt down the stairs and using momentum and all the force he could muster, he planted both hands on Messier's chest and shoved.

Unstable and leaning in the wrong direction, Messier tumbled backward, arms whirling the air in search of elusive balance, not finding it. He landed on his back, feet pointing up the staircase. His head struck a riser with a sickening hollow thump that sounded like a person checking the ripeness of a cantaloupe. His yell of surprise dwindled into a low exhaustive moan.

The silence that followed was oppressive, the stillness unnerving. Panting hard, close to hyperventilating, Steve cut a glance toward the second-floor hallway. A faulty light bulb flickered on and off, making him believe for a beat that a guest had opened a door. He saw nobody. He scanned the lobby at the bottom the of the staircase. Saw nobody. Slowly, he knelt. Down low, Messier's body stank of unhealthy sweat. The man's open eyes showed mostly white. The cervical collar and the twist of his head reminded Steve of the predictable outcome of a hangman's noose.

Fear grew loud in his mind, stifling almost every coherent thought. The ramifications if someone caught him—a night manager investigating the noise perhaps, or the heavies returning from their private assignment—were unconceivable. He couldn't imagine how horrific an African prison would be, if local authorities found a foreigner kneeling beside a dead body.

He had to go.

He had to go now, before someone showed up with questions he couldn't answer.

A fragment of rational thought held him in place. He flipped open Messier's coat…

…and the big man's body convulsed. One leg twitched twice.

Steve yelped and recoiled. Scrabbling backward, he landed on his butt, the fear as bright and piercing as a chrome ice pick.

Messier didn't move.

Steve sucked in a couple of stabilizing breaths. He scanned the hallway again. Nobody. Slowly, he reached out and placed a shaking hand on Messier's whiskey cask chest. He felt nothing.

Dead, Steve thought. *You killed him,*

In self defense,

Wasn't self defense at the time,

I saw an opportunity,

Killed him,

Self defense...

...and then he felt a faint heartbeat beneath his palm, and then another, the rhythmic, all-important beats that meant life!

Steve's relief was as overwhelming as the fear was acute; he didn't take a second to consider why he felt such relief at Messier's survival, this Dark Sky heavy who certainly meant him harm, if not death. His only thought now, was how urgently he needed to get moving. To escape.

He *really* had to go.

He found the big man's wallet, a well-worn leather billfold thick with American dollars, cash that worked well in most third world countries when it came to everything from tips to bribes. He pocketed it all. There was no driver's licence but there were three credit cards. Two had a name Steve didn't recognize printed on them, an alias he assumed. The third was an American Express with Global Solutions written on it. He silently thanked the diligence of GSs' internal travel agency, for issuing the head of the expedition with an unlimited credit card. It joined the cash in Steve's pocket. Finally, he found Messier's phone. Using the man's index finger, he bypassed the lock screen. Forcing himself to slow down and work methodically, he spent a minute adjusting the settings. When he was certain the device would remain unlocked, he stepped over the unconscious body, descended the stairs and walked out the front door of the hotel.

He paused deep in the building's shadow. He looked left and right. Seeing nobody, he started toward the highway, walking at a pace just shy of a run. At the highway, he turned left in the direction of the little roadside shops he'd seen on the drive from the airport and then, because he couldn't help himself, he started to jog.

CHAPTER 37

IN A ROOM on the second floor of the hotel, Paige Patel stepped out of the shower. Her hair was bundled in a towel. She'd wrapped another towel around herself and knotted it on her chest. After washing off countless hours of traveling grunge, she was more than ready for bed.

Enjoying the contrasting sensation of cold ceramic tiles on her hot-out-of-the-shower feet, she walked to the window, intent on closing the narrow gap where the curtains didn't quite meet. For no discernable reason, possibly because she hadn't taken a good look earlier, she pulled one curtain aside two or three inches and peeked out at the hotel courtyard. She didn't expect to see anything. At first, she didn't. Then, as she was about to turn away, the darkness at the hotel's entrance expanded. A tall, slender piece broke off and became a person-shaped shadow. The figure looked left and right in what Paige imagined was a furtive manner and then moved cautiously into an area that was marginally brighter, thanks to a slim wedge of yellow moon. Between the individual's gait and the scant extra light, she recognized Steve Quinn.

She narrowed her eyes and leaned closer to the window, watching as he walked down the hotel laneway, deliberately remaining in the darkest pools of night. At the highway, he turned left and broke into a run.

She pulled her gaze away from the window and looked at the desk where her cell phone was charging. How Steve had escaped Messier's strict observance was a mystery. Since he had, Messier and his colleagues needed to know. They needed to find him. They needed to get him back. Her job demanded she alert them.

She didn't move.

Privately, Paige felt Ethan Turner had asked too much of Steve too quickly. Setting aside the Covid-28 mission, most of Dark Sky's projects could be explained and, where needed, burnished. Burnished or not, insisting Steve accept them as a way to rehabilitate the world before it became a hell-scape similar to Over-there, was unrealistic. It was an emotional ride too arduous for a stable mind to process, never mind the fragile psyche of an individual who'd experienced a life-altering tragedy, followed closely by the knowledge that a multiverse existed. If he couldn't accept Dark Sky before he knew about Covid-28, he certainly couldn't accept it afterward. Not in Paige's estimation, and she understood…

Paige considered the Covid-28 strategy abhorrent. Her opinion, however, was irrelevant. As a small cog on the Dark Sky gear wheel, she was without influence or input when it came to making decisions of magnitude. She was not integral to Covid-28. It was happening with or without her, therefore, she wasn't responsible for it, nor was she accountable to it. There was nothing she could do about it, which made minimizing it and compartmentalizing it easier, much to her growing shame.

Her gaze remained on her phone and the call she was required to make.

Steve's question, *will I be disappeared*, danced in front of her, like a bright red tube-man flapping his plastic arms at a used car dealership. It demanded her attention. It demanded an answer. Until she'd met him and was forced to face the question head-on, she'd held it as a theoretical concept. An organization capable of creating and using Covid-28 would certainly assassinate a whistleblower, but *why would they?* Killing was unnecessary because, what would a whistleblower say?

Who would he tell? Who'd believe him? She understood this rationale represented avoidance on her part. A safety net. But without direct knowledge that Dark Sky killed to protect itself, it was easy for the question, *will I be disappeared,* to remain theoretical.

His question wouldn't leave her alone. It had torn her safety net to tatters. He'd turned theory into reality and made it personal. And since it had become real and personal and couldn't be ignored, neither could the multitude of deaths in Africa.

As they always do, rationalizations, justifications, and avoidance had reached their inevitable zenith. All that was left was the manner in which Paige chose to deal with them. Her cheeks burned with shameful heat. Her eyes moistened. She dropped her chin to her chest, knowing what she had to do.

Blinking to clear the moisture from her eyes, she picked up her phone with trembling hands. She worked the side-buttons in sequence until the Power Off message appeared. With only the merest hesitancy, she swiped right with her thumb, killing the phone. The screen turned black. She tossed the dead device on the desk. Smiling through her tears, she whispered, "Good luck," and then tugged the curtains together, sealing the gap.

The towels she'd wrapped around herself fell to the floor. She crawled onto the bed, secured the mosquito net behind her, and slid beneath the sheet. The air conditioner hummed its quiet white noise. After twenty-plus hours of travel, she thought the bed was more amazingly comfortable than anything she'd ever slept in before. It didn't cross her mind that unloading some of the acidic guilt she'd been carrying might have had something to do with how quickly she fell asleep. The small smile was still on her lips.

CHAPTER 38

AN UNFATHOMABLE TIME later, a repetitive thumping dragged Paige out of deep unconsciousness. It took over a minute for her to realize someone was knocking on her door. She considered ignoring the intrusion but judged by the intensity, that whoever was knocking so relentlessly, didn't plan on going away. She groaned and blinked and found the fortitude to crawl out from beneath the sheet. It took another minute of effort to locate and don the oversized T-shirt she typically slept in when travelling.

She unlocked and opened the door.

Turner's Dark Sky employees stood in the hallway, staring at her. The one in the front—his name was Spencer—still had his arm raised, fist ready for another round of determined door-knocking. They'd all changed out of their collared shirts, slacks and coats. Now they wore sneakers, baggy cargo shorts and in turn, a Nike, an Under Armour and a New Balance tech shirt. She wondered where they'd gone and for what purpose, and how they'd found time to change out of their travelling clothes. Powerful men with identical buzz cuts, aggressive postures and eyes full of worry, they were practically clones, aside from the brand names. She could only distinguish Spencer from the other two because he was the solitary black man on the crew…and wasn't that something an HR expert could never admit out loud?

Spencer said, "You alone?"

"What do you want?"

"Messier is hurt. Hurt bad. We can't find Quinn."

Paige flinched in surprise. Her eyes widened. She gasped and an involuntary hand flew to her mouth. She immediately understood the contradiction the three men displayed in their posture: anger about their friend's condition battled the strain they felt about Steve's disappearance. She also understood the subtext in Spencer's question, *you alone?*

"You think he's in here? With me?" She stepped back, opened the door wide and said, "Help yourself."

Although she wasn't aware of it, her unscripted reaction disguised the fact that she knew Steve was gone. It effectively allayed Spencer's suspicious mind. Looking faintly embarrassed, he nodded. "Thank you. Not necessary. I had to ask."

"What happened to Brian?"

"He fell down the stairs—

"I'm betting he was pushed," one of the clones said.

"—and bashed his head. He's got vertigo so bad he can't walk. We had to carry him to his room. Even that was too much motion; he puked on me. He can't handle light. Not even the lamp beside the bed. He said it makes him feel like his head is going to explode."

Paige blew out a long breath. She said, "What do you need? What can I do?"

"Nothing at this point," Spencer said. "We've got to find him. Unfamiliar African town in the middle of the night? He couldn't have gone far."

She heard the need for reassurance in his statement, the trace of desperation in his voice. It made sense. Turner would go feral if they couldn't track Steve down. She said, "I'll be here if you need me." With as much conviction as she could muster, she said for a second time that night, "Good luck," and then closed her door.

CHAPTER 39

FEAR AND ADRENALINE carried Steve only so far, before the eighty-two-degree air and the sixty percent humidity, forced an end to his crazed sprint. Hands on hips, he gasped and gulped for what felt like a lifetime but in reality, was little more than sixty seconds. After regaining his breath, he started walking at a more sustainable pace, putting distance between himself and the hotel.

On his right-hand side, single-story buildings paralleled the highway. A Vodacom shop with bars on the windows, a store-front advertising Toyotas and Nissans, another promoting a safari company, felt ominous in their looming, rundown condition. One ramshackle structure of corrugated metal, plywood scraps and wooden pallets reminded him of the Toughs shanty town Over-there. The stink of burning garbage wafted in and out of his nose. Vehicles traveling in both directions passed him, everything from full size busses to motorcycles carrying two, sometimes three passengers. Several three-wheeled bajajis (commonly referred to as tuk-tuks), slowed as they drove by, in hopes of capturing a fare. Steve waved them off. The convenience store he'd seen on the drive from the airport to the hotel wasn't far away and for the time being, he preferred the anonymity.

As it turned out, the store was farther away than he remembered. In the darkness, the unfamiliarity of his surroundings and the speed of the Land Cruiser in which they'd travelled, conspired to stretch time and distance. Eventually though, he saw the flickering barrel fire and the cluster of buildings he had in mind.

The store wasn't any wider than a single car garage, the kind people used for storage because it's too small to park a vehicle inside. A counter stretched across the front and bumped into a refrigerator filled with water, beer and soda. Bags of potato chips were clipped to a ceiling beam with brightly colored clothes pegs. Behind the counter, a young man watched a video—Steve thought it might be Top Gun: Maverick—on large cell phone, a Pro or a Max or something equally pretentious. His eyes barely left the screen when Steve opened the cooler and pulled out a dewy Coca-Cola. He cracked the top and drained half the bottle before taking a breath. He emptied the second half more slowly, put the empty on the counter and waited until the young guy canted his head away from his movie and looked at him curiously.

The guy said, "Hey man, how's it?"

Pleasantly surprised at the friendly tone—he was expecting indifference, possibly irritation for the interruption—Steve nodded at the phone in the guy's hand and said, "Nice phone. Like mine." He showed the guy the phone he'd taken from Messier. "I need a charging cord."

"No problem." The guy found the appropriate cord, put it on the counter beside the empty Coca-Cola bottle and asked, "Anything else?"

"I need a place to plug in for a couple of hours."

The guy pulled back in surprise, the earlier curiosity turning to confusion, like, *I don't understand what this foreigner is saying.*

Steve maintained an affable smile while inside, his nerves churned…

Keeping the young guy eye locked, he plucked a one-hundred-dollar bill out of Messier's roll of cash. "That's for the Coke and the cord." He pulled out a second one-hundred-dollar bill. Making sure the guy saw it, Steve pointed over his shoulder to the back of the store, where a beaded curtain filled a doorframe. He didn't know what was back there. Maybe nothing more than a storeroom, but he had Messier's cash to gamble with. He was betting the space was used for more than crates of inventory. He placed the second bill on top of the first. He tapped them with two fingers. The guy watched with wide eyes; Steve had his full attention. "This one is for electrical power. You watch your program. I'll charge my phone. When it hits one hundred percent, I'll give you another bill. In return, you'll call me a taxi to the airport. Sound good?"

The young guy wavered for a second, probably debating whether or not he'd get in trouble for doing this foreigner with more money than brains, a favor. He must have decided the risk was worth the money. He said, "Sounds good." He flipped up a quarter section of the counter top, creating access to a narrow corridor leading from the front of the store to the beaded curtain in the rear.

Steve walked to the back and swept the curtain aside.

As he expected, the back half of the "single car garage" was a storage facility. It was also a break room and an apartment. A table with two chairs faced a flat screen television hanging on the wall. There was a hot plate, a miniature refrigerator, a sink containing a plastic basin full of dirty dishes. Instead of a sofa, a single cot lived in one corner. The rest of the space was filled with cases of water, beer and soda, as well as cardboard cartons with labels such as Old Dutch and others with printing he didn't recognize. It took only a few seconds to scan the room and deem it suitable for his requirements.

He plugged in Messier's phone and started surfing the world wide web, searching for, finding and then copying and pasting into the phone, the email addresses of as many public figures, journalists and politicians as he could find. He didn't filter aggressively. If an address looked like it might make it to someone with power, influence or a voice, he added it to his growing list. He was under no illusions. A high percentage of the emails he'd send would not land, a point Paige made and he'd argued against, while silently agreeing with her. But he also thought some would land.

The young guy earned himself another fifty when he poked his head through the beaded curtain to see if Steve wanted anything. Steve asked for a Red Bull. He had momentum on his side but the shot of sugary energy the Coca-Cola had given him had run out and there was plenty more work to do before he left for the airport.

He kept an eye on the clock.

When he judged his list extensive enough, he began creating the email. He used talk-to-text, in order to get as much information about Dark Sky and its activities written down as fast as possible. He dictated the story as Paige told it to him, carefully excluding the bits about the Passage and the parallel world. As he wrote, a childhood story weirdly resurfaced, about a five-year-old girl named Josephine…

Once upon a time, Josephine spotted the most beautiful red apple she'd ever seen. Josephine loved apples. This apple was in a fruit basket on her grandmother's dining room table. She picked it out of the basket and held it close, admiring how flawless it seemed. Shiny and bright, it looked as though it had been painted just for her. She knew it wasn't meant to be eaten. As part of the centerpiece, it was there to look pretty. But Josephine also knew how delightful the first crunchy bite would taste.

She couldn't help herself.

She bit into the apple with excitement. As soon as she bit down, she knew something was wrong. The apple was soft and mushy inside. It tasted dry and mealy. Where was the crisp sweetness she expected? She'd picked the apple because it looked perfect on the outside, but the inside was rotten.

Josephine's grandmother wasn't angry. Of course she wasn't. This was a children's story and therefore, the lesson was subtle as a starving Rottweiler.

Grandma crouched down to Josephine's level and said gently, "Jojo, it's not always the outside that matters. Sometimes things aren't perfect, no matter how nice they look. Other times the best things are hidden inside, even if they don't look perfect at first."

Steve blinked away the surprising prickly sensation in the back of his eyes, and shook his head at his own silliness. It was probably exhaustion and the accumulating emotions of the last several days—maybe the last five months—but somehow Josephine's Red Apple had more of an impact than a children's story had any right to have. He missed Over-there far more than it warranted.

He proofread his email several times. He corrected punctuation and spelling where needed. It probably wouldn't destroy Dark Sky but it was more apt to be taken seriously and it had a better chance of bringing the organization to its knees, if the people reading it believed it was written by a literate adult, not an adolescent Tik Tocker.

Three hours after he started with the address search, when his eyes were blurring with fatigue, he set the alarm on his borrowed phone. He knew it was good practice to wait several hours between writing an email and sending it. In this case, he thought that rule was doubly important. Paige had said that with an ever-growing population, there were proportionally more smart people being born into the world, even if the world never learned who they were. What she hadn't mentioned—but what stood to reason—was that the converse was also true: a proportionate number of idiots were also being born. These people weren't hidden or unrecognized. They were everywhere, all the time. For them, ignoring the worsening state of the planet was their default setting; building was hard, destroying easy…

…and it was them who gave Steve pause and made him wonder if Dark Sky might be doing the right thing, despite the cost.

He needed to sleep on his email.

He stretched out on the cot. After a short nap, he'd re-read it a final time and then take a cab to the airport. He'd leave Moshi on the first available flight, wherever it happened to be going.

CHAPTER 40

AFTER PAIGE SHUT the door to her hotel room, Spencer and the two Dark Sky heavies put their heads together. Within seconds, confirmation bias set in: they collectively ruled out the airport as Steve's destination. At that time of night, as late as it was, there'd be no flights and therefore nowhere for him to go. In all likelihood, the terminal building would be dark and locked up tight. The airport was almost twenty miles away from the town of Moshi. Buses, on the other hand, were all over the roads. Everything from large inter-city coaches, to ubiquitous bajajis, to scores of lane-splitting motorcycles, filled the roads to bursting. Ignoring an orchestra of pointless horn-honking, this frenzied mess converged on, and diverged from, the main bus station, located less than a mile away from the hotel in which they were staying. The Dark Sky heavies reasonably assumed that an escapee, trying to get as far away as fast as possible, could board one of the modern, Wi-Fi equipped coaches and vanish into the chaos within minutes.

The bus stand was their first stop.

It was less a building than two large parking lots separated by a low row of vendors beneath umbrellas and shops with Fanta and Sprite billboards on the roofs. One parking lot was filled with dozens of small buses and minivans used for short distance destinations. The other side was devoted to the full-sized coaches. None of the Dark Sky men could figure out which bus was going where, or determine which one was leaving within minutes, or which one was parked for the night. The schedule and organization in the station was beyond them. In desperation, they started handing out American twenty-dollar bills like they were two-bite Snickers at Halloween, giving cash to anyone who spoke English and might have seen a foreigner, other than themselves.

They were unsuccessful, in part because handing out free money drew people toward them like fleas to dogs, whether the fleas had information to sell or not. Usually not. It also raised the attention of nearby police officers. Although paying a cop to turn a blind eye may have been possible, none of the three wanted to put that possibility to the test. Not now. Not after meeting a local Dark Sky contact earlier in the evening and spending an exorbitant amount of money on the hand gun each man now carried, well concealed in his oversized cargo shorts.

An hour after they started, they took a break in a restaurant not far from the bus stand. Over cans of ice-cold Kilimanjaro Premium Lager, they once again, put their heads together. None of the them had slept. All of them were sweaty, hungry, angry about Messier's condition and worried about the repercussions they'd face if they didn't find Quinn. When Turner's name came up, they avoided each other's eyes. The undercurrent of anxiety was making them increasingly frantic, all of which made their next idea seem more reasonable than it was. Maybe Quinn had chosen to hide in a different hotel. There weren't many hotels in town, but as with any city, not all of them showed up on an Expedia search. There were Air B and Bs to consider. A thorough search wouldn't happen quickly.

One heavy stayed near the bus station and kept an eye peeled. Just in case.

Spencer and the second heavy began canvasing the town's hotels, again without success. Dawn was only a short time away when Spencer acknowledged defeat; he didn't know where Quinn had gone. He didn't know where to look next. The only remaining idea he had was the idea he'd already dismissed.

With futile hope overshadowing them, Spencer and Heavy Two took a taxi the twenty miles to the airport. When they arrived, they saw a widebody airplane parked on the tarmac. Spencer's partner told him it was an Edelweiss Air A330. Spencer cut him a thin-lipped smile. He didn't care—he was long past giving two fucks what kind of airplane it was—but the sight of it gave him a much-needed shot of optimism.

Maybe, he'd spot Quinn arriving at the airport. He'd snatch him as he climbed out of a taxi, grab him before he joined the check-in lineup, and then... The next part of Spencer's plan was unformulated. He just wanted Quinn back, in custody before he spoke to Turner and determined if there was a new mission statement, now that Messier was incapacitated. There wasn't much time. Even with a Do Not Disturb tag hanging on the door knob, housekeeping was going to want access to Messier's room, where they'd find a seriously injured individual who couldn't tolerate motion, light or noise. In all likelihood, they'd raise holy-oh-fuck. Spencer didn't want to be anywhere close to Moshi when that happened.

The Moshi airport terminal building was open. Inside he found an early-rising Edelweiss agent tapping away at a computer keyboard beneath a sign that read, "Edelweiss Air Check-in." The agent looked up and greeted them with a smile, happy for the company, it seemed. He told Spencer the jet on the tarmac had landed late the night before. It would depart again in a few hours. In fact, it was the first available flight out of Moshi, scheduled to depart for Dar es Salaam at nine. Check-in opened at six-thirty.

A buzz of confidence widened Spencer's smile.

After perusing every accessible corner of the terminal building, the two restless Dark Sky employees walked outside with time to kill. Like boys do at every airport in the world, Spencer and Heavy Two strolled to the fence separating them from the secure part of the airport. They clung to the chain-link and peered through the holes, watching as a small twin-engine airplane taxied away from a hanger on the other side of the airport. It lined up at the end of the runway.

Sounding like a swarm of angry mosquitos, the power came up and the twin accelerated down the runway. Seconds later, it leapt into the air.

Spencer looked at Heavy Two and scowled, his hopeful mood disintegrating. He instructed his colleague to remain in the Moshi terminal building. Just in case. Then he took another taxi around the airport perimeter, to the hanger from which the twin had departed. He found a sign reading "Office" screwed to the side of the building, climbed the stairs and entered a small, tidy waiting room. The agent behind the check-in counter introduced himself as Regan. With a glowing, white-toothed smile, he wished Spencer a good morning and asked how he could help.

Spencer wasn't sure why everyone in Moshi was so friendly. Maybe it was because he was as black as the locals and their initial thought when they saw him was that he was a local too. Or, maybe it was because Tanzania was an all-round friendly place. Whatever the reason for all the geniality, it was gazelle-fucking irritating at oh-dark-thirty in the morning, after being awake for more hours than he could count on both hands and feet. He kept his tone pleasant though—pleasant got things done—and asked, "That little airplane, the one that just took off? Where's it going?"

Regan answered in a tone that was both mildly offended and quietly proud. "That's not a 'little airplane.' That's a Beech 200. That's our newest aircraft."

Keeping the easy-going expression on his face, Spencer raised his hands apologetically. "A Beech 200. Right," he said, wondering why everyone wanted him to know what kind of airplane was parked, landing, or taking off the Moshi airport. "Can you tell me where it's going?"

"Nairobi. The people on it are part of a medical task force. Doctors and scientists and what not." He lowered his voice. "Because of Covid-28. They're trying to figure out if it started in a slum. Or if it's connected to a slum. Kibera in Nairobi is the largest urban slum in Africa."

Spencer nodded his understanding. As tasty as that bite of trivia was, he didn't give two fucks. Not right then. Turner's wrath was on his mind; it would be far worse than Kibera if they didn't find Steve Quinn. He asked, "How many people on the airplane?"

"Six," Regan said. "They had a day off in their schedule. They're going on safari. That's why they left so early. They chartered the Beechcraft." He paused. After a second he amended his statement. "Seven people. One gentleman showed up at the last minute. He wanted to go with them." Sounding impressed he continued, "He gave everybody one-hundred American dollars. He *really* wanted to go with them."

"Nairobi, huh?"

"Serengeti National Park first. They'll stop at Ndutu. Visit the elephants, giraffes and zebras. Later, they'll fly to Nairobi."

"Any chance you got another Beech 200? I'd like to go to Ndu…" Spencer stumbled over the pronunciation.

Regan helpfully rescued him. "Ndutu. No, Sir. Sadly, no." He brightened. "We have a Cessna Caravan. Slower than the Beechcraft. The flight would take ninety minutes. But," he added reassuringly, "the Caravan is just as safe. You could be airborne in sixty minutes. Once the pilots wake up and get here and fuel the airplane."

Spencer shook his head. "Not good enough. Airborne in forty-five."

Regan frowned and rubbed his chin and agreed, forty-five minutes was indeed better (and entirely possible), if the pilots did their safety checks quickly and efficiently.

Ninety minutes later, Spencer boarded the Caravan, and took off for Ndutu airstrip.

CHAPTER 41

IN THE VAST grassy savanna region of northern Tanzania, a Beech 200 carrying six tourists and Steve Quinn landed with a gentle bump on the Ndutu airstrip. It completed a sharp one-eighty and back-tracked toward a small building with a green roof that served as the airstrip's terminal. Lined up on one side of the building was a row of trucks that provided transportation to lodges and camps, and one that was reserved for the six guests bound on an all-day safari.

The truck drivers clustered together beneath a Tanzanian flag fluttering listlessly on a short pole in front of the building, watching as the Beechcraft rolled to a stop. The engines wound down. The propellers stopped rotating. The first officer (thanks to Tamara's job, Steve had a sense of how aviation worked and knew they preferred to be called "captain" and "first officer" rather than pilot and co-pilot), walked down the narrow aisle in a stoop toward the back of the airplane. He unlatched the air-stair door and pushed it open. A hydraulic snubber lowered it slowly to the ground.

Steve waited while the medical task force, who'd initially refused to allow him on their charter and then changed their minds when he started handing out cash, deplaned. When they were gone, he shuffled to the front of the Beechcraft in a crouch of his own. He introduced himself to the captain in the left seat before the man had a chance to deplane himself. He thanked him for the ride and said, as nice as the park appeared, he'd prefer to visit Dar es Salaam.

Steve knew the Beechcraft was going to Nairobi later in the day. He'd considered sticking with it. After mulling it over, he dismissed the idea, figuring that would be akin to leaving a trail of white bread crumbs for Dark Sky to follow. A different destination seemed like good misdirection; he wasn't convinced that Paige was correct when she claimed he wouldn't be disappeared or otherwise "managed" with extreme prejudice. Those options seemed more likely than being fired or furloughed and then ushered out the door with a gold watch in hand.

The captain replied with a nod and said yes, Dar es Salaam was a nice town, a place everyone would enjoy. Either deliberately or cluelessly, he acted as though he didn't know what was coming next.

Steve asked the captain to fly him to Dar es Salaam.

Looking suitably regretful, the captain said flying to Dar es Salaam was quite impossible. He already had passengers. They were visiting the park, as Mr. Steve must know. In a few hours, when they finished taking photos of elephants, giraffes, and zebras, he was flying them to Nairobi. Mr. Steve *had* to understand; these guests took priority.

Steve recognized a negotiation when he heard one. His bargain-hunting mother had taught him well. In this case, though, he didn't have time to play the haggling game. He remained politely insistent. He told the captain he could pay for the flight, and showed him the corporate American Express card to prove his claim. He then peeled five one-hundred-dollar bills off Messier's bankroll. The cash was for the pilots to split, he said. Three hundred for the captain, because he was the man with authority. The decision-maker. The first officer could have the remaining two. The money, he explained, was a thank you. A "bonus" nobody need know about. All the captain had to do to earn it was make a phone call to head office and say he'd lined up another charter. If he left without delay, he'd be back at Ndutu an hour or more before he had to depart for Nairobi with his six original passengers.

Steve suspected that if the captain's boss heard the company could fly a second charter within the constraints of the first, the extra revenue would be too enticing to refuse. Doubling up made overwhelming commercial sense.

His supposition was correct.

Half an hour after the Beechcraft landed at Ndutu, it was airborne again, heading southeast with Steve as its only passenger. It passed the Cessna Caravan containing Spencer, who was flying in the opposite direction, toward the Ndutu airstrip.

The pilots, all of whom worked for the same company and thus knew each other, chatted on a discrete radio frequency for three or four minutes about where they'd meet for dinner the following night. One bragged about his new cell phone. Another bragged about a recent date. Neither thought of discussing the reason for their respective charters. Charters kept them in rice and ugali; the reasons were irrelevant. The Beech 200 captain made a deliberate point to avoid discussing his passenger. He didn't want the conversation sneaking up on the five hundred dollars he'd been given. He'd told his first officer the bonus was two hundred and generously given him half.

Steve planned on getting on the first available flight out of Dar es Salaam, so long as it had connecting flights to the United States. Fortunately, there were several flights to choose from, one of them being a KLM Boeing 777 bound directly to Amsterdam. Quietly thanking the Global Solutions Corporate Amex, he purchased a ticket.

Ten hours after boarding the 777 in Dar es Salaam, he was scanning a departures board in Schiphol Airport, searching for flights to the United States.

He didn't have time to make the first flight bound to Los Angeles.

His second choice to Chicago O'Hare was full.

His third option had available seats. He put the Amex to work again and bought a one-way ticket to Atlanta's Hartsfield-Jackson airport on Delta, with a continuing connection all the way to Portland, Oregon.

If he'd been less intent on putting as much distance between himself and Dark Sky's heavies and had paid more attention to the various television sets in Schiphol's bars and lounges, he would have seen snippets on CNN and BBC about a developing situation that was, as of yet, short on facts but potentially earth-shattering, involving a heretofore unknown entity called Dark Sky. Paige was *almost* correct when she said nobody would pay attention to a whistleblower because the claims would be too farfetched. Given any other scenario, she would have been one hundred percent correct. But in this case, the world was *already* staring at Africa and demanding answers. The assertions in Steve's email didn't have to generate momentum. Significant momentum had already been building when he hit the Send button.

The flight from Amsterdam to Atlanta took ten and a half hours. Steve couldn't know that, during that time, at least half the emails he sent vanished straight into Spam folders. Others bypassed Spam and landed in in-boxes. Most of these were subsequently trashed, unopened, although some were tagged with an Unread label and immediately forgotten.

A low double-digit percentage of his emails, however, were opened.

Journalists reached out to their political contacts for details and confirmation. Their skepticism was high—how much credence could a person put on an unsigned bulk email—but curiosity is a journalist's stock in trade. They had to show at least minimal interest. When their calls were met with stiff-armed "No comments," their investigative ears perked up.

Some of the emails were opened by low-level staffers, who (in all likelihood), had vendettas against their more influential bosses, or were trying to bulk up their own contact list for future opportunities—which suddenly seemed closer than they had a day before. The emails were swiftly forwarded to journalists whom the staffers trusted, further increasing the story's level of veracity.

Occasionally, a high-level politician opened the email. That person, with years of backhanded experience, started looking for ways to insulate himself from something that smelled like a surefire scandal. Guilty or not, they had large salaries and valuable pensions to protect, so they found ways to subtly foist scrutiny on their political enemies.

Essentially, a tropical depression began with Steve's email at the epicenter.

By the time he landed in Oregon, some thirty-six excruciating hours after leaving Moshi in the Beech 200, the tropical depression had grown into a shitstorm of epic proportions.

CHAPTER 42

THE EPIC SHITSTORM that Steve created blew up on television, radio, and social media all over the world. Investigative committees from Australia to Zambia were immediately launched. Politicians of every stripe covered themselves in deniability. In Africa, the Zimbabwean president made a statement saying he had nothing to do with infecting the vast Harare slum. Protesters were unconvinced. Thousands stormed parliament, overran it, set it alight, and killed three ministers before the rest of the government escaped via the same underground tunnel through which the president had evacuated the compound when the protests began.

The Chinese government made a monumental event out of arresting everyone in sight at a Shenyang factory they claimed was the source of "critical drone components." Nobody knew if their response was staged or genuine. Everyone believed it was classic Chinese misdirection: if Beijing avoided all mention of Covid-28, that *proved* they had nothing to do with its predecessor, Covid-19, a claim China continued to fervently maintain and nobody believed.

In a desperate attempt to divert attention, the hugely unpopular Canadian Prime Minister, who was weathering *another* scandal that should have landed him in prison, claimed that the opposition party's denial of Climate Change had caused the genocide. Sobbing, he made melodramatic apologies to his innumerable African friends, people whom fact checkers couldn't find and doubted existed.

The tempest was of little concern to Steve. The fallout would settle where it did. Change would happen, or it wouldn't. As Paige said, Dark Sky would continue in different iterations in countries other than the United States. He felt he'd done as much as he could to restore a percentage of humanity into a world that had forsaken it. His concern was Ethan Turner.

Turner had vanished when the shitstorm struck. Steve guessed that when a guy who worked at the highest level of a clandestine spy organization decided to disappear, he stayed disappeared until he chose to re-emerge. When that happened, Steve wanted to be long gone, hidden, and inaccessible, as far from Turner's retribution as he could get. As far as Steve knew, Turner was the only person in the world who knew the identity of the "unknown source" that had set the shitstorm in motion. He wouldn't take Dark Sky's exposure lightly.

Steve had a second, equally pressing concern. He'd holed up in a no-name hotel that happily took payment in cash. Now Messier's money was all but gone. In a day or two, he'd have nowhere to go, and no money to get there. After purchasing his airfare to the West Coast, he'd stopped using the corporate American Express for fear it would draw attention to himself. Other than the clothes on his back, his only possession was the passport Turner had given him, and it was as useless as the Amex.

Basic survival had become as problematic as Turner's certain retribution.

Steve could only see one way out, an improbable idea based on a throwaway statement that Paige had made and he'd weirdly remembered. They were on the Boeing Soundwave at the time. She was explaining Dark Sky's mission. He'd interrupted and said the world she was describing wasn't beautiful. It was a goblin, wearing lipstick and eye shadow. He preferred home, where ugly wasn't hiding behind a mask. She replied, "Going home is never as easy as retracing your steps, is it Sweet Pea?"

He remembered her statement, because she seldom said anything so muddy. Even her descriptions of thin spots, the Passage, and alternate worlds—phenomena that sounded more like fiction than reality—were clear and precise. It made him wonder… what if she wasn't waxing poetic? Maybe all he had to do, in order to return to the exhausted Over-there world where he had a safe haven, an income and a place to live, was retrace his steps. Thinking about it, though, Steve realized that retracing his steps wasn't as simple as it sounded.

Where did he start?

How far did he have to backtrack?

How accurate did he have to be?

He didn't feel he could delay. Hanging around in this shiny, rotten world, hoping Turner didn't resurface while he tried deciphering Paige's exact meaning, wasn't something he could afford, literally or figuratively. He had to get away. It had to happen soon. He had to get it right the first time.

Lacking a definitive starting point, he decided to accurately recreate the night he and Paige had met. It was as good a starting point as any and better than most. Prior to meeting her, his life Over-there had been plodding along normally. Five tequila poppers later, he woke up in Tamara's fancy apartment, and his bizarre, alternate-reality life began.

As far as he could see, there were only two things he couldn't replicate about the night they met: Paige's presence and the red pill. Hopefully, the red pill wasn't significant. She'd told him it was supposed to help him tolerate the Space Between. Presumably, if he manned up, he could walk through the alley without the pill's help. Sadly, there was nothing he could do about her absence. If he needed her, if he tried slipping from one world into the next without her, and it didn't work, he was fresh out of ideas.

He walked into Dak's on Thursday night, as nervous as he'd ever been. "Where the Streets Have No Name," was playing on the sound system when he sat down on what was becoming a familiar chair, up against the cube-shaped bar in the middle of the room. The raised stage was empty, as were most of the low tables around the perimeter.

A male bartender appeared from the other side of the cube and asked what he wanted.

Steve wanted Lynn. A week ago, Lynn was working Thursday night. Her absence was another missing element, the third in what he acknowledged was becoming an absurd fantasy rather than a rational course of action. He ordered an IPA. Asked, "Where's Lynn tonight?"

"Sorry, my man," the bartender replied. "She's off. Some problem with a kid." He shrugged and made an exasperated face, like *I'm tired of dealing with staffing issues.* "Tonight, you've got me. I'm Rodney."

Steve nodded unhappily. Like a closing door, at a certain point would the gap become too skinny to squeeze through? With luck, the missing elements weren't cumulative. He said, "Rodney, you know how to make a tequila popper?" Just the word "tequila" conjured up the smell and the taste of the alcohol. His stomach did a slow cautionary roll, reminding him of the previous week's hangover. He ignored the warning. Tequila poppers were part of the ritual.

Rodney answered, "Nothing to it. You want one?"

Steve ordered three. Rodney laughed and said, "Serious business, my man."

Rodney didn't know the half of it.

Dak's slowly started filling up. Steve wanted to enjoy the bar's increasing energy, the girls in their short skirts and high heels, more palatable drinks, the Stones and Bon Jovi, and Heart on the sound system. Unfortunately, the upbeat vibe wasn't working for him. He was too wired, too intent on what needed to happen to have any fun.

Five poppers in (Rodney had gone from amusement to concern, like, *really my man, another one?)* the song Steve was waiting for started to play.

A-weema-weh.

A-weema-weh.

Hardly classic rock, but memorable all the same.

Gratefully, he pushed away what little remained of his IPA. He rose on steadier legs than he expected, nowhere near as drunk as he should have been after the poppers, what with adrenaline counteracting the alcohol in his system. He walked out Dak's front door, turned right, and headed toward Tamara's apartment, or, Over-there, the scabby one-bedroom apartment.

At the Metro station, he stood at the top of the escalator and watched it carry people into its depths for a minute or two. With a smile, he remembered the flash of surprise on Paige's face when he didn't invite her home with him. They'd had quite a time that night, talking silliness, owning a helicopter, a stupid fast car, living in Gotham City. He'd sung to her, and she hadn't laughed at him.

When he judged he'd replicated that part of the night sufficiently, he started walking toward what he'd inadvertently begun thinking of as the "gateway," dragging his heels as growing dread pushed nerves aside. The alley was next. No red pill to counteract its menace this time.

Despite his slow pace, it appeared in front of him, radiating all the malice he remembered. As if to emphasize the danger, a thin arc of moon slid out from behind a cloud. It flashed sickly yellow light on smashed upper windows, making them glow like jagged spit-shiny fangs. Beneath the windows, small piles of shattered glass lay in puddles on the alley floor. A beaten dumpster and a tire run down to the cord leaned against a blackened cinderblock wall. Wind-blown fast-food wrappers, trapped in a rusty shopping cart, flapped as though caught in a breeze Steve couldn't feel. Boarded-over lower windows were covered in dripping, hastily painted graffiti.

"Nothing down there but trash," Steve said aloud, trying to convince himself of something he knew to be false. He leaned slightly left. A hint of a shimmering mirage appeared out of nowhere. It stretched from one side of the alley to the other, like waves of heat radiating off an asphalt highway. He straightened. The indistinct mirage disappeared. He tilted his head a degree to the right. The mirage reappeared.

Steve's gently rolling stomach became wildly turbulent. His dry mouth filled with queasy saliva.

He forced himself to step into the alley. Every instinct pushed him back with an insistence that felt physical, as if a giant hand were planted firmly on his chest. The rancid stink of garbage, urine, and poisonous waste emanating from the wet sludge in the gutter caught in the back of his throat. He told himself to walk fast—get it over with—but every step remained little more than a shuffle.

He kept moving.

The slice of moon disappeared. The sky darkened. A light rain began falling, slicking down his hair and dripping off his forehead, his nose. Behind him, something squalled high and shrill. He whirled. The toe of one sneaker tagged an empty beer can. It clattered across the uneven concrete. A rat scurried from one side of the alley to the other, squeaking in startled outrage. Steve's eyes jumped from one impenetrable shadow to the next, searching for a door that was surely swinging open on rusty hinges, and the unknown horror slithering out of the building toward him.

He'd never felt as sick.

The buildings on either side leaned in, tightening the claustrophobic darkness surrounding him. There was no more graffiti. Urban philosophers didn't venture this far from the safety of traffic and streetlights. He bit his lip, clenched his fists, and blinked rain and tears out of his eyes. He pushed forward resolutely, one small step after another, past the shopping cart, the dumpster, the worn-out tire…

… until he walked unscathed out of the oppressive blackness.

Trembling, bent over with hands on knees for balance, the claustrophobia disappeared in an instant. The nauseous feeling diminished by the second. Something else had changed too: the air he breathed smelled dirty.

He straightened, wiped the back of his hand across his mouth, and pushed his wet hair off his forehead. He looked to his left, recognizing the silhouette of his building, standing tall against the night sky. In the distance to his right, a tiny orange light danced. Steve guessed it to be the forty-five-gallon barrel fire in front of the Tough's little community. The yellow Labrador retriever shuffled out of the shadows. Damp and ragged, ribs showing beneath his sparse and patchy coat, he dispelled any doubt as to Steve's location.

His mad plan had worked.

Laughing with palpable relief, he squatted down and offered the back of his hand for the dog to sniff, unreasonably pleased to see the mangy beast again. He scratched it between the ears, and swore the dog responded with a happy grin. "Good to see you again, Dawg. That's what I'm going to call you. Dawg." He repeated, "It's good to see you."

CHAPTER 43

WITH DAWG TRAILING along in his curious sideways shuffle, his snout inches off the ground, his head swinging in an optimistic pendulum, Steve headed home. In the distance, city lights reflected off low clouds and drizzle. Thankfully, the electrical power was on in his quadrant of the city. He walked past the leaking dumpsters at the rear of his building, the stink of garbage riper and stronger than he remembered after a week of clean air. He keyed his way in and entered the building, holding the door open for Dawg, who hesitated until Steve said, "It's up to you."

Once inside, Steve stared at the steel fire door that opened onto the staircase. He blew out a tired sigh, not thrilled about having to climb to the fourteenth floor (thirteenth, according to Elaina Cosma), and then back down one, uncertain if that part of the replication was required. There was no getting around how much he enjoyed the functioning elevator in Tamara's building.

With vain expectancy, he stabbed the Up button. Why not try? It couldn't hurt.

While he waited for the elevator to arrive, he scanned the length of the hallway and cracked a weak smile. The walls were scuffed, the paint dirty. The dim bulbs in the wall sconces flickered. There'd be no saltwater aquarium or pool table in the lobby. A narrow band of light sliced out from beneath Elaina's door. Dawg snuffled the stains on the threadbare carpeting, most likely enjoying the scents he discovered, odors he wouldn't have found on the polished marble floor in the other world's version of the building.

The elevator announced its prompt arrival with a soft bing-bong chime. The doors split open silently. Surprised, Steve held back for a second or two, doubt bubbling in the back of his brain. Was he really home, or was he caught in some other-world way station?

Behind him, reflected in the mirror on the back wall of the elevator, Elaina's door opened. The lady stepped out of her office. "Mr. Steve," she said.

He exhaled a quiet breath of relief. Her Eastern-European accent grounded him and convinced him he was back where he belonged. By extension, it reassured him that even in this "failure" of a world in which so much was broken, some things could still move in the right direction, even small things, like elevator repairs.

"Welcome back," Elaina said. "You were gone long time."

Tonight, she wore a tight dress that stopped well above her knees, heavy black eyeliner, wet red lipstick, and matching talon-like fingernails. He didn't notice any telltale seams beneath the fabric of her dress. The familiar headband was in place, containing her thick hair in a loose tumble on top of her head. An oversized leather handbag hung from the crook of her arm. She pulled her office door shut behind her. Walking on spiky black high heels, she joined him in the elevator, slowing momentarily when she spotted Dawg. She gave the dog a brief scowl and then said, "The repair people finally fix elevator. Is nice. It works all the time now."

Steve couldn't tell if she was pleased or proud. He suspected both. "It is nice," he agreed slowly, curious as to why she'd joined him in the elevator. He wondered if she'd decided to be more aggressive, like, *fingers on his arm didn't work last time, so this time I'll follow him into his apartment without offering a reason.*

He had to admit, she looked good. Overdone, but not unattractive, which seemed to be her jam. She smelled sweet and floral, making him imagine the other world after a cleansing spring rain. As he had when Elaina showed him the apartment, he continued to find her mildly intimidating for no definable reason. He backed away from her, trying to be casual about it, trying to create space inside the confines of the elevator. Elaina stuck close, allowing their legs to touch, their arms, their shoulders. Ascending past the fourth floor, she said a friend had given her a present. Would he like to see it? While she talked, she rummaged around in her handbag, apparently looking for her friend's gift.

More curious about the reason she joined him in the elevator than the gift, he said, "Sure. Why not?"

She glanced up and shot Dawg another narrow-eyed glare. "What's with the mutt?"

Sitting in the opposite corner, Dawg looked back at her with his head cocked distrustfully. His hackles rose, and he rumbled, low in his chest.

"We're buddies." Steve shrugged. "He's a Labrador retriever. You don't like dogs?"

"I don't like rabid fucking mutty dogs."

Steve tilted his head at her answer. Something was wrong. Different. Trying to pinpoint the sudden change in her manner, he said warily, "What did you want to show me, Elaina?"

She pulled something out of her handbag. He caught a bare glimpse of it—a plastic device, black in color, two shiny chrome probes on one end—a moment before she shoved it harshly into the soft area between his hip and ribs. Holding it firmly in place, she said, in perfectly unaccented English, "The thing is, my name is Jenny Payne." She twisted the device, grinding it into his side. "In case you're curious, this is a stun gun. Did you think Dark Sky would forgive and forget?"

The elevator settled silently on the fourteenth floor. The doors cycled open. Steve swallowed. Something clicked in his throat. Fear filled his heart, chasing away the curiosity.

CHAPTER 44

THEY WALKED DOWN the hallway in silence, Jenny Payne clinging to Steve's arm, the stun gun jammed tightly into his kidneys. His front door stood ajar two or three inches. The interior lights were turned on, creating a bright vertical band separating the hallway from the apartment. He pushed the door the rest of the way open and stepped inside on rubbery legs. Glued to his side, Jenny Payne used the stun gun to nudge him forward, into the center of the living room. Dawg followed. He sniffed the kitchen baseboards in search of tasty crumbs, did three unconcerned circles beneath the table and then fell asleep with his snout on his paws.

Steve's mouth was ash dry. He managed to ask, "What now?" somehow keeping the tremor out of his voice.

Ethan Turner stepped out of the bedroom. "Now, Steve, you and I are going to talk." He held Tamara's pistol in one hand, up near his shoulder. Wobbling it from side to side, he said, "In the night stand? Kind of a cliché, don't you think?" He cut his eyes to Jenny Payne. "Hit him."

Jenny Payne said, "Gladly," and squeezed the trigger.

A rattling sound filled the apartment.

A small part of a second before he collapsed in convulsions, Steve asked himself what he'd done to incite such hostility in Jenny Payne.

The first thing he registered when awareness returned, was a heavy weight on his chest. He blinked his eyes open. Jenny Payne sat astride him, pinning his arms to his side with her knees. Her short dress had ridden up her smooth thighs. Steve was absently aware that he'd been wrong earlier. She was wearing underwear, an insignificant ribbon of lacy black silk too small to create panty lines. She held a vial of honey colored fluid in one hand, a syringe in the other.

She asked him, "How was that for you? It was fucking spectacular for me." She held the vial upside down and stabbed the needle into it. Making sure Steve got a good look, she slowly pulled out the plunger and sucked half the liquid from the vial into the barrel of the syringe. She withdrew the needle. Long and fine, it gleamed ominously under the overhead light. Mimicking movie doctors, she flicked her scarlet fingernail against the barrel to remove the air bubbles and then spritzed a tiny amount of liquid into the air. A glistening amber drop clung to the tip of the needle.

Steve's eyes were wide. Terror twisted inside him. His jaw worked from side to side. In a croaky stammer he said, "What is it?"

"You know how a nurse says, 'This won't hurt?'" Jenny Payne's smile was ghastly. "Yeah, not so much."

Seconds stretched into eternity. Steve's vision narrowed; two small grey tunnels focused solely on the needle's stainless-steel glint. His heart thumped a wild, erratic beat making him feel small and vulnerable. With Jenny Payne's weight on his chest and rising panic choking him, every inhalation was a struggle.

Slowly, she lowered the syringe with its poisoned content, until it disappeared from his sightline. He rolled his head to the side in a frenzied effort to see through watery eyes. "Get it away from me," he said, the words high-pitched, garbled, useless. The sharp sting of the needle piercing the skin of his shoulder forced a shudder up and down his spine. Then the weight on his chest eased as Jenny Payne stood, swung a slim leg over top of him and walked away, in one nimble motion.

Sitting backwards on a kitchen chair, Turner watched with a smile bereft of good humor. One arm lay casually across the back rail, a ludicrously oversized watch on his wrist. His opposite arm dangled down the back of the chair, Tamara's pistol in hand. The laser site she'd attached below the barrel blinked a lethal red dot on and off the discolored carpet, as he toggled the power switch back and forth with his index finger. A couch cushion rested casually on his lap.

Steve blinked several times, clearing his vision. The cushion scared him as much as the amber fluid Jenny Payne had injected into his arm. He understood the cushion's purpose. A cushion made an ideal makeshift silencer. Without it, *maybe* Turner was only using the pistol as an intimidation device. *Maybe* he wouldn't use the weapon as it was designed to be used. But the cushion sitting so comfortably on Turner's lap made a mockery of those *"maybes."* He was going to use the pistol.

Steve rolled onto his belly, pushed himself to his hands and knees and crawled to the sofa. He pulled himself up, while every muscle in his body silently screamed, *what the fuck was that,* while his shoulder throbbed monstrously at the injection point, while his mind jittered all over the place in a futile effort to find a way out of the situation.

Turner said, "I have to admit, Steve. I underestimated you. I don't know how you got past Messier. And the thin spot? How'd you figure it out? This shit-house is the last place I expected to find you." He let his eyes roam around the scabby apartment, shook his head, hiked his shoulders. "Doesn't matter at this point, does it?"

On the other side of the room, Jenny Payne sat on the floor with her legs tucked beneath her. She had pried open one of his uncle's boxes and was unpacking it one item at a time, examining each item she removed with interest. When she pulled a slave-girl Princess Leia action figure (still in the original blister pack), out of the box, she gave her head a little shake and muttered, "Star Wars geeks."

Turner said, "Jenny, sweetheart? You want to quit fuckin' around and put on some music?"

She set Leia aside and held up a November '94 Playboy magazine, safely preserved in a clear plastic sleeve. On the cover, Pamela Anderson looked out at the world with sleepy eyes and pouty lips. Jenny Payne said, "He's got some cool stuff here." She lay the magazine down, found the power button on a nearby dock and pressed the On button. Tuned to a classic rock station, the music started, Sammy Hagar (or Van Halen, depending on your point of view), asking, "Why Can't this be Love?"

Turner said, "You realize what you've done, Steve? A decades old legacy, destroyed. Years of work, destroyed. Future projects, destroyed or in jeopardy. As for me? My future is over. I can't go back. Someone's got to be held accountable. It's usually not the guy on top of the mountain. Usually, the right-hand man takes the bullet. That's me. In this case, I doubt I'll be enough. The president might have to resign. A president hasn't resigned in disgrace since 1974. Congratulations. You're single handedly responsible for that." His voice grew harsher. "I'd like to hurt you. Get old school on your ass. Wire your balls to a car battery. Like that. Circumstances make that impossible. We're still going to play the retribution game."

He narrowed his eyes, seemed to think and then said, "When I joined Dark Sky, the gentleman who recruited me suggested I assemble a team. People I trust. Messier, for instance. And Jenny. Jenny has a thing for Messier. Would that be fair to say, Jenny? You have a thing for our bedridden associate?"

Jenny Payne looked up from the pages of a Sergeant Rock comic book. She said, "It's mutual." She gave Steve a wicked glare. The way her thick black hair was bundled and secured in place with the headband, made her look like a diabolical queen wearing an obsidian crown.

As Steve watched, her face blurred and melted into a grotesque mask. A spike of brittle fear stabbed him in the heart. He looked quickly away, and felt the fear magnify as the apartment walls began to ripple and billow around him. The floor rose and fell like the surface of the ocean beneath a lazy afternoon breeze. His inner ears couldn't determine why there was no motion in a room that was in flux and a surging tide of nausea forced oily sweat to bead on his forehead, scalp and lower back.

Turner's attention remained focused on Steve. "In Afghanistan, I had success with what weak-minded people and left-wing cry-babies refer to as 'enhanced interrogation techniques.' Jenny helped in that regard. Did I mention she's a physician? She came up with this opiate cocktail." He pinched his fingers together, held them up near the side of his head and then rapidly spread them apart. At the same time, he made an exploding mouth sound. "Mind blowing. Literally. It takes the fear a person naturally feels and amplifies it. Gives it edges. Makes it real. You ever see the drooling, empty lumps in a dementia hospital? People pissing themselves in wheel chairs? That's all that was left of the towel-heads by the end." He said this with satisfaction, punctuating his statement with, "I guarantee one goddamn thing. None of them were emptying their AKs into Americans anymore."

Jenny Payne held up a stainless-steel hip flask from the Bowmore distillery in Scotland. "I'm keeping this."

"He's not going to care," Turner said, without looking at her. He studied his deliberately masculine wrist watch, as if he didn't know precisely how long it took for Jenny Payne's cocktail to take full effect. Then he told Steve, "You won't end up a drooling, empty lump. Jenny only gave you half a dose. This isn't an interrogation. I'm more interested in seeing you suffer than asking questions. Goddamn righteous prick."

Steve's terror was demonic now, a brutal relentless assault on every sense, layered on top of the absolute certainty that Turner was moments away from shooting him with Tamara's pistol. The room around him continued to roll in languid, erratic loops. His understanding of the music had virtually disappeared. He heard only the occasional recognizable fragment (now it was Don't Stop Believin'), beneath harsh static and shrill feedback. His mind's eye was filled with colliding, split-second tableaus that fractured and reassembled themselves into different horrific patterns…

a car wreck that turns an elite athlete into a paraplegic,

the hollow-eyes and distended bellies of starving children in war-torn countries,

an uncontrolled airliner plummeting out of the sky, and the shared knowledge of three hundred passengers—from the retired couple returning home from a dream vacation, distraughtly holding hands for the last time, to the recently engaged flight attendant in her jump seat, weeping silent helpless tears—that death was an eternal instant away.

In the basement of Steve's mind, in a corner where a sliver of coherent thought still shone brightly, he thanked every real and imaginary God in the universe, for the mercy of half a dose. He couldn't imagine the ordeal being worse than it already was…

…and then Turner, who'd honed his expertise in the desert and knew exactly what to say to shatter minds, spoke a few more words and made the ordeal much, much worse. He said, "Let's get your journey into the ether started, shall we? Paige Patel didn't make it home from Africa."

The magic of Jenny Payne's cocktail became instantly apparent.

The nightmarish bedlam in Steve's mind, organized itself. Every face in every saturated psychedelic image, became Paige's face. It was an immobile Paige hooked up to tubes and a breathing machine, her large dark eyes full of desolate awareness.

Paige in a long, single-file line of diseased people trudging along a metal gantry, their clanging footsteps carrying them inexorably to the end of the gangplank, where one by one, they leapt into a white-hot incinerator, because nobody recovered from Dark Sky's Covid-28 virus.

Paige lying dead in the septic sludge of an African slum, while bloated flies feasted on her sightless eyes and dogs ravaged her body.

Moaning, frantically repeating, "No, no, no…" Steve squeezed his eyes shut. With all the supreme concentration he could muster, he sought the bright spot, found it, reached for it. From the bottom of somewhere damp and slithering, he heard Turner say, "A little more volume, Jenny. The screaming is about to start."

Jenny Payne cranked the volume knob clockwise.

The instantly recognizable notes of Queen's, "Under Pressure" punched through the static and feedback...

ding,

ding,

ding,

da-da,

ding,

ding...

Startled, Dawg lurched to his feet, back rounded, large head scanning the room, sparse hair on his neck bristling,

and, Jenny Payne said, "Filthy fuckin' mutt," and cocked her arm and threw the stainless hip flask at him. It bounced off the dog's muzzle. Dawg yipped in surprise and then growling angrily, he leapt at her,

and she recoiled with a shriek, beating ineffectively at the snarling dog's chest,

and Turner, with the pistol in one hand and the couch cushion silencer in the other, watched the spectacle like it was a Discovery Channel documentary,

and Steve, focusing on the light and thanking Jenny Payne for her restraint with the hallucinogenic, straightened his legs and arched his back and pushed with his feet, and jackknifed over the sofa, hands scrambling for the shotgun stowed in the Couch Cradle, screaming expletives in abject terror, screaming Paige's name with inconsolable loss, and Freddy Mercury sang louder and louder and louder,

"Give love,

give love,

give love..."

and Steve came up, swinging the barrel of the shotgun across the back of the sofa, bellowing nothing but incoherent noise,

and Turner, a comical look of surprise on his face, raised Tamara's pistol and pulled the trigger three times, and a neat round divot appeared in the wall behind Steve and chips of cinder block and dust filled the air, and the second bullet popped a spider-webbed hole in the window, and the third, no longer thwarted by the startle effect, slammed into Steve just below his collar bone, and his feet tangled, and falling, with the left side of his body broken, he lined up the Shake Awake red dot site, highlighting Turner's chest, and squeezed the trigger, heard the boom, felt the shotgun's recoil hammer him in the shoulder,

and Turner flew backward off the chair, slammed into the wall and slid down the brickwork, his startled expression going slack, and to Steve's over-stimulated mind, the undulating wall behind Turner wept blood and the wooden splinters of what remained of the chair fluttered to the floor like carrion birds to a corpse,

and Jenny Payne howled,

and Dawg growled low in his throat,

and Freddy Mercury sang, "Under pressure,

under pressure,

under pressure..."

EPILOGUE

THE PARAMEDICS ARRIVED a good ten minutes before the police. Professionals that they were, they recognized a person in the throes of an overdose. They immediately shot Steve with Naloxone. The magic of *that* drug brought him back to himself in seconds.

A neighbor that Steve had seen but never met was inside his apartment, leaning against a wall. He wore a green paisley robe and red paisley slippers. His hair was in disarray, his eyes puffy with sleep. He had a compact Smith and Wesson carbine clenched tightly to his side. His hand was on the polymer grip, his index finger resting along the frame, ready to go hot at the slightest provocation. With his opposite hand, he held a cell phone against his ear. As far as Steve could tell with his ears ringing from the gunshots, the neighbor was describing the bloody scene to a police dispatcher. Off to the side, Jenny Payne whimpered beneath a growling Dawg, who straddled her with bared teeth and drooly jowls.

The police arrived while the paramedics were cleaning, dressing, and stitching the wound in Steve's shoulder. They left shortly thereafter. The cops stayed most of the night. It took them longer to sort out the details than it did after the previous shooting in the building. They had trouble reconciling the inconsistencies. Ethan Turner didn't look like the typical home invader, what with his designer clothes and expensive wristwatch. His weapon of choice was a pistol that belonged inside the apartment he'd invaded. He wasn't carrying an ID.

Steve claimed complete ignorance as to Turner's identity. If he admitted to knowing the man, he was flinging open the door to many dozens of questions. Describing his association with Turner, where he'd come from, and why he was here now, was plainly impossible.

The neighbor with the Smith and Wesson (rightfully nervous, the cops had insisted he put the rifle away), sped the investigative process up when he vouched for Steve and added that he, too, had never before seen the home invader. Then he slowed the investigation down when he vouched for Elaina, telling the cops that she was the building's manager, having taken over from lazy Charlie Houston when Charlie went on vacation, or retired or had otherwise gone missing without fanfare.

"She's not the manager," Steve interrupted hotly. "She stunned me. And drugged me! Her name isn't Elaina. It's Jenny Payne. She let the guy into my apartment. The lunatic."

Cops being cops, they didn't want to hear that part. *They* decided who was and who wasn't a lunatic, not the victim. However, there were enough discrepancies between Steve's story, the neighbor's collaborating story, and Jenny Payne's version of events that when the cops finally left, they took her with them. They thought a more in-depth interview was required. Silently, Steve figured they'd have their hands full with her. They'd be lucky to pry a word out of her mouth.

By that point, the eastern sky had started to brighten. Steve was jacked on adrenaline and whatever painkillers the paramedics had fed him. Sleep was out of the question. When the crash came, he assumed it would hit hard, and he'd sleep for a couple of days straight. Before that happened, though, a strange sense of nostalgia for a world he hadn't much liked a week ago had wrapped its rosy red glow around him. He didn't need proof to confirm that he was back where he belonged—that wasn't in doubt—but the nostalgia demanded he experience his environment in the same way a loving wife might walk behind her husband, trailing light fingers across his shoulder… he was with her, present, in the moment and the moment was real.

With his arm suspended in a sling and Dawg padding along beside him, head drifting from side to side, Steve headed for the elevator. He thought he'd visit CompuTech and confirm his employment status. After being gone for a week without notice or permission, he suspected it might be in jeopardy. He hoped the bullet hole in his shoulder would buy him some consideration with his supervisor.

The elevator carried him to the lobby with silent speed. Out on the street, he crouched, rubbed the yellow dog's ears, and said, "I'll be back later. I'll bring food. You want to sleep inside again tonight, it's up to you."

He started walking.

Instead of crossing the street to avoid the three-shack shanty town, as he'd habitually done in the past, he headed straight for it. As he drew close, the Tough he thought of as the tiny community's mayor, pushed a ragged blue tarpaulin aside and stepped out. Wearing his ever-present ball cap and hoodie, he straightened, squared his shoulders, and stared at Steve out of hard black eyes.

Steve didn't find him as intimidating as he might have a week ago, before his confrontation with Messier. He held up his undamaged arm, palm open near his shoulder, kind of a wave, kind of a gesture of appeasement. "Morning," he said. "I've walked by your place before. I should have stopped and said hello. I'm Steve."

The Tough said nothing for a second or two, and then his hard stare and rigid posture softened. "Don." He pushed the brim of his cap up with an index finger. "They call me Mexico Don. You were in high spirits the other night, yeah? That was you?"

"Yeah. That was me. I met a girl."

"That'll do it." Don nodded. "For a while."

"'Mexico Don?'"

"I used to winter in Cancun. I operated fishing charters. My boat sank in tropical Storm Gamma." He shrugged. "It wasn't insured."

"I went to Cancun once." It was Steve's turn to nod. They stood in companiable silence for a few seconds, with memories of Cancun between them, and then Steve said, "Anyway, it was good meeting you, Don. I'll catch you later."

Mexico Don said, "Later," and held out a friendly fist.

Steve bumped it with his own clenched fist.

He kept walking.

Approaching the alley, he slowed and then stopped, refusing to let its evil vibrations shove him away. He thought about Paige and a wan smile crossed his face as he remembered the way she had leaned into her Indian accent when she was imitating her mother, the way she could be so serious one moment and allow the constant undercurrent of fun to bubble up the next, the sexy Meghan Markle messy bun, the juvenile nose ring, so contradictory to the intelligent individual she was, her perfect posture, smooth mocha skin…

It wasn't the poisoned air leaching out of the alley that shortened his breath and hollowed him out.

He saw her beam at him, and he watched her spin away, her voluminous skirt billowing out from her legs, giving him a glimpse of those kick-ass, high-heeled boots, and then she was walking away, growing smaller, smaller. As the sound of tapping heels faded into the distance, he called after her, and she said over her shoulder, in that lovely blended accent, "I know. I miss you too, Sweet Pea."

Steve swallowed hard and swiped the back of his hand across his moist eyes. What was Turner implying when he said Paige didn't make it home from Africa? What had he done to her? His mind drifted back to the hallucinations and all the sickening possibilities that Jenny Payne's drug had shown him. He forced himself to shut the visions down before they gained traction. Turner had surely lied. It felt like something he'd do. It was probable, in fact, bitter, and spiteful as he was at the end.

Steve stared contemplatively down the alley's dark length.

Would it work again, this thin spot, this gateway that gave him access to a different world? If he forced himself to walk into the alley, would he walk out the other side into a parallel America in which Paige was alive?

Was that feasible?

He scratched his unshaven cheek with slow thoughtfulness.

The End

www.ingramcontent.com/pod-product-compliance
Lightning Source LLC
LaVergne TN
LVHW091029080826
845145LV00002B/412

* 9 7 8 1 9 9 9 4 4 2 3 4 7 *